Praise for *The Si*

"Rice's portrayal of the imperfec
their emotional struggles will strike a chord in every mother, daughter, or sister." —*Marie Claire*

"Popular Rice, in her mellifluous style, captures the essence of family and sisterhood as each character deals with love and loss." —*Booklist*

"Rice's writing effortlessly conveys the way family can bind as well as buoy us, reminding us that when the sea of life gets too choppy, by setting our prows toward the places that made us, we will find a safe harbor. Another winner from one of America's most beloved authors." —*BookPage*

"The moving story of three sisters reuniting and learning about love, loss, and family." —*Life and Style*

"Atmospheric and deeply moving . . . a spellbinder." —*Irish Voice*

"Rice enriches familiar themes of family, failure, redemption, and romance with a watercolor-lovely portrait of Martha's Vineyard and sketches of the tug-of-war between sea and sand, rich and poor, development and preservation characteristic of the island." —*Publishers Weekly*

"Compelling . . . a satisfying and worthwhile ride." —*Library Journal*

Praise for the novels of Luanne Rice

"Exciting, emotional, terrific. What more could you want?"
—*The New York Times Book Review*

"A light, sure touch."   —*Time*

"An appealing writer much loved by her fans."
—*The Daily News*

"Rice has an elegant style, a sharp eye, and a real warmth. In her hands families, and their values . . . seem worth cherishing."   —*San Francisco Chronicle*

"Rice writes unabashedly for women, imbuing her tales with romance and rock-strong relationships."
—*Chicago Sun-Times*

"Rice's great strength is in creating realistic characters readers care about."   —*The Denver Post*

"Ms. Rice shares Anne Tyler's ability to portray offbeat, fey characters winningly."   —*The Atlanta Journal-Constitution*

"Rice's trademarks are fine writing, a good eye for small detail, and an uncanny way of conveying the mysterious glue that holds families together."
—*Kirkus Reviews* (starred review)

"Luanne Rice has a talent for navigating the emotions that range through familial bonds, from love and respect to anger. . . . A beautiful blend of love and humor, with a little bit of magic thrown in."   —*The Denver Post*

PENGUIN BOOKS

THE SILVER BOAT

Luanne Rice is the author of thirty novels, twenty-two of which have been *New York Times* bestsellers. Five of her novels have become movies or miniseries, and two of her short pieces were featured in off-Broadway productions. There are more than twenty-two million copies of her books in print in twenty-four territories around the world. A native of Connecticut, she divides her time between New York City and southern California.

The Silver Boat

Luanne Rice

PENGUIN BOOKS

PENGUIN BOOKS

Published by the Penguin Group

Penguin Group (USA) Inc., 375 Hudson Street, New York, New York 10014, U.S.A.
Penguin Group (Canada), 90 Eglinton Avenue East, Suite 700, Toronto, Ontario,
Canada M4P 2Y3 (a division of Pearson Penguin Canada Inc.)
Penguin Books Ltd, 80 Strand, London WC2R 0RL, England
Penguin Ireland, 25 St. Stephen's Green, Dublin 2, Ireland (a division of Penguin Books Ltd)
Penguin Books Australia Ltd, 250 Camberwell Road, Camberwell, Victoria 3124,
Australia (a division of Pearson Australia Group Pty Ltd)
Penguin Books India Pvt Ltd, 11 Community Centre, Panchsheel Park, New Delhi – 110 017, India
Penguin Group (NZ), 67 Apollo Drive, Rosedale, Auckland 0632,
New Zealand (a division of Pearson New Zealand Ltd)
Penguin Books (South Africa) (Pty) Ltd, 24 Sturdee Avenue,
Rosebank, Johannesburg 2196, South Africa

Penguin Books Ltd, Registered Offices:
80 Strand, London WC2R 0RL, England

First published in the United States of America by Viking Penguin,
a member of Penguin Group (USA) Inc. 2011
Published in Penguin Books 2012

1 3 5 7 9 10 8 6 4 2

A Pamela Dorman / Penguin Book

PUBLISHER'S NOTE: *This is a work of fiction. Names, characters, places, and incidents either
are the product of the author's imagination or are used fictitiously, and any resemblance to actual
persons, living or dead, business establishments, events, or locales is entirely coincidental.*

THE LIBRARY OF CONGRESS HAS CATALOGED THE HARDCOVER EDITION AS FOLLOWS:
Rice, Luanne.
The silver boat / Luanne Rice.
p. cm.
ISBN 978-0-670-02250-2 (hc.)
ISBN 978-0-14-312103-9 (pbk.)
1. Sisters—Fiction.   2. Irish American families—Fiction.
3. Martha's Vineyard (Mass.)—Fiction.   4. Domestic fiction.   I. Title.
PS3568.I289S54 2011
813'.54—dc22   2010044290

Printed in the United States of America
Set in Sabon LT Std
Designed by Amy Hill

For Jessie Cantrell, Mike O'Gorman,
Sarah Walker, and Ted O'Gorman

ACKNOWLEDGMENTS

As always, I am grateful to Andrea Cirillo.

My sincere gratitude also goes to the teams at Pamela Dorman Books/ Viking and Penguin Books, especially to Pam Dorman, Julie Miesionczek, Clare Ferraro, Kathryn Court, Dick Heffernan, Norman Lidofsky and their fantastic sales teams, Lindsay Prevette, Carolyn Coleburn, Nancy Sheppard, Andrew Duncan, Rachelle Andujar, Stephen Morrison, John Fagan, Maureen Donnelly, Hal Fessenden, Leigh Butler, Roseanne Serra, and Amy Hill.

Much gratitude to Ron Bernstein.

Thank you to Amelia Onorato for showing me the process of creating a graphic novel.

I am thankful to Jessie Cantrell and Mike O'Gorman. My cats would especially like to thank Ted O'Gorman and Hallie Clarke.

Many thanks to Adrian Kinloch.

Thank you to Audrey O'Brien Loggia for sharing the Vineyard, Galway, and St. Clerans with me.

Sending good wishes to James Lee in Ireland, with thanks for all the wonderful places he showed me.

PART I

Three white frosts on three successive mornings were taken by old-time Vineyarders as a sort of scriptural ending of winter and beginning of spring.

HENRY BEETLE HOUGH

CHAPTER ONE

Dar McCarthy sat on the granite step of her mother's rambling, gray-shingled house, listening to surf break beyond the pond. There had been a gale last night, driving in wild ocean waves, and through the salt pond's wide bight she could see gray-green seawater tower and crash, the foam bright white in the first morning light.

Last night's high wind had blown out all the clouds, and the dawn sky was turning what Delia used to call "happy blue." The sun hadn't yet melted the frost, which glimmered on the old stone walls and spiky brown grass, the lilac branches and the stone Buddha in the herb garden. Her mother's ancient cats skulked home from a night of hiding under the barn, looking tufty and tiny and old.

"What did you catch?" she asked. They ignored her as usual, rubbing at the screen door to be let in, leaving snags of gray fur in the wire mesh. Dar obliged them, reaching up to twist the brass knob behind her head. As the five cats ran in, Scup, her mother's black Lab, ambled out. He made a quick round of the yard, padding paw prints in the frost, then came to sit beside her on the step. They leaned into each other.

Scup nosed her hand with his white muzzle. He was thin; she could feel the ridge of his spine. She petted him for a while, and then he barked. She had promised him a car ride. Standing, she patted the pockets of her down vest to make sure she had her car keys.

They never locked this house, called Daggett's Way centuries before Dar was born, and she never locked the Hideaway, her tiny yellow beach cottage at the west end of her family's fifteen-acre property on the Atlantic Ocean in Chilmark, Massachusetts.

Opening the hatchback of her teal blue Subaru, she let Scup in and smelled the fresh air. Daffodils were ready to bloom in clumps around the yard and by the corner of the weathered shingle house; tiny buds had formed on tips of the lilac bushes. After a long, cold Martha's Vineyard winter, April was here. Dar's hands felt icy, so she closed the hatch and jammed them in her pockets. She was shivering not only from the morning chill.

She knew this feeling so well, from when she was twelve; everything that mattered in life was about to give way. Back then she'd had no real preparation, but now small warnings were everywhere: bills, deadlines, contracts, constant and unwanted calls and e-mails from Island Properties.

Climbing into the car, she discovered that Scup had jumped into the passenger seat. She looked into his deep brown eyes and wondered if he sensed impending change. He had seen the boxes she had been collecting from Alley's and the Chilmark Store.

Pulling out the driveway onto South Road, she knew she was early to meet the ferry. She turned right, passing the cemetery, driving along the oak- and stone-wall-lined road, seeing the sun rise over the trees. One car came toward her, heading west—another year-rounder. They both waved. She turned into the parking lot at Alley's Store, scanned the trucks for Andy Mayhew's. There it was, dirty white with a hoist in back and his logo painted on the door.

She climbed the porch steps, looked for Andy but didn't see him, said hi to everyone standing around drinking coffee. Stopping at the bulletin board, she riffled through all the business cards and notices until she found a note written on a thick card embossed with Harrison Thaxter's family crest; this was how they communicated.

When are the girls arriving? he'd scrawled in fountain pen. Reaching for the pencil dangling from the board by a string, she wrote back, *Today!* Then, not knowing whether he'd be by any time soon, she added, *(Friday, April 9th)*.

"When's he going to get a phone?" Andy asked, handing her a large steaming black coffee.

"When's he going to get a house?" she asked.

They both chuckled. Andy, Harrison, the McCarthy sisters, and a tight group of friends had grown up here—first summering on the island, then some of them digging in and becoming year-rounders.

"You okay?" Andy asked, standing close, their arms touching.

"Yes," she said. "Going to pick up my sisters. I can't wait."

"You sure about that?" he asked. He was tall, and the top of her head just grazed his chin.

"Pretty sure," she said, giving him a big smile, as if they hadn't talked about this last night, as if her sheets might not still be warm from where they'd slept. "It's going to be hard, getting ready to leave all this."

"You don't have to—" he began.

"Thanks, Andy," she said, putting her finger to his lips.

"You want me to come with you?" he asked.

She shook her head. "You have a stone wall to repair."

"I found some pretty granite, covered with lichens," he said. "Will you come see later?"

"I'll try," she said. "It's going to be sister time for the foreseeable future."

He started to say something else but stopped himself.

"What?" she asked, but he shook his head.

"See you tonight," he said.

They pressed each other's hands, and she made her way back to the car. Backing out of the parking lot, she rolled down the window to wave. Sipping coffee, she let the chilly air in.

Dar arrived in Vineyard Haven just in time to see the nine o'clock boat rounding West Chop and slicing through the harbor. Gulls cried, circling the upper deck. No matter what time of year, she always felt delight and expectancy, seeing the ferry pull in. Anyone at all might be aboard, but this time she knew for sure—Rory and Delia.

She and Scup jumped out of the car, stood aside the car lane. The MV *Island Home* screeched and squeaked, thumping back and forth between the huge barnacled, creosoted pilings. Chains rattled as the ferry's metal ramp was lowered, and Dar peered into the dark hold, her heart beating fast.

Vehicles began to off-load. She held her breath. This was the Steamship Authority's newest ferry. Dar, her sisters, and their mother had stood on this dock, listening to Carly Simon, her son Ben Taylor, Kate Taylor, and others singing to welcome the new boat. Dar had done a drawing of the scene, given it to the captain. He'd flattered her, looking for her signature.

"An original Dar McCarthy," he'd said. "My daughters won't believe it."

"Tell them I'll draw them on deck in my next installment."

"Wow," he'd said. "That better be a promise."

"It is," she'd said, and she'd kept her word, putting the ferry and the captain's children in a scene in her next graphic novel.

And now, here came Delia, driving her green Volvo wagon, waving out the open window. Dar waved back, noticing Delia's granddaughter, Vanessa, beaming from her car seat in back, as well as the fact that Rory and her kids weren't in the car.

Dar followed Delia over to an empty spot, hopped inside, and hugged her youngest sister. They rocked back and forth, not wanting to let go. Vanessa held a doll in the crook of her arm and shouted, "Hellohellohellohello!"

"Hello, Vanessa!" Dar said. "Hello, hello! Where is Rory?"

"Oh God," Delia said. "I've been up since three, and I need a whole lot of coffee before I get into that. She wanted to take her own car. Can we go home, and then I'll tell you? Have you heard from Pete? Oh, never mind that now. Let's just get home, and we can talk."

"Of course," Dar said. She held her sister's hand, not wanting to let go or get out of the car. But Scup was waiting, and they were blocking traffic, so Dar blew Vanessa a kiss and ran back to her own car.

. . .

Delia Monaghan led the way. She talked to Vanessa, pointing out landmarks.

"That's where my best friend, Amy, lives in the summer, and that's the old oak—see all the big, winding branches, all the way down to the ground and up again—we all used to climb, and that's the creek where your daddy used to catch crabs and herring."

"My daddy!" Vanessa said.

Delia met her eyes in the rearview mirror and smiled. "That's right. Daddy." She kept driving, was fine till they passed Chilmark Cemetery; glancing down the hill, she tried to find her mother's grave. She could almost see herself and her sisters and half the island residents standing there in the October light. Summer people had returned to the Vineyard, and her fellow winter residents had gathered to say good-bye to Tilly McCarthy. Everyone had been there except Pete.

"Oh, Mom," Delia said. The funeral was the last time she and her sisters had seen each other. They usually gathered on the island for Thanksgiving and Christmas, but this period without their mother, and the reality of what was to come, had been too much to bear; they'd each celebrated in their own way.

Delia had spent hers with her husband and granddaughter—Vanessa's mother was only eighteen, pregnant again with another man's baby, and took every possible chance for Delia to babysit.

Rory had spent the holidays with her three children, and not with her husband.

Dar had probably gotten together with Andy Mayhew; Delia could not figure out that relationship. It had lasted forever, but no one was getting married or moving in together.

Delia pulled herself together before turning in to her mother's driveway. The sight of the big old house filled her with yearning and made her think of childhood—her own and Pete's, and now Vanessa's. She could just see her mother, tall and sturdy, dressed in faded jeans and a linen shirt, white hair short and practical under a wide-brimmed sun hat.

What a great mother she'd been, basically raising the girls on her own after their father had left. The whole situation had left the family stunned and devastated, but Tilly McCarthy had always tried to keep her daughters' hopes up. Those linen shirts in beach colors—blue for sea and sky, green for marsh grass, orange for sunsets, deep pink for the beach roses that grew along the path to the beach—those colors chased the darkness in their house, let her daughters think, sometimes at least, that life was good and bright.

She'd invent special, magical occasions. The girls would come down for breakfast and find clues on the table. Cut-out stars meant that night they'd be going down to the beach, spreading blankets on the cold sand, gazing up at the sky to learn constellations and watch for shooting stars.

Three watercolor brushes tied with ribbons of marsh grass hinted that she'd planned an artists' expedition; they'd pile into the station wagon and find a cove, or salt marsh, or hilltop. Unloading easels, watercolor pads ordered from Sennelier in Paris, miniature Winsor & Newton watercolor kits for each of them, they would set up and paint *en plein air*, an all-girl version of late-twentieth-century Impressionists. Only Dar would stick with her paintings; Delia and Rory would get bored and wander off, exploring. Their mother didn't mind, as long as everyone had fun.

"Well, here we are," Delia said, unbuckling Vanessa's car seat.

Dar walked over, and they gave each other a long hug. "Hi, Vanessa!" Dar said.

"Beach!" Vanessa said.

"Yes, soon we'll go down to the beach," Delia said.

The kitchen was chilly, so Dar threw a few logs into the woodstove. Delia looked around. When they used to come to open the house each Memorial Day, they'd have to sweep out dead wasps and mouse droppings and broken acorns dropped down the chimneys by squirrels. Once they'd found a complete fish skeleton in the fireplace and could only imagine an osprey had lost its grip flying overhead.

"Oh my God," Delia said, going to hug Dar as she made coffee. Her older sister felt lean, almost skinny; she'd always been that way, as if following some private, inner asceticism. Delia felt fat by comparison, folds of flesh and pudgy wrists. She pulled away and instantly felt thinner. "You have no idea how much I've been dying to talk to you in person. The phone just doesn't cut it."

"I know," Dar said, putting two scones in a pan. The oven groaned as it heated up.

"Mom never gave in to the microwave I bought her," Delia said.

"She liked things as old and original as she could keep them," Dar said.

"Oh, Mom," Delia said. "She tried to hold on to everything, balancing all the while. Imagine being stuck between Grandmother and her English ways, and Dad sounding like he'd never left county Cork."

"Yep," Dar said, watching Vanessa clutching her doll, playing on the floor with Scup. "We'd come here and be blue-collar girls in a silver spoon world."

Delia laughed. Scup came over, tail wagging, and she leaned over to pet him. "Mangy old guy," she said. "His poor tail doesn't have any hair left on it. What are we going to do with him?"

"I'll keep him and the cats," Dar said.

"And where will that be?" Delia asked.

"I'm working on it," Dar said. "Where's Rory?"

"Coming on a later boat," Delia said. "Something to do with Jonathan."

"She'll get here when she can." Dar paused. Tell me about Pete," she said.

Delia closed her eyes, remembered the day two and a half years ago when she'd driven Pete, her only child, to the airport. He'd dropped out of American University mid-semester. Delia and Jim had lost the tuition money they'd paid, and Jim felt betrayed and furious. Pete had spent three summers crabbing with the watermen out of Kent Island in Chesapeake Bay. But after leaving college, he decided to try his luck fishing in Alaska.

The pay was good, he said. He could reimburse his parents. She believed him; she'd never doubted his integrity. But two days after he flew to Anchorage, a sheriff arrived at their house just outside Annapolis, bearing court papers for Pete, naming him in a paternity suit.

"He's missing all this time with Vanessa," Delia said. "She's nearly two."

"I know," Dar said, setting the coffee mugs down.

"Do you talk to him?" Delia asked, grabbing her mug, half dreading the answer.

"He calls me sometimes."

"He calls me, too," Delia said. "At home, when he knows I'm

at work, and at work when he knows I'm home. He can't stand to talk to me."

"It's not you," Dar said. "He can't stand himself."

"My son is all the way up in Alaska, fishing in wicked weather . . . that's when he can get on a boat. The fishermen up there are so suspicious of outsiders."

They were silent for a moment; Dar was thinking of dangers of storms, of what could happen to a person on a boat at sea. Delia couldn't separate the past; it filled her thoughts and dreams with fear.

"They're big, steel-hulled trawlers," Delia heard herself say.

"That's good. Well, the guys are probably territorial like the fishermen here," Dar said. "And the watermen on the Bay, right?"

"I know, but I worry about him being cold and hungry. He makes good money when some captain is desperate for crew and signs him on—but he can't count on it. I'm worried when he's on a boat, and nearly as much when he's not. He's one step away from welfare. Sometimes I think he doesn't want to work, so Maryland can't attach his wages for child support."

Dar moved her chair closer. "He's figuring it all out," Dar said. "I'm not defending him, but I know he's going to come around. He's got too much of you in him to keep doing this."

Delia shook her head hard.

"You're the most responsible person I know," Dar said.

"You mean boring."

"Never," Dar said. "Just steady and good."

To Delia, coming from her cool, willowy, offbeat older sister, that still sounded dull as hell. But she gave Dar a smile, to let her think she'd accepted the compliment.

Neither of them had mentioned their father or his dangerous sea voyage. They didn't have to, because the story lived inside them, made them who they were. Whenever Delia picked up one of Dar's graphic novels, she saw exactly how haunted their lives had been. Dar expressed mystery enough for all three sisters.

Now they'd come to clean out their family's house, and Delia wondered what surprises they would find, what leftover evidence of love, loss, and the great big question that remained.

Dar could almost see them on the beach: herself, her sisters, and baby Pete: the first grandchild, her first nephew. Building sand-castles, playing in the shallow water, showing him how to use a plastic shovel and pail, tilting the striped umbrella so he could nap in the shade. The summer he was two, they'd taken him on the Flying Horses in Oak Bluffs, for Mad Martha's ice cream in Edgartown. Jim, Delia's husband, rarely came to the Vineyard; he considered it too snobby and preferred to stay home.

As Pete got older, Dar and her sisters had taught him to swim and bodysurf. When he was thirteen, Dar and Andy had helped him catch his first wave on a long board. They'd shown him the best surf-casting spots at sunrise and sunset, watched him catch his first striper. Harrison had welcomed him aboard his Hatteras Sportfish so Pete could enter the island's bluefish tournament, taught him to tie knots, shown him how to sail on his family's Herreshoff 12.

By then Pete was ready to race at the yacht club, and he found some friends with a Rhodes 19. Dar had loved when he'd admitted racing and the yacht club weren't for him; he'd rather just let the wind take him, not have to worry about competition or who had the most expensive gear.

As Pete's aunt, Dar saw it her duty and blessing to pass on to him all the beach, nature, and maritime things she'd always loved. So much had come from her father, and she'd tell him about Mike McCarthy, what a great father and boatbuilder he had been. His hands had been permanently rough and creased, and she was proud of his carpentry and hard work.

Dreaming back to a much younger time, the summer she was eleven, Dar remembered being with her parents on the beach. She saw herself and sisters bodysurfing the crests of long waves, swimming out with their mother again and again, thrilled by every perfect, curling wave carrying them over the white sand bottom. Her father, used to the saw-edged rocks of southwestern Ireland, had wanted to run in and rescue his daughters every time.

They'd run out of the water, completely chilled, and lie on blankets up in the dunes, where the sun baked down and the wind was screened by beach grass. Their mother would have brought a picnic, and they'd all dig in. She had loved seeing her parents side by side in their low beach chairs, her mother completely in her element, her father awkward in bathing trunks and sunglasses, as if he'd rather be in his work boots and overalls, planing a plank, joining it to the next on the boat he was building. Dar had loved that her mother tried teaching him to relax.

The McCarthy family lived between two worlds. Getting off the ferry, they'd leave one life behind and enter another one. Throughout the school year in their small house in Noank, Connecticut, Dar would watch her mother pretending not to have grown up rich and trying to get used to balancing the checkbook and packing her husband's and children's lunches every day. But when summer came and they returned to the big house on the salt pond, the wide porch, and cocktails at sunset, she again inhabited her realm. Dar and her sisters joyfully joined in, and their father had his own reasons.

Dar, her sisters, and their best friends would ride their bikes twenty miles into Edgartown. They'd spend the day sailing, and if it got too late, their mother would pick them and their bikes up in the station wagon. They would ride to Menemsha, talk to the guys on their fishing boats, eat lobster rolls on the dock. Rainy days, they would huddle under the porch roof and learn how to make and mend sails, using waxed thread and vintage leather sailmaker's palms, talking nonstop.

Community Center dances were sweet, wild, and romantic. A local band would play, and everyone would dance. Dar remembered her racing heart, the intensity of slow dances, usually with Andy, pressing their bodies together, hardly able to breathe, never wanting it to stop. But it always did—the dance would end, and it would be time to go home. Dar always wished for happiness to last, for all love and good things to stay the same, but she had received early proof that they never did.

The year she was twelve, Dar's life as she knew it ended. Her body kept moving, but her spirit had flown away, after her father. Her parents separated that winter, and that summer he sailed to Ireland on a boat he'd built. He made one call home from a port in Kerry, but then he disappeared somewhere off the craggy, razor-sharp rock coast between Dunmore Head and county Cork.

Dar alone had watched her father sail away, in the clear light after a rainstorm, and as if she'd been his keeper, for a long time she'd felt it was her fault he didn't return.

Rocking her in her arms one of the worst nights, Dar's mother had tried to soothe her. She explained what Dar already knew: that her father had come to the Vineyard as a young man, looking for a tract of land his Irish grandfather claimed was his birthright. He'd fallen in love and married her mother, had children, spent years building boats, but he'd never forgotten his initial reason for coming to the Vineyard.

"Sweetheart," her mother said, "your father was driven by something inside. Do you know what that means?"

Dar listened, not wanting to let on that she did.

"A feeling so strong, it began to matter to him more than anything else in the world."

"Did he go back to Ireland to get away from us?" Dar asked.

"No," her mother answered. "The opposite. He had this idea that if he went, and brought back proof about his land, that we would value him better, love him more."

"I could never love him more," Dar said, but her mother didn't reply. Maybe their love had already been tested too much; his resentment and determination had pushed her away. Only twelve, Dar had observed and taken in the way her parents' closeness had swirled and dissipated, like a beach being eaten away by winter storms, over that last year.

Dar had seen what "driven" meant. She remembered her father walking this property belonging to his wife's mother. She'd gone with him so many times, exploring all fifteen acres, from the gorse hedge at the land's eastern end to the yellow shack, known as the Hideaway, at the westernmost. They'd walked from South Road to the edge of the salt pond, searching for surveyors' markings and stakes.

"What do they look like?" she'd asked, walking beside him.

"A crosshatch on a boulder, an iron stake or maybe a granite post."

"What do they do?"

"They mark where one person's property ends and another's begins."

"But this is all Grandmother's," Dar had said. "Why are we looking here?"

"Because you never know what you might find."

She'd glanced up, scared by the intensity in his eyes. "I'm no one special," he said. "A boatbuilder. But there's a treasure right here, Dar. Straight from our ancestors, a land grant from the king of England."

"Dad, you're Irish," she'd said. That had brought a dark smile to his face.

"Exactly."

Feelings too much for Dar overtook her, and it was on that walk with her father that Dulse began to materialize.

CHAPTER TWO

Rory McCarthy Chase was now aiming for the noon ferry, but it was looking less and less likely they'd make it. She'd started off late at seven a.m., driving along I-95 from Old Lyme, Connecticut, knowing there was no way she'd meet Delia for the nine o'clock boat. She'd called Jonathan at one in the morning, losing all hope of falling back to sleep.

"Come with us," she'd said, as if it were a normal conversation at a polite hour. "The Vineyard is where we started. Let's go back there, start fresh, forget all that's happened."

"Rory," he'd said, groggy and slurry, "I know you. You can't forget all that's happened. It's hurt you too much."

"At least you admit it," she said.

"See what I mean?"

"No, it's late, I'm just so tired . . ."

"Should you be driving tomorrow?"

"Drive us," she said. "That's how we always used to do it. You'd drive, and I'd play games with the kids. We'll miss you too much. How can we go without you?"

"Rory," he said slowly, waking up. "We're separated. I still . . . I still care for you. But I'm the one hurting you, and I can't also be the one to comfort you. Go out there, be with your sisters. Let Sylvia, Jenny, and Obadiah have fun on the beach, play with Vanessa. Let their aunts spoil them. And you too, okay?"

"Do you really love her?" Rory asked.

"Alys is beside the point," Jonathan said. "But yes. I do."

Rory let out a shriek. She hung up and lay awake analyzing every word they'd said, and why Jonathan had lost his mind, and how she was convinced his falling in love with someone young had to do with all the money they'd lost in the art market crash and how his fragile male ego couldn't hack it, and how sad it was, and how much she still loved him, and how sad *that* was. Around four she fell into a thin sleep.

Finally they were on the road, having grabbed breakfast at the Niantic Burger King drive-through. The traffic on I-95 was light, and as soon as they turned onto I-195 in Providence the highway was lined with scrub pines, filling the car with their spicy scent that had always reminded Rory of family vacations. Even before Jonathan . . .

"Why didn't Daddy come?" Jenny asked, having held the question inside for over an hour.

"Well," Rory began.

"Because he's with Alys now," Obadiah said.

"I hate her," Jenny said.

"Honey, don't say 'hate,'" Rory said. She kept both hands firmly on the wheel, leaning forward as if it could get them to the ferry faster. She remembered the mysteries of her mother and father's separation—no one, especially Irish Catholics and English bluebloods—talked about such things back then. But her mother had been so good to her daughters, easing them as carefully as possible through most of it. Rory aspired to that.

"Your father still loves you," Sylvia said. "That is the important part."

Rory gave Sylvia—her wise oldest child from her first marriage, even that a rebound from one of her and Jonathan's breakups—a grateful glance in the rearview mirror.

"But he loves Alys more," Jenny said. "Or he'd be with us."

"Breakups have nothing to do with children," Sylvia said, and Rory recognized her own words, spoken long ago.

"That's true," Rory said. "Daddy loves you as much as ever, and he always will." She tried really hard to smile as she drove, to reassure Jenny, eight, and Obadiah, nine, that their half sister Sylvia, fourteen, knew what she was talking about.

Now, finally reaching Woods Hole, Rory drove into the standby line. It wasn't too bad, and Dave the deckhand waved them onto the noon boat with moments to spare. The horn blew and the crew began casting off even before Rory and the kids were out of their car. The hold smelled of exhaust and salt air. Everyone hurried up the staircase to stand on deck.

They lined the rail, watching Nobska Light and the Woods Hole Oceanographic Institution recede, then turning to face forward and watch the Vineyard get closer. The wind in their faces was brisk, but the sun felt warm. In spite of everything, Rory felt the excitement of going home.

· · ·

Dar took a break while Delia fed Vanessa her lunch, and took Scup back to her place. An eighth of a mile from the farmhouse, through acres that had been in her mother's family for hundreds of years, they ran through tall grass, past lilacs, through breaks in crisscrossing stone walls, past the old cellar hole, through a small grove of gnarly apple trees, all the way to the ramshackle one-story beach cottage her family had always called the Hideaway.

Built of pine, on stilts in case the salt pond overflowed, with an outdoor shower hooked up only from June through October and a perpetually sandy floor, it had been a place for the family to keep their beach things, to change and take a shower in the sun.

When Dar had moved full-time to the Vineyard the fall after art school, she'd insulated and re-roofed the Hideaway wearing painter's pants, a Mad Martha's T-shirt, a Red Sox cap, and latex gloves to keep her fingers safe from the stinging pink fiberglass.

She'd offered beers to anyone who wanted to help her, and the day had turned into a party with all her friends left on the island post–Labor Day. They'd painted the cottage yellow, and Andy had built her a small porch that she loved.

Now, inside, she quickly checked her e-mail. This place was geeked out; she had an iPhone charging; a seventeen-inch Mac-Book Pro and a MacBook Air; and her old silver Wacom CTE-640 digital drawing tablet, one edge held together with duct tape. Her Japanese publisher had given her a newer one as a gift, but Dar was attached to the old model and the stories that had come out of it.

The least technical and most important parts of her space were the view across the salt pond to the Atlantic Ocean and her memories of times her family had come back here after spending all day at the beach. Dulse hovered behind the cobweb above, wanting to be called down. Dar didn't glance up. Scrolling through her e-mails, she knew what she would find.

There it was—the Realtor's latest plea to let the new owners and their architect stop in during their children's spring break, so they could start construction right after the closing.

Dar gave Scup a biscuit. She opened the window beside her bed and felt the sea breeze. For half a second she thought about the spring ritual of putting screens in the windows here and at the farmhouse. It wouldn't be her problem this year.

Walking back to the big house, she tried to practice Tonglen. She went on yearly retreats to an island north of Nova Scotia, meditating and learning to let go. She had gotten her mother into Tibetan Buddhism during her last few years, and it had given her a measure of acceptance and peace while her heart slowly failed. Tonglen was a way to develop compassion for other people by breathing in their hot, tarry pain and breathing out cool, blue love. Picturing the new owners and their architect, she got stuck in the hot tar.

By the time she reached the farmhouse, she was cool enough to smile at the sight of Rory's old blue wagon.

"Hey!" she called as she walked into the kitchen.

Rory and Delia were sitting at the table, but Rory jumped up at the sight of her. "Darrah McCarthy, you are a sight for sore eyes!"

"Same to you, Rory-girl," Dar said as they slammed into each other for a hug.

"Me too!" Delia said, working her way into the circle.

Dar was taller than both, and her arms wrapped around them. She felt as if she were trying to hold on to the moon. Small and bright as it waxed and waned up in the sky, but it escaped once a month, turning the nights black. She kept her sisters close, wanting them to stay hugging as long as possible, as if that could stave off what was coming.

"Someone's been smoking," Delia said, breaking apart.

"Remind me not to hug you again," Rory said, shaking her short dark hair as if she could get the smoke out of it.

"I didn't mean it that way," Delia said. "I'm thinking of Mom, heart disease. I love you and want you to live forever."

"Amen to that," Rory said. "For all of us."

"Speaking of 'amen,'" Delia said, "it just feels so weird to me to see the Buddha out in the garden."

"Well, Dad took Catholicism with him when he left," Rory said. "At least as far as I'm concerned. Is it too early for beers?"

"The sun's over the yardarm!" Delia said.

Rory opened two Heinekens and a Diet Coke for Dar. They all clinked and drank.

"Where are the kids?" Dar asked.

"The beach."

"Vanessa is so pretty," Rory said. "What's her mother like?"

"She's beautiful, eighteen, lives on the Internet," Delia said.

"Is there a chance she and Pete could get back together?" Rory asked.

"Uh, no," Delia said.

"Well, I'm sure he's making a lot of money up there, socking it away for Vanessa's education. I've heard of crab fishermen pulling in a hundred grand a winter."

"We know someone who *wanted* to go there," Dar said. "As a brilliant moneymaking scheme."

"Harrison," her sisters said at once.

"A little too much work, though," Rory added. "Actually fishing."

The mention of their childhood friend lightened everybody up. Harrison had once come up with an idea for a guide called "The Lazy Man's Guide to Life." But he knew he'd never write it, because it would take work and he enjoyed being lazy too much. Dar took out the snapper blue fillets she'd broiled the night before, and Delia found one of their grandmother's brown crockery bowls in the back of the cupboard.

Rory cut slices of lemon on the butcher-block table, then squeezed them over the fish while Delia drizzled pale green olive oil and ground pepper and sea salt into the bluefish salad.

Dar laid out slices of Rickard's bread she'd bought at Cronig's last night. While her sisters made bluefish sandwiches for each other and Sylvia, she found peanut butter and strawberry rhubarb jam for Jenny and Obadiah. They packed everything into a wicker basket, pulled on sweaters and fleeces, grabbed the two plaid wool picnic blankets, and went out to find the kids.

They walked across the wide open field toward the beach. The frost had melted in the warm sunshine, but they saw footprints in the dry brown grass. Following them down the hill, around the pond, they spotted the salt-bleached boardwalk thrown into the reeds by a winter storm.

"We'll have to get that back in place," Delia said.

"Not this year," Dar said.

"You know what?" Rory asked. "Can we call a moratorium

on the new owners and the whole moving thing for at least a day? I want to enjoy getting together without it turning into a wake."

"Good plan," Dar said, not able to avoid thinking of the Realtor's latest e-mail.

"Denial has its place," Delia said.

They continued on, walking down the sandy path between two sharply wind-sculpted dunes. The blue ocean glimmered, and before Dar could spot her nieces and nephew, she heard them shout from down the beach.

"Aunt Dar!" Obadiah yelled, skidding in at her feet, then scrambling up for a hug. "We saw someone naked!"

"It's true," Jenny said.

"Ah, spring comes to Lucy Vincent Beach. What have you two huge people done with my little niece and nephew?"

"We're us!" Obadiah said.

"Oh my God, you are," Dar said. Then she turned to Sylvia, who was standing back and seeming shy. "Silvy, you're so beautiful."

"I'm not," she said, kissing Dar.

"You completely are," Dar said. "You look just like your mother."

Dark hair, blue eyes; they all shared the same coloring, but Sylvia had Rory's spark, an almost-hidden ready-for-anything wildness. Dar thought back to when they'd been kids, how every boy on the Vineyard had wanted Rory. Huge blue eyes, long tan legs, and the tiniest bikini sold on Circuit Avenue.

Rory and Harrison had been best friends and ringleaders for fun and trouble; they'd pile into Harrison's father's vintage Cadillac Eldorado, top down, a moveable party in a red-leather interior, driving all over the island, picking up and dropping off friends as they went.

Dar remembered how proud Harrison seemed to have Rory up front beside him. She'd light his cigarettes for him, make sure the radio was tuned to the right station, never stop laughing at his effortless humor. They weren't romantic, but they weren't unromantic, either. It had been a great sexy monster of suppressed desire.

Dar gazed at her sister now. Still lovely, she'd kept plenty of that mysterious spark. Rory walked beside Sylvia, talking low, laughing at something Silvy said. Dar wished she had her sketchpad.

They all headed for the warmest spot, up in the dunes—bright with sun, sheltered from the sea breeze. Sylvia and Rory spread out the blankets; Delia took Vanessa from Dar, who opened the picnic basket. She passed out blue ironware picnic plates and faded floral cloth napkins.

Andy surprised her and came down to meet them.

"Well, look who's here!" he said, walking over in construction boots and Carhartt jacket.

"Andy, hi!"

"Good to see you, Mayhew," Rory said.

"Back at you, Chase."

Dar smiled, made room for him on the blanket, gave him half her sandwich. He nodded, thanking her, and they smiled at each other. They kissed, and Dar felt her sisters watching.

"How's everyone's winter been?" he asked.

"Jim's business was slow," Delia said. "But we're hoping things brighten up this spring."

"Pretty much the same here," Andy said. "Building slowed down more than I'd expected. It's picking up, though."

"Things will get better," Delia said. "They always do."

"What's the story with Harrison?" Rory asked. "He actually sent out Christmas cards with a picture of a wreath on a huge garage door."

"At least he's festive," Andy said.

"Eternally so," Rory said. "Thank God for that. But seriously—where is he living?"

"Let's just say he's downsized," Dar said.

"Yeah, he had some legal bills back in January," Andy said.

They all knew the latest story. Harrison had gotten caught breaking into Town Hall to steal back the bronze bust of his father, Harrison Thaxter, Sr.—known for local philanthropy in better days—which had been auctioned off at the foreclosure sale two years earlier. The cops would have gone easy on him if he'd just returned it, but Harrison had taken the bust off-island, hidden it somewhere and refused to reveal its whereabouts.

"They said it's a second infraction," Andy said.

"The *dogs*?" Rory asked.

"What about the dogs?" Obadiah asked. "Which ones?"

"Harrison's," Rory said. "He loved his dogs a lot. He just probably should have kept them on a leash more. They kept running away."

"Did they ever get back home?" Jenny asked.

"Uh-huh," Rory said, giving a reassuring hug without telling the kids the story.

Four years ago Harrison's father's very old dachshunds had taken off yet again, found by Animal Control hunting rabbits in someone's garden. Fines for previous incidents had piled up, and the officer wouldn't release Fred and Rose without full payment.

So Harrison had driven to the shelter after midnight, used a ladder to haul himself over the tall chain-link kennel fence, spraining an ankle on the way down, knelt, and squeezed his bulky frame through the swinging rubber dog flap to take his dogs right out the front door.

"Oh, Harrison," Delia said. "Can't he ever just do things by the book?"

"Never has, never will," Andy said. "He probably doesn't even know what the book says."

"Yeah, he does," Rory said, choked up. "He just doesn't care. Loving his father and his dogs means more to him than the rules."

"Try telling the town that," Delia said.

"When can we see Uncle Harrison?" Jenny asked.

"Soon," Rory promised.

"Are there sharks in the water here?" Obadiah asked, shielding his eyes as he looked out to sea.

"Sometimes," Andy said.

"Daddy said he used to surf right over them," Obadiah said. "Blue sharks and makos, and once a great white."

"I doubt that about a great white," Rory said.

"Just because Dad said it?" Obadiah asked.

"There was one trapped in a salt pond on Cuttyhunk a couple of summers ago," Andy said. "Full-size."

"I don't mind about sharks," Obadiah said. "I can't wait to learn to surf over them. Dad said he'd teach me. We're lucky, because even though we have to sell Granny's house, Jenny and I can still come to the Vineyard to stay with Gram and Pop."

"Daddy says we'll always have the Vineyard," Jenny said.

"That's true," Rory said.

"But I don't get it," Jenny said. "How can *we* have it, when you won't?"

"Oh, sweetheart. It has to do with taxes. Money. Sometimes people can't afford to hold on to things they love."

"Just like Harrison," Andy said.

"Just like," Rory agreed, and once more Dar wished she had her sketchpad to capture the look in her sister's eyes.

CHAPTER THREE

Family togetherness and impending change brought Dar's father back to her again. That night she dreamed of him, young and darkly handsome. She was twelve, and they were standing on the dock in Menemsha Harbor, just a few miles away. The dream felt real as life, the details the same, the questions the same.

He'd come to America from Cork. He'd worked at boatyards from Southwest Harbor, Maine, to Tiverton, Rhode Island, always aiming to save money and make his way for a long stay on Martha's Vineyard. People teased him, saying fate had led him straight to Mathilda "Tilly" Daggett. He would come right out and say yes, it had, courtesy of King Charles I.

The tilt of Tilly's mother's chin said it all: she was convinced her son-in-law's attraction had been to Daggett's Way and not Tilly's heart. From Dar's youngest days she had picked up on friction between her grandmother and father. It made her want to defend him even when, on the outside, things seemed okay. The family would have dinner together. Her grandmother would ask her father to grill the steak. What should have been normal felt as if she was ordering him around. It didn't help, the way he'd pace her land after dinner, staring at the ground even after it was too dark to see anything.

Whether at the Vineyard or back home in Noank, Connecticut, her parents always argued about money. Whispers from their bedroom with the door closed, in the front seat of the car when they thought their daughters were asleep, and the way the dining room table was always covered with bills, just like a jigsaw puzzle, Tilly trying to figure out how to put it all together, Michael refusing to accept any help from his wife or her mother.

That Memorial Day had been the worst of all. Dar's parents had been separated for months. Her father had worked double-time, finishing the sailboat he'd been building for two years.

He'd used a friend's boathouse, across Menemsha Bight, a waterlogged shack that swayed with the tide. He'd taken the ferry alone to the Vineyard on winter weekends, leaving the family behind in Noank.

In spite of the separation, he took Tilly out for the first sail; Dar had watched her parents leave the harbor, heeling over as they sailed into Vineyard Sound and out of sight. The sky had been bright blue, no clouds. But by the time they returned, her mother was red-eyed, and her father looked set and determined.

"Was Mom crying?" Dar asked when her mother walked down the dock, leaving them alone.

He didn't answer, just checked on the lines, making sure they'd been properly cleated.

"Doesn't she like the boat?" Dar pressed.

"Of course she does," he said, gazing at his masterpiece: twenty-eight feet long, the hull and cabin painted oyster white; the mast, boom, and other brightwork varnished golden brown.

"This boat's not like the others you make," Dar said.

"Because she's our family's alone. I built her for us and not for pay."

Her father had taken Dar sailing before—but always on other people's boats. He was so good, they'd hire him to design and build their boats, then hire him again to teach them everything he knew about sailing and the sea.

"My grandfather would be proud and I don't say that lightly," he said.

"Why wouldn't you say it lightly?" Dar asked.

"Well, I don't like to brag. But I learned to be a carpenter in his shop, and no work was too fine for the old man. He could be critical. Very tough. But he taught me all his tricks. Will you look at that fairing?"

"Fairing?" Dar asked.

"Sanded so finely you can't see the seams."

"She's the most beautiful boat I've ever seen."

"Her name is *Irish Darling,* after my darling Dar."

"Really?"

He nodded. "Yes. And after your mother and sisters. With a name like that, she could easily sail from Menemsha to Cork," he said. "Across the Atlantic and straight into Kinsale Harbor."

"I want to go to Ireland," Dar said.

"You will, Dar. I promise, someday. Not this summer, but soon. Once I bring back the proof."

"The proof of what?"

"Of our birthright."

"I still don't get it, Daddy."

"Oh, it's a fairy tale about a troublemaker."

"Is the troublemaker bad?" Dar asked.

Her father laughed in a way that gave her chills and made her beam. Even at twelve, Dar had magical threads running through her veins, picking up every sensation and emotion in her family. When her father laughed, there was nothing better.

"No, not at all," he said. "Some of the best people are trouble-makers."

"Really?" she asked.

"Certainly."

"Can we go on board?" Dar said. Her father lifted her down from the dock and she went straight to exploring. She tried opening all the cabinets and hanging lockers, got the hang of the secret latch on each one. He'd sanded everything so carefully, made the wood fit even the tightest spots, painted the surface with glowing amber varnish, created narrow shelves above the berths so they would have a place to keep their books and notebooks and paints.

"Can you find the hiding place?" he asked.

"For a person to hide in?" she asked.

He laughed. "No. Smaller."

She'd looked in every drawer and cabinet, reaching back, closing her eyes, feeling for spots that weren't supposed to be there.

Again he'd laughed, watching her try to figure it out. Finally he showed her: the deck looked solid, made of teak and holly. But if you pressed one tiny square of wood, a block of floor lifted out, leaving a hole just deep enough to hide passports, tickets, tide tables, and a brass sextant.

"It's so cool," she said, hugging him, smelling the familiar mixture of smoke, sawdust, and varnish.

In the dream she felt him drifting away, not only his body but his mind, as if he had already left to cross the ocean, and Dar's chest ached, wondering how any document, no matter how important to him, could make him leave. She had woken up, sweating in a panic.

Most of the year, Dar's family lived in a cozy, gray-shingled, blue-shuttered house in the harbor town of Noank, Connecticut: a bus ride to school, a bike ride to the boatyard where her father worked. Her grandmother had bought the house for her parents soon after Dar was born.

But in Dar's artwork, their normal little house morphed. She wrote a series of graphic novels about Dulse, a girl whose father disappeared from her life—despite his promises—just as Dar's had from hers. Scenes of black, white, and gray; perpetual winter, dirty snow, ice across Mystic River and the contours of Noank Harbor.

The dream-house's windows overlooked a cove full of swans frozen into the ice. Dar floated through the rooms like a ghost, dissolved into vapor just as she had the day her parents separated. They didn't call it that; they just said he was going to sleep at the boatyard for a while. But Dar knew.

Then they said he was going to take a trip to Ireland. Dar had almost felt relieved. Maybe he could get that document and come home and everything would be better.

But things got worse and eventually fell apart. He sailed across the Atlantic, called once to say he'd made it to Ireland, and then never came home again.

Dar's bones had turned to water, and her skin had become as fragile as cobwebs. She had broken open, and she felt as if her heart had been stolen by one of the bald eagles that flew down from the Arctic every winter.

Their grandmother had come down to Noank from Boston. Dar remembered that she never cried or even looked sad—as if her mission was to lift the mood of her family, get them back on the right track, heal the children's sorrow, drinking endless cups of tea.

In Dar's dreams and her drawings of Dulse, her grandmother wore a crown. Her father used to complain about the Noank cottage, saying it wasn't the gift he so much minded, but the fact that his mother-in-law constantly reminded him from whom it had come—that he hadn't bought and paid for it.

Dar's dream spirit flew outside, down to the cove where she and her father had walked at night, to look up at the sky and learn about the stars. Lights glowed in town and the harbor, making the darkness hazy. He'd pointed out his favorite constellation, Orion, and she'd shown him hers, the Pleiades—sisters clustered together.

Waking suddenly before dawn, she forgot where she was and that she was solid, human, older than her father had been when he'd left. Andy slept beside her. She eased out of bed, pulled on jeans and a sweatshirt, grabbed a warm fleece blanket, and went outside to sit. Scup followed her, took a turn around the frost-coated yard, spread himself at her feet.

This was her discipline, morning and night. She sat on a low teak bench between the Hideaway and the beach path, watching the eastern sky lighten to lavender, bright stars swinging so low they seemed to brush the field and sea. It took time for her to settle, but finally she began to follow her breath, noticing as it went in and out. Soon she stopped noticing the cold and the sound of the waves breaking offshore.

Impermanence; all things must pass.

The need to accept the unacceptable had led her to this practice. She had been wild and sad, swinging back and forth, close to losing herself forever. She had done everything possible to numb herself, protect herself from the pain—drinking and taking refuge in her work, as if they could protect her from every loss, fear, and worry.

At first she'd wait until five to drink: a scotch while going over that day's work. Then wine with dinner, liter bottles of white wine, so many she'd started to feel ashamed about putting them out for collection. Scotch became vodka because it tasted cleaner and she hoped it would help what had become murderous hangovers.

Midnight phone calls she wouldn't remember; she'd wake in the morning and see her chicken-scratch handwriting on a pad beside the bed, unfamiliar area codes, illegibly doodled names. Once she'd hit redial, heard an old boyfriend's voice, and hung up softly, feeling mortified.

A heavy snowstorm when she shouldn't have been driving, arriving home after a Christmas party, tripping over a rock in the yard, waking up the next morning covered with snow. Left side of her face black and blue, temple cut with a line of frozen blood on her cheek, and instead of calling 911 she'd gone to the freezer for the Stoli, poured a tall glass and sat by the window staring at the whiteout.

But the worst part of drinking hadn't been the injuries, dramatic near-misses, embarrassing phone calls. It had been the long, slow loss of herself. Dar had cut herself off from friends, family, and life the best she could. She drank to feel alive, and then she drank to feel numb. There was no middle ground. Her hand began to tremble as she drew. Worst of all, the stories disappeared. Dulse went underground, and between hangovers and blackouts, Dar couldn't find her.

Sitting on the bench now, she wrapped the blanket tighter. With every breath she let her shoulders drop a little more. She found herself opening up, exposing her tender heart, feeling deep sadness. The contact was fresh and raw, but it was reality. For so long stillness had amplified her fears. She'd felt empty and alone, panicking and jumping up from the bench or cushion at the first painful feeling.

Two weeks after falling in the snow, she'd started going to Alcoholics Anonymous—a morning meeting at the hospital in Oak Bluffs. That was fifteen years ago. Andy had gotten sober there, too. Two people who needed solitude joining a group to save their own lives. Now Dar mixed it up, attending the early meeting less frequently. There were meetings all over the island, different times of day, whenever she felt like going.

When she was finished her meditation, the sky was deep blue. Standing, she stretched, and so did Scup. She went back inside the Hideaway to find Andy still asleep. She stared at him for a moment. They were both loners, had never tried to live together, but it thrilled her to see him in her bed.

She leaned down to kiss him, and he rolled over and pulled the covers back. He was long, weathered, with a sexy sideways grin, and he was hard. She stood by the bed, undoing her buttons, letting her clothes drop to the floor. He stared at her body, and she liked it.

He took her hand, pulled her into bed. He kissed her, one hand on the back of her head, then moved his mouth down her neck, shoulders, to her breasts. Her nipples tingled, and she could barely lie still. She eased her way down, took him in her mouth. He moaned, and she wanted to drive him crazy.

She felt him starting to come, and backed off. He was still on his back, so she climbed on top of him, so wet he slipped right inside her. He cupped her breasts in his rough hands, and she began to move in tight circles. She tried to slow down, but he wouldn't let her, and she didn't really want to. Arms thrown around his neck, she lowered her chest to his, moving her hips hard up and down. He made an aching sound and she did too as she felt everything inside her hot and melting.

She climbed under the covers and he wrapped them tight around her. They stared into each other's eyes. Andy had lines in his face and around his green eyes. His brown hair was going gray, but he still reminded her of the boy she'd grown up with. They'd hung out every summer, but it wasn't until five years ago that their friendship had become something more.

"Good morning," he said. "Did that just ruin your meditation?"

"Made it better."

"Last night you were talking in your sleep."

"What did I say?"

He smiled and shook his head. "Words I couldn't understand."

The language of Dulse, Dar thought. They climbed out of bed, took a shower together. She wanted to make love again, and it was obvious he did, too. But they had to get going.

"Can I take you for a ride before your sisters are up?" he asked when they'd dried off and gotten dressed. "Show you the stone wall?"

"Yes," she said, and they headed out.

He opened his truck door, and she and Scup climbed in. Andy drove out the driveway, tires crunching the frosty ground. He stopped at Alley's Store to pick up coffees, and Dar checked to see whether Harrison had replied to her note—he hadn't. Back in the truck, Andy headed down a private lane in West Tisbury.

Dar was silent. She needed to see Andy a lot, almost every night. But there were other times when she required solitude, when she had to go deep into herself, nature, and the memories that drove her work. On nights like that, she couldn't be with him. He was the same way. He needed his life alone in his pine cabin. It made her sad sometimes, that they couldn't give each other more.

He drove along, under a canopy of bare oak branches. The deeper woods were filled with tall pines. A vernal pool lay in a hollow, the still, dark water glistening with cold light.

Andy parked the truck, and Dar and Scup followed him down a path covered with pine needles and fallen leaves, taking care not to slip on the frosty surface. At the bottom was a rushing stream, icily coursing from a melting pond. They crossed the water, made their way up the opposite side, stood at the edge of a seemingly endless field.

"This was one of the original island farms," he said. "That's its millpond."

"Where's the house?" she asked.

"No house right now. Just a cellar hole and this pond. And the wall . . ."

"I suppose the new owner plans to fill the pond, maybe dig a swimming pool, and build a sprawling mansion bigger than the one he has in Greenwich."

"No mansion," Andy said. "He just wanted the wall repaired. Wait till you see."

They climbed the hill opposite the pond, and there it was, massive and sturdy stones cut from granite, covered with silver-green lichens and glistening frost. It looked as if it had been there forever, sprung from the glacier that had formed the Vineyard.

"Which part did you repair?" Dar asked, examining closely.

"You can't tell?" he asked. "Then I've done something good."

"You have," she said. "It looks entirely eighteenth century."

"Earlier," he said. "Sixteen hundreds."

"Wow, Andy. I can't tell the difference."

Andy took that in with some pride. Then, steering her through the cracked wooden gate, he said, "This is what I really wanted to show you."

She gazed down at a four-foot-diameter doughnut-shaped piece of granite. Kneeling down, she felt the rough surface.

"The millstone?" she asked.

"That's right," he said.

"What did they mill?"

He knelt down beside her, foraged around the wheel, held up a few petrified kernels of corn. "Big cornfield here, once stretching halfway back to Alley's. Of course, the property's been cut up half a dozen times. The untouched part right here is five acres."

He held her hand as they both got up. They heard Scup foraging through fallen oak leaves.

"Thanks for showing me all this," she said. "Especially now."

"I figured you needed to know there's still some parts of the island left untouched. Or almost so," he said, glancing at the wall and millstone.

He drove her back, dropped her in the farmhouse driveway. She kissed him for a long time, holding tight, wishing they could go back to the Hideaway. Instead she jumped out of the truck, and she and Scup ran toward the house.

CHAPTER FOUR

Delia stood at the kitchen sink, sipping coffee. She and Rory had stayed up late in their pajamas, talking by the fire. They'd remembered late nights long ago, parties that could last till dawn.

At Christmas and New Year's, the guests would gather round the big fireplace in the living room; hot July nights they'd spill out into the yard, drinking Tilly McCarthy's signature summer cocktail, Moët & Chandon mixed with fresh peach juice. Happy, lively times.

Delia peered out the kitchen window, glimpsed a white truck through the hedge. It pulled into the driveway, and Delia saw Dar kiss Andy and come toward the house.

"Good morning," she said, kissing Dar as she walked in. "Didn't Andy want to come in?"

"He had to get to work."

Dar poured herself coffee. Was it wrong of Delia to want Dar to have someone in her life? Not that everything with Jim ran smoothly, far from it, but it helped knowing someone was there, the person you loved and cared about, the one who loved you back.

"Are you okay?" Delia asked.

"Yes," Dar said.

Delia wondered. Was she really? Was it possible? They'd all been raised to think that marriage and children were the way. Their father leaving had done a good job of slicing Dar to pieces. Rory and Delia had been stronger, or somehow better able to seal it off. Practicality helped. Delia took out her checklist and years of their mother's bank statements, ready to get down to business.

"Are we ready for this?" Delia asked.

Dar shook her head.

"It has to be done. I've looked through every account, watched the balance fall as her health care bills piled up."

"I know, I was here," Dar said.

Delia felt hot, but she took a deep breath. Each sister had helped in her own way, but it was true: Dar had been present the whole time.

"Sorry," Dar said. "I didn't mean it that way. I just remember how hard it was to write the checks every month, seeing her money drain away. I was afraid it would run out before her heart stopped. We were lucky to be able to keep her at home till the end."

"I know how much it meant to her," Delia said. "Between you and the private duty nurses . . . She was lucky, Dar, wasn't she? To be able to stay here? To have had the means? Grandmother made so much possible, when you think about it."

"Yes," Dar said. "The other world." That's what they used to call it, their grandmother's big houses and proper ways.

"You know what I was remembering?" Delia asked. "Mom's parties. They were so wild and wonderful."

Dar leaned against the counter, arms folded. She wore skinny jeans and a long black sweater, and even though her dark hair was still damp, to Delia she looked raffishly elegant.

"Those parties were Mom's way of whistling in the dark," Dar said. "She never had them before Dad left, but afterwards she surrounded herself with as many people as she could, pulling her friends close so she could forget . . ."

Delia knew this was Dar's sacred territory. "Don't you think she forgot him long ago? They were separated by the time he left."

"No," Dar said. "She hoped he'd come back. I know she did."

You did, Delia wanted to say. For Delia and Rory, survival had meant accepting that their father wasn't coming home. He'd crossed the Atlantic—that much of the mystery had been solved.

Nearly a month after leaving the Vineyard, he'd called from the very edge of West Kerry, Ireland, where he'd sculled into an outermost harbor, rudder damaged and sails torn to shreds in a wild gale. One phone call home, one minute each for his wife, Rory, and Delia. Five minutes for Dar. And they never heard from him again. He'd made it to Ireland with still a fair way to sail to get around the treacherous coast to Cork, and that was all they knew.

"Dar . . ."

"It's okay," Dar said.

"All right, then," Delia said, tapping her pad. "Let's get down to this. It's waterfront property. The reassessments were brutal."

"Mom never anticipated how high they'd be."

"Do you think she knew before she died that we'd have to sell?"

"She dreaded it," Dar said. "But she was too weak to really deal; she wanted to believe we'd be able to keep this place forever."

Glancing at the accounts, a thought crossed Delia's mind: if they sold Daggett's Way, there would be money left over. She could use her share to help ease her family's financial strain, give Pete whatever he needed to get him back on the right track. Money didn't matter to her a bit, except for how it might help fix her family.

"I'm up," Rory announced, heading straight for the coffeepot. "Have you figured it all out without me? Good, let's go to the beach!"

"Good morning," Delia said.

"Sleep well?" Dar asked.

"Yes. I only called Jonathan once."

"Why'd you call him at all?" Delia asked.

Rory held the mug between her hands, blowing on the hot coffee. "Well, it's not as if the gallery is doing well in this economy, but I was thinking maybe we still had a painting of our own worth selling, to raise tax money. We don't."

"But it was a good excuse to call him," Dar said.

"Forget it, okay? What are we going to do about the money?"

"It's bad, you guys," Delia said, staring at the checkbook. "No matter how we figure it, there's not enough here. I guess we could talk to the tax assessor, try to work out a payment plan."

"With what?" Rory asked.

"I know," Dar said. "That's the problem."

"Look, it's not going to get solved this minute."

"It's not going to be solved at all," Delia said. "I'm just facing facts."

"Delia," Dar said.

"Stay calm, everybody," Rory said. "We need a break. What are we going to do today?"

"I thought we'd go see Harrison," Dar said.

"Oh, yeah," Rory said, and they all started to smile. "The day's shaping up already."

They left the kids home. Sylvia was fine with babysitting and taking a break from the adults. Dar took the long way, driving through Chilmark to Menemsha, out past the Coast Guard station and fish markets to the end of the road. A trawler chugged out of the harbor.

Across the white-capped bight was Lobsterville, a long, narrow sand spit where her family had picnicked on warm summer nights, waiting to watch the sun set and the moon rise. Dar and her sisters stared across the water at the broken, tilting pilings, remains of the dock from which their father had left.

"Now it's time to be happy," Rory said. "Don't forget—*happy*. No melancholic silences until the witching hour."

"I'm in sheer bliss," Delia said.

Dar glanced in the rearview mirror to see if she was being sarcastic. Rory, sitting beside her up front, lit a cigarette and blew out smoke rings.

Delia made a show of opening the back windows so the car was suddenly filled with chilly salt air. Dar had quit smoking at twenty, but it had been an early bond with Rory—that plus piercing each other's ears, numbing the lobes and outer edges with ice cubes, taking slugs of whiskey to kill the pain, and using a thick sewing needle to do the deed, then hanging tiny gold hoops bought in Oak Bluffs in each hole.

Dar made a U-turn at the dead end, drove back through Menemsha and Chilmark, through wooded back roads that led toward Oak Bluffs. The air smelled of bright pine and earthy oak. This was another land, removed from the beach, and from the towns. Nearly deserted except for the occasional cabin tucked back in the woods—one of which belonged to Andy—it felt remote and spooky.

"I can't see Harrison living back here," Rory said.

"Tell me he's bought forty acres, planning to build a replica of his parents' house in Edgartown," Delia said.

"Not quite," Dar said.

"He looked the same as ever at Mom's funeral," Rory said.

Dar pictured how he'd looked that day. Blue blazer, white shirt, yacht club tie, khakis, Top-Siders, heavier than ever, wiping away tears, mourning his "other mother."

Dar flipped on her signal, even though there was no traffic in either direction. She turned right just past a sign for Island Storage and then wound along a sandy road that led to rows of storage units.

"What's this?" Delia asked. "I thought we agreed not to store any of Mom's stuff."

"Exactly," Rory said. "Forget the side trip, and let's go see Harrison."

Dar drove in a looping zigzag, up a small hill. Narrow metal compartments lined the road, but as it climbed higher, the units became larger, built of concrete. Dar always got lost in here, but she spotted the satellite dish on top of one flat roof, aimed toward it, and found Harrison in a satin robe flopped like a beached whale on a hardware store folding webbed chaise longue.

"Welcome!" he said, clambering up.

"Holy fucking shit," Rory said, getting out of the car. "You've got to be kidding me."

Harrison welcomed her, and then Delia, pulling them into a huge Harrison-style hug.

The unit's overhead garage door was open, and Delia peered inside. Dar watched her take it in: the four-poster bed; three vintage guitars and two fiddles, gifts from someone he'd done some work for, hanging on the wall; an antique partners desk intricately carved with dolphins and scallop shells; the gilded chairs that had once adorned the living room of his parents' Beacon Hill apartment.

"Is this where you hide your family's treasures?" Delia asked.

"Hell no," Harrison said. "Didn't Dar tell you? It's where I live, baby."

"You live in a storage unit," Rory said in a flat voice.

"Yes!" Harrison said. "It costs a hundred dollars a month—fully tax deductible. Come on in."

"I can't believe it," Rory said. "This can't be real."

"I'm rich in many, many ways," he said in his deep baritone.

Dar trailed behind as Harrison showed her sisters his flat-screen TV, his computer, his small bathroom.

"How is this possible in a storage unit?" Delia asked.

"It's industrial, baby," he said. "Think loft space, Manhattan in the eighties. Light industry welcome. Electricity, running water. Satellite TV. I rent under the name of Thaxter Enterprises."

"Which does what?"

"Sails, drinks, and romances the ladies," he said.

Dar knew the first two were true, but it had been a while since Harrison had romanced anyone. He never complained, but she knew he had fallen far. He wasn't Icarus, but his father had been—gambling the old money away, melting his wings at the Monaco and Las Vegas roulette tables, crashing to earth.

After his father's sudden death, Harrison had been left with debts and the reality of his father's bank taking possession of the Boston apartment and the summer place on Water Street in Edgartown. He didn't advertise his financial situation; Dar was one of his few confidantes.

"But there's no shower," Delia said, looking into the bathroom.

"For that I go to the yacht club! Which is where I'm taking the McCarthy sisters for lunch right now. Just let me change."

Rory rode with Harrison in his navy blue panel truck, and Dar and Delia followed. Delia was full of questions, including how he managed to afford the yacht club if he was living in a place worse than a trailer park, and Dar kept telling her to ask Harrison. They drove down Main Street in Edgartown, past sea captains' white clapboard houses and the brick courthouse, boutiques and cafés.

Dar parked behind Harrison, who looked more jaunty than she'd seen him all winter, in chinos, a red polo shirt, and a dark green fleece she'd given him for Christmas. He clinked as he walked, pockets full of keys. When they got to the yacht club, Delia shook the gate, puzzled.

"It's closed," she said, disappointed. "I forgot—it closes for the winter, doesn't it?"

"Reopens in May," Harrison said, his tone jolly. "The commodore left the water on so I can shower."

He used a key to unlock the gate, held it open for the sisters, and guided them onto the sun-drenched dock. They sat in a row, legs dangling over the harbor, just as they'd done as kids waiting for sailing lessons, and then regattas. Dar noticed Harrison snuggling close to Rory; it was an open secret, the fact he had always loved her.

"Guess we can't have lunch if it's closed," Delia said.

Harrison reached into his fleece pockets and pulled out three half-pint bottles of Benedictine and Brandy. "Lunch!" he said. "Sorry, Dar."

"No problem," she said, watching them all unscrew the caps and clink.

"To all the good times," Rory said, staring into Harrison's eyes.

"Yes," Dar said, but Delia bowed her head.

"I'll have none of that!" Harrison said, jostling her. "No sadness on my dock. So our parents spent all the money, taxes ate up my house and are about to eat up yours, but so what? The sunshine is free, the harbor is free—well, except for moorings. Don't let the taxman get you down! Rent the unit next to me. The beaches don't care if you live on the waterfront or you live on the light industrial way. Summer is coming."

"But how do you afford your 'home' and your club?" Delia pressed.

"Man with a van, baby," he said. "I still specialize in delivering rare instruments. Surprising number of collectors here on the island. Just last week I had a vintage Martin guitar, 000-45, tiny little thing worth a fat six figures, on the seat beside me."

"Did you strum it?" Rory asked. "Come on, I know you did."

"Hell yeah! Sounded about as sweet as a guitar can sound. Even though I can't play."

"Who bought it?" Delia asked.

"A guy in DC, big house off Embassy Row. Works for the government by day, gigs at the Hawk and Dove by night."

"So cool, love," Rory said. "This is genius. Getting drunk together like the old days. Before lunch, no less, on the day before we have to start packing."

"Look," Dar said, pointing overhead. A pair of snowy egrets flew low to the water, on their way to Chappaquiddick. They raised up to clear the *On Time*, the small ferry plying the channel between Edgartown and Chappy, then disappeared behind scrub pines.

"Dad," Rory said, setting her bottle down.

"Do you remember?" Dar asked.

"I remember your dad," Harrison said. "He was the coolest. Knew more about boats than anyone."

"He'd tell us stories about egrets," Dar said. She fell silent, wondering if her sisters had the same memories. He would sit on the porch steps, staring out at the salt pond. At the edge of the sparkling water were shorebirds, and his favorites were the lanky, gawky blue herons and snowy egrets.

He'd make up stories about egrets who fell in love for life, migrated down dangerous air currents to the West Indies, returning to the same pond every summer. He said they recognized the McCarthys, and their offspring did, and they would never forget—the snowy egrets of Chilmark Pond and the McCarthy family were connected by love and history forever.

"Why would he tell us stories like that," Delia said quietly, "and then just sail off?"

"He meant to return," Rory said. "With his Holy Grail, or whatever."

"His 'birthright,' " Delia said.

"What good was it to him if he bottomed out on a shoal?" Rory asked.

"Your father was a great sailor," Harrison said, gulping half his bottle, putting his arm around Rory. "Here's to Michael McCarthy, no matter where he may be!"

"Cheers to him," Rory said.

"I still remember sailing with him," Harrison said.

Dar felt herself levitating. She saw the scene as Dulse would, and when she returned home, she would write and illustrate it verbatim. The boy of privilege who lived in a storage unit; three sisters haunted by the father who had sailed away and never returned.

Two more egrets flew across the harbor, this time toward Katama. As in Dar's life, egrets played a strong role in her graphic novels. They were known as messengers, all-knowing spirits, pure of heart, with long white necks, bright eyes, and black bills and legs.

Dulse sometimes flew on their backs, letting the strong white birds fly her over low hills covered with silver sage and purple heather, into caves lining sea lochs, searching for fishing nets caught on the craggy rocks. Dulse pulled the nets into the sunlight, combed through them for fish bones, whale baleen, iridescent jingle shells, mother-of-pearl, anything that sparkled. Luminosity, whether in the sky or waves or objects delivered by the sea, always delivered a message to Dulse from her father.

"Dar, are you awake?"

She opened her eyes, saw her sisters and Harrison gazing at her.

"What did I miss?" she asked.

"Nothing," Harrison said. "Absolutely nothing. We're drinking in the sun, and we're together. Life is good. Isn't it?"

They all smiled, answer enough.

CHAPTER FIVE

The next morning a fog bank rolled in from the east, melting the last frost and coating cobwebs with silver drops of water, making the house and everything in it damp and chilly. Today was packing day. Coffee percolated, the teakettle whistled, and Dar lit the woodstove.

Delia, Dar, and Rory's children hauled the boxes from various hiding places. Sylvia and Obadiah were in charge of putting the moving-company boxes together with heavy-duty tape. Jenny sat on the kitchen floor with Vanessa, tearing newspaper into smaller squares, perfect for wrapping the smallest items.

"We should separate boxes and write our names on them," Delia said. "So we know who's getting what."

"I would like the duck decoys," Obadiah said quietly.

"I think your grandmother would want that," Dar said.

"Where's your mother, anyway?" Delia asked Obadiah.

"Uh, talking to Dad on the phone," he said.

"She found something really incriminating in his e-mail!" Jenny said.

"What do you mean?" Dar asked.

"Rory hacks into his e-mail," Delia said.

"What did she find?" Obadiah asked.

"That he and A-L-Y-S were having an *affair* even before he moved out," Jenny said, her whole body shivering with a sob. "I can't stand saying her name, so I *spell* it!"

"Oh, honey," Dar said, hugging her.

"It's terrible," Jenny wept.

"What is terrible?" Rory asked, tearing into the room.

"Nothing," Obadiah said quickly, as if wanting to protect her.

"No secrets. Tell me."

"*You* have secrets!" Jenny said, her voice rising toward hysteria.

"Aunt Dar said I could have the duck decoys!" Obadiah cried out, making such a heartbreakingly desperate attempt to change the subject he began to shake.

"Your father probably has plenty of duck decoys," Rory said. "In his parents' house just a mile from here. I'm sure he'd let you use them."

Obadiah turned as if she'd slapped him, sensitive to his parents' breakup and the tensions of his mother and aunts. Jenny sobbed as her brother ran from the kitchen. Then Rory exhaled hard and went after him.

Dar stoked the woodstove, trying to warm the room. Everyone's grief was heavier than fog. Her heart cracked, one more window in an old house being broken. She looked around, reading the room as a cautionary love story—the old oak and maple furniture, the paintings, drawings the girls had done when they were little, shells collected on beach walks, stored in old glass milk bottles. Their mother and grandmother had thrown away nothing.

For Dulse, man-made objects meant nothing. She foraged the beach and woods for shells and pebbles. Iridescence poured from the sky, through silver-edged clouds, turning shell and bone into treasure, and she absorbed her lost father's love through her fragile skin.

Looking around the kitchen, Dar knew that "things" mattered. Sea glass, channeled whelks, and driftwood gathered on family walks were just as important as other family heirlooms. She took a deep breath; they had to start somewhere. She reached for a small pewter dory on a mahogany shelf above her grandmother's spoon collection, then held the boat up. "Who would like this?"

No one spoke. Dar supposed they all harbored secret wishes, their own private desires for a piece of this paradise. Rory walked in, arm around Obadiah. Both mother's and son's blue eyes were bereft. *I hate myself*, Rory mouthed silently to her sisters.

"Here's an idea," Delia said. "What if we took pieces of masking tape, wrote our names on them, and put them on whatever we want?"

"What if two people want the same thing?" Jenny asked.

"We'll duel," Delia said.

"We could play darts and the winner gets it," Rory said.

Everyone approved the masking tape idea. As they spread throughout the big old farmhouse, Dar put James Taylor on the kitchen stereo and turned on all the house speakers. She was still holding the small dory; it felt warm in her hand. Her father had left it here; he'd once told her it came from his grandfather's boat shed in Cork. She wrote her name on a piece of masking tape and stuck it on.

The third day of packing, Rory went to her old room and looked around. The brass bed, the patchwork quilt, the chest of drawers she and Dar had painted with mermaids and whales, one of her grandmother's handmade rugs braided from their cast-off wool skirts and jackets, a framed watercolor her mother had done of Rory and her sisters playing on the beach. She sat down heavily. Being in this house made her feel even more tied to Jonathan.

They'd hung out together in groups one whole summer, but they'd fallen in love at a beach bonfire, far out on the acres of private dunes and pristine beach known as Squibnocket Associates. There were only one hundred member families, and Jonathan's and Rory's were two of them.

Kids clustered around the fire, including Harrison, Delia, and a bunch of friends. The moon had risen, spilling silver over the waves, onto Nomans Land, the island just offshore. Rory stood on the tide line, ankle deep in frothy water.

She felt Jonathan before she saw him. He stood so close, his breath on her neck like a warm breeze.

"What are you looking at?" he asked.

"Nomans Land," she said.

"The navy used it for bombing practice," he said.

"As if I didn't know. I live right down the beach."

"I know where you live," he said. He put his arm around her

waist and led her away, as if from danger. They walked a hundred yards, bare feet in the effervescent white wash, far enough from the group that the fire's crackle was lost in the sound of waves. Glancing back once, she saw the glow. A few minutes later, Jonathan eased her down onto the hard sand.

He held her face in his hands, stared deeply into her eyes. She laughed nervously as if they were playing at being older than they were, but he didn't even smile. He pushed the hair back from her face, caressed her cheek, lowered his mouth to hers.

The kiss was so hot, she nearly cried out. He reached under her embroidered cotton top, and she felt his hand on her breast. Second base, and he was turning her inside out, nerve endings sizzling. The waves washed up to their knees, tide coming in. Next thing she knew, they were doused with salt water, laughing.

"Oops," he said.

"Didn't see that one coming," she said.

They crawled up the beach, fumbled with each other's shorts. Jonathan wasn't wearing underwear, and she was startled, fascinated, and slightly grossed out.

"Is this your first time?" he asked, lying on top of her, his scalding hot erection pressed against her belly.

She nodded, wondering whether it was his first time too, holding back the question because she knew somehow it wasn't.

"You're more beautiful than any girl on the island."

"What a line," she said.

"You don't believe me?"

She didn't respond, and he kissed her lips. He pushed himself inside her, and she thought she would split in half. But then it started to feel good in a sparkly-creepy way, and she bit her lip until she tasted blood. The chilly sea breeze blew across their soaked bodies, but his chest was hot as he held her tight.

From that moment on, Rory was in love. They stayed together through his graduations from Deerfield and Trinity, hers from Fitch High School and Connecticut College, with a major in marine biology.

He cheated on her. At the end of that very first summer, with a nanny for a family in West Chop. In prep school, with a Miss Porter's girl who'd gone to Deerfield for a dance. At Trinity, with his pretty art history teaching assistant. Rory knew.

She had a way of figuring it all out. He'd sound different on the phone, look sheepish when they saw each other, touch her tentatively as if expecting to be slapped down.

She'd go through his pockets, wallet, datebook, address book. When she'd find a new girl's name written in, or tickets to a play or movie he hadn't told her about, or a cocktail napkin with a stupid haiku written on it, she'd hate him. She'd confront him, and she'd cry—and he'd soothe her, saying the girl had come on to him, he'd tried to resist, it meant nothing.

She broke up with him "for good" the October after college graduation. She couldn't bear the worry and piercing sense of betrayal. They'd get together for brief interludes, but her lack of trust was strong, and he felt constantly scrutinized and attacked. Three summers later they broke up again "for good."

Loneliness for him made Rory feel desperate, as if she'd be alone forever. It was the worst feeling, as if she were hollow, as if she didn't even exist without someone to love her.

That's the state she'd been in when she met Alex, a Brazilian fisherman on a boat at Menemsha, where she had gone to make

notes on the fishery, hoping to get into a graduate program at
Scripps. Alexander Fortuna was very tall, lean, tan, serious. He
appeared brooding, but when he looked at Rory, his black eyes
were so sexy, his smile so bright. He planned to use his fishing
money for med school, to become a surgeon. He'd already graduated from UMass-Dartmouth, the first member of his family to
get a college degree.

She'd been intrigued, wanted to fall in love. Alex was tender,
treated her as if she was brilliant. He encouraged her desire to go
to graduate school, something Jonathan had never done.

Between Alex's fishing trips to Georges Bank, Rory got pregnant with Sylvia. When he returned, he began looking for houses
on the island. They rented a tiny one owned by his fishing boat
captain, on the hill facing Menemsha Harbor. She had Sylvia, and
tried so hard to love her life with Alex, but it didn't work: she still
loved Jonathan.

By then, Jonathan's parents couldn't stand her. But Rory's
sisters and mother were behind her, no matter what. They'd
adored Alex, but her grandmother had never stopped pushing
for Jonathan. She had liked the idea of two Vineyard power clans
being united—the Daggetts and the Chases. She dismissed the
McCarthy connection, negating Rory's Irishness. Rory would
marry Jonathan, and the children would be WASPs through and
through.

Abigail Daggett negotiated things out with Jonathan's parents,
and Rory and he had a Vineyard wedding under a white tent at
Daggett's Way, with the after-party on the same private beach
where she'd lost her virginity. They lived summers on the island,
winters in Old Lyme, where Jonathan, initially bankrolled by his

parents, opened an art gallery specializing in the Old Lyme school of American Impressionists and Tonalists.

Once they got married, he seemed to settle down and be faithful and content. He was good to Sylvia. Rory remained on guard the first few years, keeping the idea of study at Scripps in La Jolla as an escape hatch, until Obadiah and Jenny were born. She fell into bliss, raising her children in the village.

She walked them to school, later taught them to ride their bikes to the tennis courts. She'd walk to Jonathan's gallery nearly every day to bring him lunch. It was her idea for the gallery to branch out, showing contemporary landscape and portrait artists, having openings that would attract the entire town.

She didn't know when the cheating began again. He swore it hadn't happened until Alys started as gallery intern, just over a year ago. The market had fallen apart, and Jonathan had said they were lucky to have someone willing to work for next to nothing. Rory had agreed; she'd liked Alys at first.

Young, blond, newly graduated from a curatorial master's program at Bard, Alys was smart and brought new ideas about hanging and marketing exhibitions. And then Jonathan took her to New York's Winter Antiques Show at the Park Avenue Armory, a weeklong must-attend event for art and antique dealers. He'd always had a booth.

Rory checked his pockets when he got home. She found a receipt from the St. Regis Hotel—deluxe room plus dinner for two, champagne in the room, and room service breakfast for two. The sight of it had made her eyes swim. She couldn't believe it, had been so sure he'd never hurt her again.

When she confronted Jonathan, he didn't deny it. He told her he was moving out; he and Alys had found a place in Hadlyme. It was just a few miles up the Connecticut River; he could see the children every weekend.

"You can't! They aren't ready for you and a girlfriend, Jonathan. Neither am I," Rory had said. He told her that if she was unreasonable about the kids, he could get a court order for temporary shared custody. But he backed off.

Rory was blindsided by all of it. She fell back into her old ways of spying on him; tracking him silently, through e-mails and texts, gave her a feeling of warped power. She'd known his passwords for years; he had kept them under his blotter on the antique rolltop desk her grandmother had given him when they'd gotten married.

Now her laptop sat innocently on the unmade bed. It called her as if she were possessed. Glancing into the hall, she saw that Delia was in her room, Sylvie in hers. She heard Obadiah and Jenny talking to Vanessa in the master bedroom. Safe.

Rory logged on, then typed in Jonathan's Gmail password: *keithfarm*. Keith Farm, one of the most lovely, wide-open landscapes on the Vineyard; his parents lived just up Middle Road from the property, and Jonathan had played in the fields as a boy.

Always careful to leave no trace behind, Rory read only the e-mails he had already opened. When she found incriminating messages, she would call him and somehow get him to confess without actually confronting him. It was as if his conscience was so guilty he had to tell her the truth.

Now, clicking on the morning's e-mails, she saw that he and Alys had written back and forth five times since she'd called him, yelling that he was terrible, terrible to abandon his family just as their son was at the age to need a father most. And Jenny! Who would she have as a male role model? Some loser who leaves his family for a younger woman?

What a bitch, Alys had written in response to Jonathan's heart-felt—Rory had to admit—account of their phone call. She felt herself shaking all over, burning with rage so great she could barely control her fingertips; they tapped the air above the keys, imagining a message of hate to Alys.

"Are you busy?" Dar asked, glancing in.

"Uh, no," Rory said, slamming her laptop shut.

"What did the e-mail say?" Dar asked.

Rory just shook her head. "Don't get me started talking about her."

"Alys?" Dar asked.

"Yep."

"Can I ask you something?"

"Sure."

"Why do you do it?"

"Do what?"

"Read their e-mail."

"Because he's too stupid to change his passwords. It's almost like *asking* me to read them. I pity the fool."

"But he's *not* asking you to," Dar said. "You're worrying me."

"Please don't. This is just terrible to get through, and I'm doing my best."

Dar held out her hand, small and shaped just like Rory's, Delia's, and their mother's. Rory hesitated, then took it. They clasped fingers. Their hands fit perfectly, and the feeling was exactly as it had been when they were girls.

"Hello!" came the voice from downstairs. "Helloooooo! May we come in?"

Dar turned red, dropping Rory's hand. "Shit, I told her to keep them away from us."

She jumped off the bed, running down the stairs, Rory and Delia following close behind.

In the kitchen, surrounded by the children, stood two well-dressed women and two well-dressed men. Delia summed them up immediately; they were all from Greenwich, or Bedminster, or Chevy Chase, or some other fancy suburb. As she watched in true disbelief, Dar grabbed the elbow of the pageboy blonde in the beige suite and strong-armed her out of the kitchen, leaving Delia and Rory to make polite small talk with the other three strangers.

"I hope it's not inconvenient," the other woman—even blonder, wearing obnoxious country clothes—beige wool pants and jacket, brown jodhpur boots, and a large russet leather shoulder bag with PRADA in big gold letters. "I believe Morgan tried to contact you, but wasn't able to get a reply. And this was the only week all three of us could come!"

"Morgan?" Rory asked, sounding suspicious.

"Please, blame it on me," the tall, thin, bald man said in a clipped English accent. He wore a tailored black suit, had pale eyes and strangely dominant upper teeth. "It would have been impossible for me to come from London at any other time and still remain on schedule."

"I feel as if I'm Alice in Wonderland," Delia said, smiling and offering her hand. "I have no idea what anyone is talking about. I'm Delia Monaghan, and this is my sister Rory Chase."

"Delia—" Rory began.

"We're the Littles," the not-so-bald man said, "and this is our architect, Jeremy Stent."

"Architect?" Delia said, still smiling, not understanding. She felt enveloped by the fog outside, as if it had entered the kitchen and swallowed her up. At the same time, her hands were shaking, as if they perceived something her brain was yet unable to face.

"Morgan *said* it would be all right," Mrs. Little said. "We really had no other choice. The children are on school vacation." She pointed out the window at two towheaded boys jumping up and down and running in excited circles. "And Jeremy has to be in Milan on Tuesday."

"But why are you *here*?" Delia asked as Dar and the now stone-faced pageboy blonde returned to the kitchen.

"I should have told you," Dar said, turning toward Delia and Rory. "I ignored the calls and e-mails, but Morgan brought her clients and their architect anyway. I'd hoped we could finish with our part before moving on to theirs . . ."

"You mean . . ." Delia started. She stared at her sister so she wouldn't immediately blow up at the strangers.

"You remember Morgan Ludlow," Dar said. "Of Island Properties. She sold our house, and these are the people who bought it."

Delia felt her blood pressure spike. To her shock, she managed to contain the fury inside. She just went to Morgan Ludlow, gently took her by the shoulders, and turned her toward the kitchen door.

"I'm sorry," Delia said, eyes on the Littles and Jeremy Stent. "But this really isn't a convenient time. It just isn't."

"But," Mrs. Little said, glowering at Morgan Ludlow, "why would you have told us it would be fine if it wasn't?"

"Please, Dar," Morgan said as Delia pushed her forward. "This man flew all the way from London!"

"And he's going to tear down our house," Dar said.

"It's up to the Littles what they wish to do with the property . . ." Morgan said.

"We get the point," Dar said. "But for now it still belongs to us, and my sister's right. The timing isn't convenient."

Delia felt so proud of Dar—of them—the three McCarthy sisters, for sticking up for what was theirs. At least until the closing at the end of the month.

"What if the deal falls through now?" Rory asked once the strangers had left.

"I don't give a shit," Dar said. "I hope it does."

"So do I," Delia said. "I'd almost rather have the IRS get it."

The kids had hidden away, but sensing the suddenly improved mood, they returned to the kitchen asking questions. Maybe someone answered them; Delia just picked up Vanessa and held her tight. Dar cranked James on the stereo. Out the window, they saw Jeremy pacing the yard, taking notes, as if figuring out how much of the ground he could cover with construction. Morgan's large black SUV sat idling on the sandy driveway.

Dar made tomato soup and grilled cheese sandwiches. Everyone ate, agreeing it was the perfect lunch for a foggy day. Delia replayed the moment she'd put her hands on that woman's shoulders and wished she could do it all over again.

She wanted to call Jim and tell him every detail. She wanted to call Pete, tell him what he'd missed. Rory poured everyone a Diet Coke, and they all raised their glasses to toast one another. When Delia glanced out the window, the black SUV was gone.

CHAPTER SIX

Every night they would cook all their favorite island food from local markets. Each day one of the sisters took shopping duty: Menemsha Fish Market, Tisbury Farm Market, Fiddlehead Farm, Cronig's, Larson's Fish, Shiretown Meats, Soigné in Edgartown.

They'd make broiled sole, creamed spinach, tiny new potatoes. Raclette with Gruyère cheese and more new potatoes, salad with baby greens, pumpkin seeds, and pomegranate seeds. Lamb chops with rosemary potatoes and homemade mint sauce. Grilled swordfish, broccoli rabe sautéed with garlic, black quinoa mixed with chopped tomatoes. Dar would drink Pellegrino, and Rory and Delia would split a bottle of wine.

These meals were both comforting and delicious, especially for the time they spent cooking and eating and cleaning up together. As the week went on, the quality of food remained as high as ever. But the sisters, and even the kids, started to droop from all the packing. They knew what was coming. And even delicious food couldn't drive it away.

One night Dar skipped dinner with her sisters. She just felt too dusty, and cold, and old. She had spent another whole day boxing up childhood and family memories. Her back and shoulders ached, her hands felt rough and sore, and her entire body was coated with a thin, sticky film of dust. She stood twenty minutes under the hottest shower possible, washing her hair and just letting the water pour over her.

Closing her eyes, she thought of the mystery of water, of how it surrounded the island and created deep glacial pools, and how the fog was a cloud that hadn't rained yet, how water had been the inspiration for Dulse.

She turned off the taps, dried herself, and put on a black V-neck T-shirt and loose black cotton pants. Sitting down, she stared in an unfocused way at the miniature metal dory that had come from her great-grandfather's boathouse in Cork.

She reached for her storyboard notebook. Her mind swirled with ideas, inspired by the pain and delights of the day: finding their grandmother's Kewpie dolls wrapped in baby blankets, in an intricately carved hope chest. The visiting architect was a reminder that things would change, and soon. Dar had decided to create a character after him, a dark lord named Argideen after an Irish river near Timoleague in West Cork.

Staring at the blank page, she could almost see her characters coming alive. The sheets of opaque white vellum paper were eight and a half by eleven inches, glued on the left side. The ink forming six cells per page, a grid and notation area within each cell, was non-photo blue so that the grid lines could be eliminated when scanned into graphics software.

She always started with pencil sketches, favoring yellow Bic mechanical pencils with .5 or .7 lead. Long ago her mother had bought her a beautiful pair of Mont Blanc pencils, and although Dar felt sentimental about the gift, she loved the way the cheaper pencil fit her hand, and the way Bic erasers never smudged.

After sketching, she'd start her line art by going in with Pigma Sensei Manga drawing pens—archival quality, and shipped from Japan—using thicker strokes for foreground and thinner lines for background. After inking, she would erase the pencil.

Dar was considered ballsy among graphic artists for working in real, not digitalized, color; few did it, because one mistake could ruin the entire page. She'd color each panel with Prismacolor markers, light to dark, mainly shades of blue. In recent years she'd started using watercolor more often. The medium seemed more appropriate to characters and story involving so much water.

Then she'd go back in with small-gauge, .2 or .3 Sakura Micron pens and crosshatch the shadows—markings so small, readers wouldn't see the lines, only sense the change of depth in the color.

Each of the six panels represented a specific aspect of the day, translated into Dulse's world. This was the first reunion of Dulse and her sisters in over a century. Because Dulse was a water spirit, motivated by grief and desire, she was very powerful. She had the ability to float overhead like a cloud, or seep through floor cracks like spilled water.

Her sisters had been under a hundred-year spell cast by their grandmother. Where was this coming from? Dar wondered as she drew. Only Dulse had been aware of their father's loss, searching for him all this time. He'd had something to prove, only he'd disappeared before telling anyone what that was. Her sisters had been turned into *Rosa rugosa*, beautiful beach roses—soft pink with green leaves and sharp thorns, lining the dunes.

Once Dulse found out, from a letter hidden in her grandmother's ebony desk, she focused all her power into rain, pouring down on the roses, washing dunes into the sea, allowing raging ocean waves to devour the beach and grab at the roses' deep, gnarled roots. The roots turned into two girls' feet, and Dulse's sisters, Heath and Finn, came back to life. Dulse coalesced into a water column, and then a girl, and she and her sisters hugged.

The next frame showed them back at their grandmother's Vineyard house. Because their grandmother was dead, the sisters would be safe there. Why was she—or her subconscious—suddenly so suspicious of her grandmother? Heath buried her bare feet in garden soil, and Finn asked for elixir made from fermented honeysuckle nectar.

Dar sat back, staring at the room she'd drawn—familiar yet alien. It looked as if it belonged in their real house—decorated in period furniture with faded cotton curtains and their grandmother's braided rugs, books in the bookcase, a stone fireplace with chimney cupboards, a wide hearth, and copper washbasin to hold kindling—yet Dar had never seen it before.

She chalked it up to dreams and imagination, and began to draw a black SUV in the yard, Argideen making his first appearance in her series. She drew him exactly as he had looked: tall, slim but muscled, bald, dressed in a Hong Kong–tailored black suit. She gave him insipid brown, almost yellow, eyes.

Dusk was falling, the last light glowing red through the mist. She heard Andy's truck on the gravel and went out to meet him. He'd been building bookcases and painting the interior of a house on Edgartown's South Summer Street, and when he kissed her he smelled of sawdust, paint, and turpentine. His painter pants and boots were stained pale, spring green.

"They're going authentic?" Dar asked.

"Yep," he said. "They went to the Historical Society to make sure their dining room walls would be in keeping with pre-colonial Edgartown."

"Rich people," she said, smiling.

"They pay my bills," he said, holding her hand, leading her to the porch. "I wish I could help you with everything."

"Oh, Andy."

"You know I'd do anything."

"I know."

They sat in the tall rocking chairs, and Dar stared out over the pond. Past the dunes, she saw waves cresting, their foam tops lavender in the twilight. Andy took her hand. They hardly ever mentioned love, but their long friendship was layered with it. She felt his closeness, and that was enough.

"Tough day?" Andy asked.

Dar nodded.

"Did you finish the first floor?"

"Pretty much. That was our goal. Some of the upstairs bedrooms, too."

"Want me to come over and help tomorrow?"

She smiled. "You have a job."

"That I do," he said. He had a wonderful, deep voice, and

sometimes he would sing to her. She was about to ask, when she heard the first sounds drifting down from Abel's Hill, up from the trees surrounding Chilmark Cemetery, from deep woods and swamps and millponds all over the island.

"Pinkletinks!" she said.

He listened and nodded. "You're right," he said.

Spring peepers: tiny tree frogs whose song sounded like tinkling bells, for one brief period in April. Only on the Vineyard were they called "pinkletinks," a name dating back to the 1600s, when Bartholomew Gosnold, the English explorer, discovered the island and named it for his daughter Martha.

Dar closed her eyes, listening to the chorus. She'd felt a little bad about not having dinner with her sisters, but now she imagined them a short walk away, hearing the same song. It united them, and she imagined them being delighted. She held Andy's hand, rocking on the front porch, listening to the peepers' high, throbbing call.

"Would you like to go to a meeting?" he asked.

"I would," she said, and got her sweater.

That night spring woke up. After dinner Rory and Delia stepped into the yard with all the kids, listening to the pinkletinks. They stood still, silent, and then everyone suddenly exploded into trying to make the same sounds: high, exuberant, trebly voices calling back to the frogs. Jenny did cartwheels and Obadiah started running around the yard, discharging tons of cooped-up energy.

"Grab your sweaters," Rory said, heading for the station wagon. "We're taking a ride!"

She and Delia sat up front, Obadiah next to Vanessa and her doll in the car seat in back, and Silvy and Jenny in the way-back third seat. Rory rolled the window down, elbow cocked outside, letting everyone savor the salt air.

At first she aimed toward Edgartown, but when she neared the airport road, she glanced at Delia.

"Detour?" she asked.

"Do you think he's there?"

"I have a feeling,"

"Where are we going?" Sylvia called as soon as she realized they were bouncing down a rutted side road.

"To pick up a surprise guest."

Rory followed the same route Dar had used, winding down the sandy pine road, turning in to the storage park, driving to the last unit on the top of the low hill. It was dark now, and she couldn't make out light coming from any of the units. But through the open car window she heard the faint sound of a baseball game.

"What is this place?" Obadiah asked, looking around. "It's kind of weird."

"Mom, it's deserted," Sylvie said.

"No, honey," Rory said. "We're here to visit Uncle Harrison."

"Yay!" Obadiah yelled, undoing his seat belt.

"This might be a mistake," Delia whispered. "Dropping in at night, unannounced, with the kids?"

"How would we announce?" Rory asked. "He doesn't have a phone." The kids were all out of the car by the time she caught a faint whiff of pot smoke. Delia made sure to slam all the doors loudly, and Rory walked over to the garage door and banged.

"Are you in there?" she called. "Your gang of admirers has come to kidnap you."

Silence. Not even the baseball game; he'd turned off the TV and was hiding inside. Then she heard two squirts from an aerosol can, clearing out the evidence. A minute later the heavy metal door was rolled up, and Harrison stood silhouetted by the blue light of his muted flat screen.

"Well, well," he said. "If it isn't my favorite gang of admirers."

"You have more than one?" Obadiah asked, grinning.

"Hah! Many more," Harrison said. "You're the third gang to stop by tonight alone."

"Why are you here?" Jenny asked.

"Here?" Harrison asked, drawing out the word as if it were the strangest thing to be asked. "I live here."

"No," Jenny said. "You live in the big white sea captain's house in Edgartown."

"With the dock!" Obadiah said. "Where you keep your boat."

Harrison gave a dismissive wave. "Anyone can live in a big white house with a dock. This is much cooler."

"It is, actually," Sylvia said, glancing inside.

"Uncle Harrison," Jenny said. "It's like a storage unit."

"Well, you're right," he said. "Many people would call it that. I prefer to call it 'home.' Would you care to come inside and watch the ball game? Red Sox versus Yankees. And I have pretzels and beer."

"We can't drink beer," Obadiah said.

"Well, you can eat pretzels, can't you?" Harrison asked.

Rory took his hand. "You're coming with us. We're heading into town for ice cream."

His eyes widened. Harrison had never been known to decline ice cream. He smacked his lips, and the kids all laughed. He wore shorts and a T-shirt, but he went inside to get a fleece and a pair of flip-flops. Everyone stood back while he pulled down the garage door.

"Stealth move," he said. "Know what I mean, Obadiah?"

"No."

"It means you don't want anyone to know you live here," Sylvie said.

"That's right, baby," Harrison said, giving her a high five. "I'm under the radar up here."

"Is it illegal?" Sylvie asked.

"What an unpleasant word. Let's not use it. Let's just say I wouldn't want this place catching on, everyone else moving in. I like it nice and private."

"It is private," Delia said.

"And so dark and quiet," Rory said, admiring the stars and the beam of Edgartown light sweeping across the sky.

"I'm riding shotgun," Harrison said, climbing in front.

Delia didn't argue, squeezing in with Obadiah and Vanessa. Rory felt Harrison take her hand after she started up the car. She glanced over, saw him grinning at her.

"Except for the fact I have three kids in back," Rory said, "this feels *so* much like old times."

"Who loves ya, baby?" Harrison asked.

As Rory backed the car around, the headlights swung low across a thicket of brush. Something gleamed in the brambles, and for an instant she thought she'd caught the eyes of a deer. But then she recognized the intelligent, dignified, familiar face of Harrison M. Thaxter, Sr., and knew she was looking at the infamous bronze bust.

She saw Harrison salute in his father's direction as they pulled away, and Rory waved, too. Harrison turned the radio on; the local station was playing reggae. He began to bop his head and sing along to "Breakfast in Bed."

"And a kiss or three . . . nothing need be said . . . no need," he sang, making the kids laugh for absolutely no reason at all except for the fact it was Harrison. Rory headed into Edgartown, parked on Water Street. She'd been holding her breath to see whether Mad Martha's was open yet for the season, and it was.

They went through the usual ritual of deciding what flavor to have, entertaining new options, but ordering old favorites: mint Oreo cream, mango sorbet, buttercrunch, sinful chocolate. Everyone but Harrison got double-scoop cones, and he asked for an extra-large hot fudge sundae with five cherries.

"Mmm," he said as they walked down Main Street toward the town dock. "Still as good as when you girls worked there."

"What girls?" Jenny asked.

"Your mother and Delia had summer jobs at Mad Martha's," Harrison said. "All the boys would have ice cream every day just to get served by them."

"Dad too?" Obadiah asked.

"Of course," Harrison said. "First in line whenever possible."

Rory knew it was true. She'd always work slowly when Jonathan came in, prolong their moments together as she assembled his favorite—two scoops of coffee on a sugar cone, chocolate jimmies on top. Hearing Harrison tell it made Rory feel happy.

"Did Aunt Dar work there, too?" Sylvia asked.

"No," Delia said. "Even her summer jobs were artistic. One lady hired her to paint tiny bagpipers on her kitchen knobs. And another paid her to tear real vines down from an old barn, because it was wrecking the windows, and to paint trompe l'oeil English ivy and morning glories there instead."

"Tromp loy?" Obadiah asked.

"It means to fool the eye," Harrison said. "Very useful word. I'd like you to write a memo on it and have it on my desk tomorrow, Obes."

The kids giggled.

When they got to the parking area overlooking the harbor, it was just as if they'd summoned Dar: there she was, sitting beside Andy in his truck, which was facing across the darkly shimmering water toward Chappaquiddick. Rory assumed they must have pulled in after going to a meeting.

Everyone surrounded the truck; Andy had his radio tuned to the same reggae station, and Harrison told him to turn it up. Handing Andy his almost-finished sundae, Harrison slipped one arm around Rory, grabbed her hand with his sticky one, and began to dance.

She didn't recognize the song, but it didn't matter. Her feet knew what to do as she leaned into Harrison, let him twirl her away, dip her and pull her close again. The music was sweet, the salt air fresh, the bell buoy ringing, and suddenly everyone was pairing up to dance.

Dar and Andy got out of the truck, began to move. Sylvia held Vanessa, whirling her around, pointing up at stars in the sky. Obadiah tried to cut in on his mother, but Harrison wouldn't let go. Instead he swept Obadiah and Jenny in with him and Rory, and the water sparkled and the dance went on.

. . .

The night had been so beautiful, and when morning came, Dar didn't want Andy to leave. She held him tight, trying to remember her dream. It had started with the bell buoy, the one they'd heard last night, tolling in the channel while the family danced. And then the dream-sound had turned to a phone ringing, with her father calling.

"What are you thinking?" Andy asked, stroking her hair.

"About my father," she said. "It's so strange. A dream that's been a nightmare before suddenly feels different."

"Why do you think?" Andy asked.

"I'm not sure. Cleaning out the house," she said. "Having my sisters and the kids here, going through all our old things. It's comforting, in a way."

"You sure did seem happy last night," Andy said.

"We were," Dar said.

"Do you think you're making peace with the idea?" he asked.

"The opposite," Dar said. "Fighting as hard as ever, but coming up with a new idea."

"Which is?"

Dar shook her head, edging more deeply against his body. "I'm not completely sure. Getting there, though."

Andy kissed her and got up to take a shower, and Dar went straight back to sleep. By the time she woke up again, the sun was streaming through the open window. The earth smelled soft, green shoots half an inch high had emerged in the gardens, and the ocean was perfectly still.

Dar sat at her drawing table. She'd begun using the small pewter dory as a pen rest, and she gave it a long look before starting to shade her most recent work. She made lines so fine, even she could barely see them; she was pleased at the job she'd done making Argideen's SUV look evil. Lost in crosshatching, she barely heard the phone.

"Hey, where are you?" Rory asked when she picked up.

"I slept late," she said.

"We all did. I think yesterday was harder than we expected."

"It was."

"Delia and I were thinking . . . would you feel like taking a walk to see Mom?"

"Yes," Dar said. "I'd love it."

The three sisters met on the road; they'd each picked a handful of dried herbs, beach grass, and lilac tips. They walked single file down the main road, turned left onto a country lane, and entered the Chilmark Cemetery. The land had small hills, granite boulders, and very old, tall trees; some of the oldest graves on the island were here, tombstones worn by time and weather, bearing carvings of death's-heads, angels of mercy, skulls and crossbones.

Colonel John Allen was buried here, having died in 1767; Mrs. Bethia Clark, whose tombstone read:

HERE LYES ye BODY
OF Mrs. BETHIAH CLARK
WIFE TO Mr. WILLIAM
CLARK DECD. FEBry. ye
22D. 1734/5 IN ye 49th
YEAR OF HER AGE

Andy had told Dar that she was a Mayhew, a distant relative, along with many other Mayhew graves in his family's plot here. Dar touched the stone as they walked past.

Over in the corner was John Belushi's grave, where his fans

regularly left bouquets, letters, poems, bottles of beer. Sometimes they left cheeseburgers, but the food attracted raccoons and the caretaker took everything away.

Approaching the graves of their mother and grandmother, Dar felt a shock wave of grief. It still seemed so new and raw, to have lost their mother last fall. The three sisters fanned out before the granite stone. The inscription was simple: her name, dates, and the words *Beloved Mother.*

Each sister took her turn placing the dry herbs, lilac branches, and tall grass by their mother's stone. They couldn't help touching it, placing their palms flat against its cold surface, as if they could somehow reach her, let her know they were there.

They'd saved some lilac branches for their grandmother's grave, just a few feet away, and spent a few minutes arranging them there before turning back to their mother.

They listened to the breeze in the trees, one of their mother's favorite island sounds. This was their first visit together since her funeral, and Dar knew they were all thinking it would be their last for a while.

"She's not in there, you know," Delia said finally. "She's in heaven. She's looking over us all the time, like a guardian angel."

Neither Dar nor Rory replied. Dar nodded to Delia, wishing it could be true.

"She's in heaven," Delia said again. "I know it."

"We believe you," Rory said in a voice that said the opposite.

They stood there for a few minutes, total silence except for the bare branches scraping overhead. The spot was peaceful and comforting. A few robins hopped around the new grass, and a downy woodpecker tapped high in an old maple.

"Mom and Dad have definitely been around this week. You know what I keep thinking?" Dar asked.

Her sisters waited.

"I know this is out of the blue," Dar said, "but could the land grant be real?"

"Are you talking about Dad's idea?" Delia said.

"Yes," Dar said, thinking of their early-evening walks. "Whether it was true or not, he was convinced that his family had been granted land here on the Vineyard."

"By some English king," Rory said.

"Talk about a pipe dream," Rory said. "A British monarch giving land in America to a poor Irish potato farmer, or whatever he was."

"Slightly far-fetched," Delia said.

Dar didn't reply. After her father was gone, she had accompanied her mother to the Chilmark Town Hall at Beetlebung Corner. The memory was vague, but she knew they'd spent an afternoon looking through land records and talking to the town clerk. Nothing had come of it.

Her mother had researched land grants. They were far from rare—land given to colonists, granted by kings, to establish settlements. In the 1700s, Spain issued land to anyone willing to settle in Florida. Revolutionary War veterans were given property by George Washington to pay them for their service.

"Besides, don't you think if there was anything to it, the Littles' real estate lawyers would have turned it up?" Rory asked.

"The title search takes awhile. That's part of why we're holding their deposit in escrow," Delia said. "Not that I believe they'll find anything. We'll be closing in a month at most."

"Dad believed it was real. It's why he went away," Dar said.

"If he'd found it, don't you think he'd have come back?" Rory asked.

"But no one thinks he even had the chance to look, right?" Delia asked. "Something happened sailing from Kerry to Cork, and he never made it."

"I know," Dar said. "But here we are, visiting Mom. We've never done the same for Dad."

"How would we even try?" Delia asked.

"We have no idea where his boat went down," Rory said.

"That's true," Dar said. "I'm not thinking of a particular spot in the sea. This morning I was drawing, and I looked at that little dory Dad took from his grandfather's boat shed . . ."

"You're thinking we should go over there?" Rory asked.

"I don't know," Dar said. "Maybe."

"*Ireland?*" Delia asked.

"What if he did have the chance to look?" Rory asked after a minute.

"For . . . ?" Delia asked.

"We think he never made it to Cork at all. But what if he did? And went looking for proof, the king's document, or whatever it was."

"He would have come home," Delia said.

"But what if he didn't find it?" Rory asked. "Whatever was eating him so badly—he had to leave his family, go looking for this thing—if he made it there safely, but couldn't put his hands on the deed, might he decide he couldn't come back?"

They stayed in the cemetery a little while longer, cleaning up the leaves around their mother's grave. Dar had always imagined her father in the ocean, his spirit in every wave. Something tugged at her memory, but she could not believe that if her father was alive, even if he'd decided not to come home, he wouldn't have let them know. He couldn't have had it in him to be so cruel.

Gathering a small pile of leaves, twigs, and pinecones, she thought of her father's pride. The look in his eyes when he'd shown her around the *Irish Darling*. All those twilight walks around her grandmother's land, looking for property markers. His determination to sail solo across the Atlantic. And the letters he'd written to Dar's mother during the months they were separated.

Dar glanced at Rory, caught her sister's sharp gaze and wondered what she was thinking. They walked home, met the kids in the yard, trying to untangle the line on an old fishing rod. An osprey flew overhead, long wings streaked black and white underneath, sticks in her beak. Everyone watched, following the hawk's progress to a nest pole across the salt pond.

"Listen," Rory said. "I'm not ready to go back inside and start packing again. Does anyone else feel like going to the beach?"

Jenny did a happy little barefoot shuffle, winding up with her arms around her mother. Obadiah ran to get the fishing rod.

"Sounds good to me," Delia said. She picked up Vanessa and turned to Dar.

"I think I'll stay here," Dar said.

She waited on the porch until she saw her sisters, the kids, and Scup troop down the beach path, and then she walked inside. The first floor was stacked with boxes, some packed and sealed, others open and half-full.

Walking slowly through each of the rooms, she let her eyes rest on every surface not already in boxes, taking in all the love and history of her complicated family. The walls, radiators, fireplaces, kitchen stove, refrigerator, woodstove, wide oak floorboards.

Dar finished looking through the Vineyard house's first floor and went up to the second, where she went through the same process, sending her gaze over every wall, brass sconce, fireplace, and other fixtures, taking her time to get where she was going.

She stepped inside her mother's room, gazed at the thin mattress of her white metal bed, peered up at the bright red, orange, and purple glass of the Murano chandelier her grandmother had brought back from a year in Italy.

By the time she got to the attic door, she took a deep breath. The old cats had come out of nowhere to gather at her feet.

Slowly opening the door, she felt the cats scoot past, slinking up the wooden stairs. The sound of paper flapping in the wind— thirty bats disturbed from their sleep by the five ancient predators. The cats chased them all to the slatted vent in the roof's peak, and the bats flew out the cracks into daylight.

"Good job," Dar said, but the cats weren't finished stalking. They slunk around the attic's perimeter, then pounced from one leather-and-brass-bound steamer trunk to another: the luggage with which Dar's grandmother had traveled as a young woman from England to Boston, to marry Archibald Daggett, Jr.

Although Dar had been up here a hundred times, played among the trunks and their contents many rainy summer days, she felt as if this were the first time. Prolonging the moment, not quite ready to find what she was after, she glanced at an old trunk filled with silk and satin gowns, moth-eaten furs, fringed silk scarves and brocade shawls, custom-made hats, soft leather boots, black satin high heels. She and her sisters had dressed up in everything.

She walked purposefully across the attic, to the stone chimney and small fireplace. The cast-iron screen, grate, and fire tools were still in place. There was a cupboard on either side of the chimney, and she tried to remember which one her mother had used.

Turning the brass latch of one, she peered inside and saw that except for a mouse skeleton caught in a cobweb, it was empty. She closed the small door, crossed the fireplace to open the other.

A blue pouch wrapped in plastic, nibbled at the corners, lay pushed back as far as it would go. She had watched her mother place it here more than two decades ago, after the Noank house was sold. Dar's stomach twisted, and she reached all the way in, grabbed the pouch by two fingers, and pulled it toward her. She held it in both hands, sat on the floor, back to the wall.

Slowing unwrapping the plastic, unzipping the soft padded blue silk pouch, she pulled out a slim stack of onionskin stationery and thin blue envelopes, held together by a rubber band that broke the instant she touched it.

The envelopes were addressed to her mother. They were written in fountain pen, as she remembered, in her father's hand. Tears caught in her throat as Dar held the letters in her lap, staring at her father's beautiful, perfect handwriting and looking at the long-ago dates and postmarks.

PART II

The great beach against which the sea continually beats.

HECTOR ST. JOHN DE CRÈVECOEUR,
WRITTEN ON A 1783 MAP OF THE VINEYARD

CHAPTER SEVEN

Knowing that one's parents wrote love letters to each other changes the way a person sees life. Dar had read her father's words long ago—back then her mother had kept the envelopes in her bedside drawer. With him living out of the house, Dar had been extra alert for any signs of good or bad between her parents, any clues to what the future might hold.

Like many oldest children, Dar had the characteristics of a good spy. The first time she'd seen her mother get the mail, hide a blue envelope in her pocket, clearly too precious to sit among the bills and circulars, Dar had known something was up. She had shadowed her mother, had seen her take the letter onto the side porch, read it with her head bent down, drinking in the words.

After a few more letters had arrived, Dar had been unable to stop herself. She'd waited for her mother to be busy in the garden, then gone upstairs and opened the drawer. Dar had felt guilty just touching the envelopes. But the sight of her father's writing, even though he was living close by at the boatyard, made her feel so homesick for him. She'd wanted to peek, just to pick up some clue about what was going on.

Dar was only twelve that year. She'd never read a love letter in her life. But her heart was so connected to her father's, she could feel the longing and sorrow he felt for what had come between him and Dar's mother. He wrote about a sunset they'd seen once, with the sky blazing red and the mainland a smoky blue outline, and how they'd held hands and known they were seeing something they would never forget, how the memory would unite them forever.

Reading those words had told Dar what she'd wanted to know. No matter what else he wrote about his desire to make her proud, give her more than she'd ever ask, be the best father to their girls, live up to his own expectations of himself, that sunset was the image Dar never forgot. She could almost see her parents silhouetted in its fiery light.

While her sisters were at the beach, she went back to the Hideaway and read all her father's letters again. He wrote so clearly, she could hear his voice. She had never known him—heard him or spoken to him—as an adult. He wrote of love and yearning; she heard shame for not having brought enough to the marriage. He hadn't set out to marry a rich girl. He had fallen in love with Tilly even as he'd stalked the land on which she lived.

Life is full of reality, no matter how talented the Irish are at avoiding it, he wrote. The truth he'd sought to avoid was that he felt ashamed of his lack of worldly goods when in the company of his mother-in-law. And he feared that no matter how deep his and Tilly's love had once been, it had changed along the way. A girl used to having everything she'd ever wanted now had to content herself with being the wife of a boatbuilder, to live in a small house provided by her mother, and to scrounge to make ends meet. *You're tiring of it, God knows I am. We—I—cannot go on in this way. I see the disappointment in your eyes*, he'd written.

Was it true or not? Knowing her mother, Dar could not believe it was. She heard desperation in her father's words—as well as a sense of resentment and a strong ambition to sail to Ireland. *I won't come back home until after I retrieve what I'm owed.*

Won't come back home: the line that had risen from memory to haunt her, sitting with her sisters at their mother's grave.

Dar stared at that letter for a long time. She looked up at the ceiling, closed her eyes until she could feel Dulse. Her hand itched to draw; it was the only way she ever made sense of emotions this strong. Moving to her desk, she opened her pad to a new page.

Her drawing summoned up a spirit of water, seaweed, bitter taste, red sunset. They weren't following any story Dar had ever drawn before; she let her pencil move, let Dulse take over.

Anger made her press down hard, break the pencil point. Twisting more lead, turning the mainland into a mountain, switching to color, outlining the slope dusky blue, dipping a brush in water, then vermilion, painting the sky blood red.

The image didn't reflect the tenderness of two people holding hands, witnessing a brilliant sunset. It boiled up from deep down inside Dar, a vision of the world—or her family—ending. She painted a midnight blue sea, lapping against the mountain's wide base, and in the middle of the water, a sailboat.

The small boat's sails caught the light of a full moon rising in the east, illuminating the way. Painting the moonlight soothed Dar's hand, made her brush more tender, let her follow the boat and not push it away, let her keep her despair yet soften toward the words her father had written decades ago—*I won't come back home*—and made her want to understand them more.

"Okay, so what are they?" Rory asked after Dar had produced the blue silk pouch, explained the basics, brought forth the envelopes for her sisters to open. "Are they love letters or good-bye letters?"

"They sound like both," Delia said, reading one.

"Mom saved them," Rory said. "They obviously meant a lot to her."

"Why didn't you ever tell us about them?" Delia asked.

"Because she was being Dulse," Rory said, and Dar knew she was right. Her sisters had always been able to accept life in a more straightforward way. Dar had had to struggle, sometimes take on the spirit of her character, make herself invisible, keep the most painful things to herself, hide them deep in memory, yet transform them into her stories.

"What if he did get to Cork?" Delia asked, restarting the conversation they'd had in the cemetery.

"How can we know?" Rory asked.

"We had that one phone call from Kerry, and then nothing. No letters from Ireland at all . . ." Delia said.

"That makes sense to me," Dar said. "If he made it to Cork, he would have been completely focused on getting his proof. He wouldn't want to give us half-assed progress reports."

"I sort of get it," Delia said. "It must have been awful, feeling he couldn't measure up. It's a little like Pete going to Alaska. He wanted to make his own money, show us he could stand up for himself. Big plans don't always work out the way people want them to."

The three of them took notes as they read the letters he'd written before he left. Any mention he had made of places in Ireland, people he could contact, dates that might matter. Dar couldn't get over the strange sensation of reading her father's letters and judging him: he had decided to sail solo across the ocean.

"Hang on," Rory said, reaching for her laptop. "Let's Google him. Michael McCarthy, Cork, Ireland . . . fifty thousand hits."

"Narrow it down. Try Cobh," Dar said. "It's pronounced 'Cove' but spelled C-O-B-H. He keeps mentioning it."

"Well, lots of McCarthys in Cobh, too. Here's McCarthy Manufacturing," Rory said, staring at the screen. "Dad was a boatbuilder, not a machinist or whatever they do at manufacturing companies."

"Just type in 'McCarthy, Cork,'" Delia suggested.

"Hmm," Rory said. "There's the McCarthy Bookshop in Skibbereen. And a list of obituaries in the *Irish Examiner* . . ." She scanned them. "Thomas McCarthy. Nuala McCarthy. No Michaels, at least this week."

"Wait," Delia said. "Shouldn't we be checking out West Kerry? That's where we last heard from him . . ."

"I know," Dar said. "But I don't remember any details about the town, or the harbor, or where he was calling from. Since we know his ultimate destination was Cork, I think it's good we're starting there."

"Whether he made it or not?" Delia asked, skeptical.

"Is there a number for the bookshop?" Dar asked.

"Yes," Rory said, reading it off.

Dar checked her watch. "It's nearly seven over there. Let's give it a try anyway." She dialed the number on the house phone, and got the *beep-beep* tone familiar from calling her British publisher. Then an answering machine picked up, with a message spoken by an Irishman. Dar barely registered the words; his accent sounded just as she remembered her father's.

"They're closed," she told her sisters.

"Shit," Delia said. "We're on the early boat tomorrow. There won't be time to call before we leave."

"Dar will call and let us know what happens," Rory said.

"I will," Dar promised.

The sisters spent the rest of the afternoon—their last before leaving the next morning—sealing boxes, loading some into their cars, setting others aside for the movers. They could barely look at each other without tearing up. Where would they congregate when this place was gone? There had never been any other place—not since they had left Noank. Dar stayed focused on the boxes, but every so often her heart flipped, thinking of the bookstore.

"That wasn't Dad's voice on the answering machine, was it?" Rory asked, half joking, glancing up from a carton carefully packed with dishes.

"No," Dar said. "He had the same accent, though. But he sounded young. Dad would be nearly eighty by now."

"What if he's alive?" Delia said. "He never found what he was 'owed,' so he didn't come back home. That's what we're all thinking, isn't it?"

Rory nodded.

"That, and could we find him in Ireland?" Dar asked.

At dusk, Andy and Harrison arrived for a farewell dinner and blowout Scrabble tournament. Andy had picked up steamers and lobsters, Harrison provided the Heineken, Rory and Sylvia made a huge salad, Delia slid stuffed potatoes back under the broiler to brown, Jenny made place cards, Obadiah was allowed to light the candles, and Vanessa looked on from her bouncy chair. Dar knew Pete should be there, so she stepped out of the kitchen to try him on her cell phone. But the call went to her nephew's voice mail, and she didn't leave a message.

The evening was warm and still, so they ate on the porch, on the long table overlooking the pond and dunes. A harrier hunted, flying low over the pink-tinged dunes. Everyone talked and laughed, pretending this wasn't the last porch dinner. The sounds of cracking lobster claws and clamshells being tossed into buckets filled the air. Melted butter dripped everywhere. Harrison got caught letting Sylvia take a sip of his beer.

"She's only fourteen!" Rory said.

"Hypocrite, my love. Remember us at fourteen?" Harrison asked.

"Shut up," Rory said with a warning glance.

"No," Harrison said. "Syl, Obes, Jenn . . . what you all need to know is that your mother was, is, and will always be the hottest woman alive."

"Hey," Delia said.

"I was getting there," Harrison said in the tone of a man who doesn't like being rushed through his stories or speeches. He took a long quaff of beer. "And your aunts are the loveliest aunts any children could ever have."

"That's not like being called hot," Delia said.

"Well. You both are. But I'm singling out Rory just for the evening. She has been much too serious this week, and she needs to remember being fourteen."

"I remember," Rory said. "Everything was wonderful except for one part. You lived in Edgartown, and I lived all the way out here, and we couldn't drive."

"Uh, except the time I did," Harrison said.

"You drove when you were fourteen?" Sylvia asked, sounding thrilled.

"Nooooo," Harrison said. "I was thirteen. Big difference. And do what I say and not what I do. That goes in all instances, not just taking your father's brand new Caddy and tooling up-island to see your lady friend."

"Did you get caught?" Obadiah asked.

"Well, eventually," Harrison said.

"What do you mean, eventually?"

"He did it all summer," Delia said. "Drove out here to see Rory."

"Yes. My parents were conveniently in Europe and had left me with the nanny."

"Anika," Rory said. "I still remember her. She was gorgeous and blond. I wanted to look like her."

"She had a little problem with power," Harrison said. "She'd lock me in my room while she made out with her surfer boyfriend on my parents' bed. But I climbed out the window every time."

"It's true," Andy said.

"And drove out here, twenty miles each way," Harrison said.

"What did your mother say?" Obadiah asked Rory. "Didn't she get mad?"

"Once again, do as I say, not as I do," Harrison said sternly. "Do you think I was stupid enough to park in the driveway where any mother or grandmother could see me? Ha. Give me some credit. I parked at the beach and walked back along the sand to get here."

"That's how you got caught," Delia said. "You didn't have a Chilmark sticker in your window."

"True," Harrison said, dipping his entire lobster tail in butter, holding it over his head to take a huge bite. He chewed for a while, butter slick on his chin, then wiped his face clean and downed the rest of his beer.

"What happened?" Jenny asked.

"Well. The Caddy got towed. The parking lot girls never gave me trouble, but one day there was this big, dumb guy who took handsome lessons. He saw I didn't have a sticker and told me I couldn't stay. But I thought, 'Man, you're just jealous of me having this cool black car, top down showing off the red leather,' and I figured he'd sit in front while I was gone and play with the steering wheel and enjoy the experience."

"But he didn't?"

"Nope. Called the cops, and they towed the Caddy. She sat in the police lot till my parents got back. Had major rain damage to the interior, thanks to the cops not making any effort at all to get the keys from me and put the top back up."

"Like it was the cops' fault!" Delia said.

"Sure as hell was!" Harrison said. "Am I right, Obes?"

Obadiah smiled and shrugged.

"It turned out okay. My father never liked the black Caddy. He'd always wanted a triple-white Eldorado, red interior. So that's what he got."

Everyone chuckled, and Sylvia asked what else he'd done when he was thirteen. Harrison told her those stories were for another night. Dinner was over, the table cleared, strawberry-rhubarb pie and coffee served, teams formed, and the Scrabble board brought out.

Darkness had fallen; instead of switching on the porch light, they lit more candles. The sound of the waves grew louder as if magically amplified at night. Dar and Andy sat on the glider, and it creaked as they rocked back and forth. They formed the word *opine*.

"Sounds like a drug," Harrison said.

"It means to express your opinion," Sylvia said.

"Whoa, smart and gorgeous," Harrison said.

Rory and Jenny laid down the word *pithy*, and Harrison and Obadiah did *itchy*, and Delia and Sylvia got a triple word score on *exempt*. They played in silence while Vanessa chattered in Delia's arms, and then Harrison lumbered out of his seat and said he had to go see a man about a horse.

"What's that mean?" Jenny asked.

"That he has to pee," Rory said.

"Why isn't he going inside the house?"

"Well, I guess he's used to things being pretty simple, living in the storage unit," Andy said as a faint smell of pot smoke mixed with the sea breeze.

The game went on, and when Harrison returned he said he just wanted to watch, but instead stretched out on a teak bench, arms folded behind his head, staring up at the ceiling. After a while, the game broke up.

No one wanted to move, or leave the porch. Andy held Dar's hand, rocking in the glider. She stared around the porch at her sisters, nephew, nieces, and Harrison. Time seemed to stop, and they all just stayed where they were, listening to the waves, holding on to the feeling of being together, wanting the evening to last forever.

The next morning dawned deep blue, with streaks of pink in the east, and the evening star balancing on the western horizon. The sisters let the kids sleep as long as possible as they shared one last coffee before ferry time. They sat at the kitchen table, hunched as close as they could get to each other.

They held hands, bowing their heads close. After so many years and happy and crazy and sad summer and winter memories, this house would no longer belong to them. They cherished every floorboard, window, brass sconce, wicker chair, every surface their family had touched.

The minutes ticked by, drew closer to ferry time. Slowly they woke the kids up, got them ready to leave. Dar poured orange juice into a silver baby's cup, and Delia gave it to Vanessa. Harrison had slept on the porch, and he took the orange juice from Dar's hand and drank from the bottle.

"Is this going to be sad?" he asked.

"What do you think?" Rory asked.

"Okay." He held his hands up as if a gun were trained on him.

"That means I have to leave. I'm going to kiss everyone now, but we're not saying good-bye. It's my rule. Got it?"

"Got it," Sylvia said, raising her cheek to be pecked.

"Good-bye!" Obadiah yelled when Harrison shook his hand.

"Obes, you are my man. Rule-breaking first thing in the morning."

"I won't say it," Jenny said.

"That's because you're sweet as sugar," Harrison said. "Okay, c'mon, Rory and Delia, over here. Quick. I can't take it much longer."

"Love you," Rory said.

"Love you more," Harrison said.

Stepping outside, they heard birds singing. Spring migration had begun, and the first warblers hopped around the trees' upper branches. Nearly overnight, the grass had turned green. The sun was rising over the pines, painting the tips of their needles orange; it was going to be an achingly beautiful day.

Harrison helped load luggage into the cars. He broke a sweat, even though the lifting wasn't heavy. Rory hugged him from behind, and his eyes filled. "Shit, get me out of here. Everyone, you know I love you. Dar, catch you later."

"Good-bye!" everyone called as he climbed into his blue van and sped away.

They heard his engine booking down South Road, fading away. The kids stood at the end of the driveway, waving until he was gone from sight.

Dar, Rory, and Delia held each other.

"This week passed so fast," Delia said. "I just wish Pete had been here! He loves—loved—it here so much."

They stood facing the house, unable to look away until Delia checked her watch, said they'd have to hurry for the ferry. They hugged again, and climbed into their cars.

Dar led the way, Scup at her side, his eyes sad and eloquent, as if he understood. She almost expected one or both of her sisters to peel off and return to the house. But they didn't, and they reached the boat on time. Dar wanted to get out of her car for one last hug, but as if her sisters couldn't handle that, they just waved, and drove onto the waiting ferry.

Dar parked in the lot, and she and Scup walked down to the ferry dock. The deckhands cast off, the captain blew the horn, and the *Island Home* began to back out of the slip. Dar scanned the decks for her sisters, but she didn't see them. Sylvia, Obadiah, and Jenny stood at the rail, waving madly, yelling, "Good-bye, Scup! Good-bye, Aunt Dar!"

"Good-bye!" Dar called to them.

She knew why her sisters weren't there. She could almost picture them in their cars, making the crossing in the hold instead of topside in the fresh air. The light was too bright, the sights too familiar, the newly conjured idea of their father too raw, and they were leaving it all behind. Dar watched the boat as long as she could, until it left the harbor and rounded West Chop, heading for Woods Hole.

Then she and Scup climbed back into her car, and even though the ferry was out of sight, she stayed right where she was, staring at the spot she'd last seen the big white boat bearing her sisters away.

CHAPTER EIGHT

Dar planned to spend that night alone in her old room in the big house. She wanted to see Andy, but even more she needed time to herself. She had the number of the McCarthy Bookshop; even though she'd tried during Irish business hours, she still got the answering machine.

Right now it didn't matter. Dulse floated in her mind, reminding her that loss was a force. It could pounce when you least expected it, surround you like a hurricane and rip your familiar life apart. Or loss could sneak up gradually, the slow march of fog creeping in.

Dulse's forces of loss had filled pages of Dar's books. She could see them coming, miles off at first, just dark specks on the horizon. She might start to believe they would never actually arrive, that the forces might decide to leave her intact.

Illness and death were two levels of loss; disappearance without explanation was another. Dar put that at the pinnacle; she assumed her father was dead, but they'd never had the chance to say good-bye or lay him to rest. There was no lichen-covered gravestone to visit, no anniversary onto which they could focus their grief and remembrance.

Dar and her sisters treasured their family's objects, but everything needed to stay right here, where it had always been. The table, the chairs, the paintings, the rugs, wouldn't make sense in any other context.

Her bones tingled, her entire body on high alert. She wanted to curl up under the covers. She wished she could wind it backwards, even if it meant reliving old events, to a time when everyone had been together.

Alone in the big house, Dar left her room and walked downstairs. The five cats had gone out to hunt. Scup lay by the kitchen door, waiting for the sisters and children to return. Dar crouched, petted him behind his ears.

"Where are we going to live?" she asked. "What are we going to do?"

At the Hideaway she'd filled a notebook with places she'd always wanted to live: Paris, Eze, Portofino, Dublin, Connemara, Donegal, Nova Scotia, Prince Edward Island, Big Sur, the San Juan Islands. Cork was at the top of the list.

How would it be to live in a small town near Cork, never knowing if she'd see her father walk past? For now, in the mood she was in, Cork was off the list. Besides, she didn't want to move at all.

Dreaming of new places was one thing, but actually leaving was another. The Vineyard was in her blood. She had never seriously wanted to live anywhere else. Besides, there was Andy.

Her cell phone rang, and as much as she didn't feel like answering, she did.

"Hello?" she said.

"Aunt Dar?"

"Pete!" she said, thrilled to hear his voice.

"I saw you called," he said. "Your number was on my cell phone. A missed call. You didn't leave a message."

"No, I know," she said. "It was our last dinner here, and I was just thinking of you so much."

"Last dinner."

"Yeah," she said.

"Shit. The sale's going through? I should have been there."

"Oh, Pete. What are you doing? Are you in trouble?"

"I'm fine."

"Your mother misses you so badly. And you have a beautiful daughter. Don't you want to take responsibility, show up for yourself?"

"You sound like AA," he said

"How would you know?" she asked.

"Uh, never mind. Let's just say I walked into a church basement once."

"You've been going?" she asked, taken off guard.

"Trying, but . . ." he said. "I'm coming home. My truck broke down outside of Denver. I wanted to get there in time to help pack up the house. To see Mom and meet . . ."

"Vanessa?"

"Yeah."

Dar held the phone, feeling a smile inside.

"That's doing the right thing," she said.

"Yeah," he said. "Finally. So, once I get my truck fixed, can I come to the Vineyard?"

"I think you should go home," she said. "To Maryland, see your parents and daughter."

"If I do that, can I drive up and say good-bye to the place?"

"Sure," Dar said. "But hurry. The closing is in two weeks."

"Okay," he said. "I've gotta get my truck fixed, and then I'll be there."

"Good, after you go home," she said. Something about his voice scared her.

She wanted to help him, to offer him money so he could get to Delia faster, but before she could say anything, the connection broke. She waited a minute, but when he didn't call back, she tried him. She got his voice mail, and this time she left a message.

"Pete, we got cut off. Call me back?"

Aside from heavy furniture, the house was almost empty, cartons stacked in the corners of each room, waiting for movers. But she opened all the first-floor windows to let the wind blow through. It smelled of ocean and new grass. She heard the pinkle-tinks singing from the swamps, ponds, and woods.

Stepping outside, she sat on the stone step facing the salt pond. Scup leaned against her. They looked up; silhouetted against the moon were Vs of geese, migrating north. She ran inside for the long brass telescope, hurried out again. Pointing the scope toward the moon, she saw clouds of other, smaller migrating birds, flying through the night: flycatchers, larks, swallows, wrens, hummingbirds, kinglets, thrushes, and so many more, back for the warm weather.

Some would land on the island, others would continue to other destinations. She knew that birds liked to return to their favorite places, were guided back year after year. They'd fly at night, find green and wooded places to land at dawn. Egrets and herons filled the ponds.

"Come on," she said to Scup. Leaving some windows open for the cats to jump back into the house, she grabbed her car keys and backed out. It was only about nine o'clock. She drove down South Road to State Road, then found the winding lane that led inland to the sandy hills and scrub trees behind Oak Bluffs.

Halfway there, her phone rang again, and it was an overjoyed, almost giddy, Delia.

"Pete's coming home!" she said. "And you don't have to pretend you don't know, because he told me he talked to you. Did you convince him?"

"He was already on his way."

"Well, I'm just so glad," Delia said. "I miss you already, Dar."

"I miss you, too," Dar said.

"Did you call the bookstore?"

"Yes. Still just the answering machine."

"Well, let me know what happens," Delia said.

"You know I will. Love you."

"Love you," Delia said.

By then Dar had pulled onto the sandy road that led to Andy's house. Gold moonlight streamed through the thick salt pines. She and Scup got out of the truck; at the sound of the door slamming, Andy came to stand outside.

Barefoot, Dar walked up the steps. She put her arms around him, and kissed him for a long time. Scup stood by, wagging his tail. After a minute Andy pushed her back just enough to see into her eyes.

"You said you wanted to be alone tonight."

"I thought I did."

"I was pretty sure you didn't," he said.

There were already bowls of water and dry dog food in the kitchen corner. Scup walked over and drank happily and sloppily. Andy's kitchen was small and efficient. Dar smelled something good simmering on the stove, but Andy led her into the living room.

It was about the size of the farmhouse mudroom, and gave into an even tighter bedroom. This had once been an old icehouse, and Andy had preserved the rough-hewn walls and timber beams. A curved whale jaw embraced an eight-pane window, looking out over the fields and trees in back.

Dar realized how rarely she'd been inside here. Usually Andy came to her. She touched the whalebone.

"What kind do you think it was?"

"A young sperm whale," he said. "My great-grandfather caught it."

She nodded. The Mayhews were an old Vineyard whaling family, just as the Daggetts, her maternal grandfather's family, had been.

The rest of the room had a green couch and lounge chair, nature books and birds nests of all sizes on shelves he'd built. Dar glanced into one finely woven nest of brown twigs and was surprised to see it lined with black hair.

"Came out of your lilac bush a few years back," he said. "After the babies had fledged and the mother had abandoned the nest."

She kept looking around, and found a photo he'd taken—on a hike last September, around the Aquinnah lighthouse and down to Lobsterville. It showed her smiling, sun glinting as she tried to shield her eyes. But you couldn't miss the affection she had for the man who'd taken the shot. She stared at it, barely able to realize that her mother had been alive at that time.

"So much has happened since then," she said.

"It hasn't all been bad," Andy said, standing beside her.

"No, it hasn't."

She stared at his collections of seagull and osprey feathers, an owl pellet, quahog and razor clam shells, a tobacco tin holding old rusty lures he'd hooked while fishing—she remembered him telling her about hauling in a fifty-two-inch striper, finding three other lures hanging from his lower lip.

Twisted driftwood, sea-polished and sun-bleached, picked up on beach walks. She felt his hands on her shoulders and turned toward him. He kissed her hard, and she pressed her body into his. He led her to the bedroom.

It was dark, the only light coming from the other room. They knew each other's bodies by heart. She reached down, felt how hard he was, lay back on his bed. Eyes closed, she felt his mouth on her, making her writhe. He was on his knees, and she held his head in her hands, arching her back.

She could have come right then, but she needed him inside her. "*Andy,*" she said. She tugged at him. Her knees fell open even more as he slid up the bed, and she felt him hot inside her. She felt his hips banging into hers, harder and harder. He reached down between their legs, touching her, and she shuddered and thrashed, and so did he.

A long time passed. She fell asleep. When she woke up, she felt him behind her, arm across her chest. He'd covered them with a quilt.

"You awake?" she asked.

"Yeah," he said. "Waiting for you to be."

"Should I go to Ireland?" she asked.

"You could," he said.

"But not now, right?" she asked. "I should wait till after the closing, and go then."

"You could do that," he agreed.

Her heart tipped over. She wanted to stay here forever. She and Scup and the cats.

He turned her around, pushed the hair back from her face, kissed her so tenderly she felt it in her toes.

"Darrah McCarthy," he said.

"I don't want to go."

"I think you have to. You and your sisters, or whichever one can pry herself loose from life with the family, go over to Ireland and turn over every damn stone till you find your father, or what happened to him."

"Really?"

"Yes," Andy said, staring into her eyes. "You know you have to, and I know you want to."

She nodded, knowing she'd just made the decision to go to Ireland. She pressed herself against Andy's body, closing her eyes tight. He felt so warm; she wanted every inch of her skin to be touching him. Invisible threads connected them, holding them in a private world that existed whether they were together or apart.

CHAPTER NINE

Over the next days, Dar called her sisters to check in and talk about the plan. They'd both hoped to accompany her, but now Delia needed to stay home and wait for Pete. Rory had called on Jonathan to take the kids and Sylvia for a week or two. He lived within their school district, so nothing would be interrupted.

"What about Alys?" Dar asked.

"Jonathan is actually seeing reason on this. He wants the kids so badly, he's telling her she has to move out until I get back."

"Good for Jonathan," Dar said.

Morgan Ludlow was out showing properties when Dar phoned, so she left word that she would be in Ireland for a few days. Morgan could contact her by phone or e-mail. Meanwhile, she could deal with the same real estate lawyer Dar's family had always used—Bart Packard, in Edgartown.

Andy said he would feed Scup and the cats. It was mid-after-noon, and he'd come by to drive her to the airport. But the sun was beating down, making it hard to tear herself away. She looked around the yard, saw all the spring chores that had to be done.

"You don't know how much I'm going to miss pulling weeds," she said. "I know every single one that comes back every year."

"You'll find other weeds," he said.

"But I don't want other weeds. I want our weeds."

"You're all right, Darrah McCarthy. You're all right."

High praise from Andy Mayhew. He drove her to the Martha's Vineyard Airport, walked her into the terminal while she checked her suitcase. He stood right beside her, as if planning to go with her. She had a moment of panic, checking to make sure she had her passport. Andy stayed calm, holding her book bag open while she searched inside.

"Got it," she said.

"That's good. You all ready now?"

She nodded.

"Have a great trip and find everything you're looking for."

"Do you think he's there?"

Andy smiled and shrugged. She looked into his weathered face, the deeply scored lines around his eyes, saw love, excitement, and integrity. He was the best man she knew.

"You better go, Dar," he said. "They're loading the plane."

"Thanks for taking care of the animals," she said.

"Don't worry about anything. They'll all be fine. See you when you get back."

They kissed, and she gave the attendant her boarding pass and walked out onto the tarmac. She boarded her Cape Air flight to Boston; it felt strange. She hadn't left the island in some time. The props began to spin, and they taxied toward the runway.

Andy had walked out the other side of the small building and was watching her go. She put her hand on the window to wave to him. The engines revved, the plane sped along the ground, then lifted up, wobbling on air currents, gaining altitude and leveling off, then straight north to Boston.

When they landed in Boston, she hurried through the concourse to Aer Lingus. Rory was already there, having driven up from Old Lyme. She'd stopped at the food court, bought sandwiches for dinner.

"How was your flight?" Rory said, hugging her.

"Short. Fine. Are we really doing this?"

"We sure are. I wish Delia could be here," Rory said. "But she's home, waiting for Pete. Standing by the kitchen window, watching for his headlights, I suppose."

"He's not home yet?" Dar asked.

Rory shook her head. "He needed his parents to wire him money to get his truck fixed. Delia knew how Jim would feel, so she did it herself."

They found seats amid a large family of freckle-faced redheads. "Black Irish," Dar heard the woman next to her mention to her husband.

Their flight was called, and they made their way onto the plane. Their seats were just forward of the wing. Rory had the window seat; Dar was stuck in the middle, next to a man speaking loudly on a cell phone. The plane filled up quickly, and soon the flight attendant was hurrying down the aisle, closing overhead bins.

The door was closed, the man turned off his cell phone, and they started moving away from the gate.

"I feel as if we're celebrating," Rory said.

"Our first time to Ireland."

The pilot announced they were next for takeoff. He revved the engines and turned onto the main runway. Dar and Rory held hands.

"Kiss and fly," Rory said, and they did.

The plane took off, banked hard right, and they were over the Atlantic. Dar leaned over as she and Rory stared down. Boston and soon the entire East Coast landmass receded from sight. Twilight was upon them.

Dar saw the endless white-capped sea spreading out to every horizon. It would take seven hours to fly across; it had taken her father a month to sail. She felt Dulse with her, ancient spirit of many sea voyages, and wished there were room in the cramped space to pull out her drawing things and start a new story.

Rory stared straight ahead, and Dar focused her gaze out the small window. The flight attendant brought the beverage cart around. Now they were above the clouds, the ocean invisible. Dar doodled images of Dulse on her napkin.

Rory brought out the bag of sandwiches. "Tomatoes, mozzarella, and basil on sourdough for both of us."

"I'm not hungry," Dar said.

"Yes, you are."

"Rory . . ."

"We need strength for what we're about to do," Rory said. "All of it. I won't even mention the Vineyard. But Dad . . . We have to stay strong to face whatever we find."

"Either way, it's not good," Dar said, turning to face her sister. "If he's alive, it means he chose to spend his life without us. And if he's dead . . . he's dead. We'll be mourning him all over."

"We've never really stopped," Rory said. "Isn't that how it goes when you just don't know?"

"It is."

Rory sipped her double scotch. "I need fortification for what lies ahead." She looked at Dar. "And behind. It's almost harder when Jonathan and I are getting along. We really saw eye to eye about Alys not being there with the kids."

"That's great."

"I don't want to be at war with him. I just want him back. It's a loop in my mind: Why did he have to leave me? We knew everything about each other. We were kids together. He'll never have that with her."

"I know," Dar said. "He must know it, too."

"He does," Rory said. "He hates what he's doing to me. But he wants out so bad, he can't seem to help it."

"You seem calmer about it than you did at the Vineyard."

"He and I have played on every inch of that island. I don't know. Maybe it's going to find Dad that's sobered me up. Maybe it's the magic of flying toward dawn over the sea. Time out of time."

"It must be hard to make marriage last," Dar said.

Rory shrugged. "I thought it was easy—you just loved each other. I'm worn down from wondering what I did wrong."

Dar could almost see Andy back home, taking care of Scup and the cats. Had they lasted so long because they'd never moved in, never made it official?

Soon the movie started, and the flight attendant came around closing the window shades. Dar left theirs open a few inches so she could look out at the stars. Rory put on headphones, engrossed in the film.

It was too black to see the sea below. She imagined her father sailing in the dark, using the stars for guidance. Had he thought about Dar on his voyage to Ireland, the talks they'd had about constellations?

She gazed at the sky; a million stars seemed balanced on the end of the wing. They were guiding her to her father. She had missed and needed him for so long.

PART III

Oh, Father dear, I oft times hear, you speak of Erin's Isle,
Her lofty hills, her valleys green, her mountains rude and wild
They say she is a lovely land, wherein a saint might dwell,
So why did you abandon her, the reason to me tell.

FROM "DEAR OLD SKIBBEREEN,"
TRADITIONAL IRISH BALLAD

CHAPTER TEN

They landed in Dublin, and Rory wished they had time to visit Trinity College, St. Stephen's Green, Four Courts, and the River Liffey. A lifetime of reading Yeats, Synge, and Joyce had taught her about Ireland, and had been her own way of staying connected to her father.

Rory knew Dar made sense of his disappearance through her drawing, and like many of Dar's readers, Rory loved Dulse and her sisters, had followed their labyrinthine paths of curiosity and sorrow through book after book. In different ways, each of the McCarthy sisters had traced their roots through poems and literature, used imagination to pierce the conundrum of Ireland and their father.

A connector flight took them to Cork. The big question was whether to rent a car and wing it, learning to drive on the left side of the road, or hire a driver. They went to the rental counter and signed out an Opel Corsa, small and, according to the agent, perfect for negotiating narrow country lanes lined with hedgerows.

"We don't encourage first-time drivers here to rent the big cars. Once you get the hang of it, come back, and you can rent anything on the lot," she said.

The sisters thanked her, took the keys, and went to find the car. It was beige and, as advertised, small.

"It looks as if we could pick it up and carry it like a suitcase," Rory said. "You know what's weird? I wanted to ask that agent lady if she knew our father. Being in Cork, I feel like asking everyone."

"I know," Dar said. "I felt the same way. Well, who drives first? It's a stick shift."

"You taught me how to drive standard. I think the honor is yours."

They stowed their luggage in the tiny trunk, then climbed into the car. Rory was glad Dar had come equipped with tour books and a complete road atlas of Ireland. Jet lag was sapping Rory's energy, but she didn't say anything. Dar seemed focused and intense, the exact way she got when she was drawing. She practiced driving through the parking lot, shifting with her left hand.

"It's like being Alice in Wonderland," Dar said. "I feel as if I drank a little potion, and right is left, and up is down, and we're driving on the wrong side of the street, only it's the correct side."

"Should we stop for tea? While in Ireland and all . . . Check into a hotel and kick jet lag with a nap?"

Dar just shot her a smile. "Put your seat back if there's room. I'm ready to drive." They stopped at a store and used their first euro to buy two cups of breakfast tea to go.

Rory sat back, amazed at Dar's skill in navigating the winding roads. As the agent had said, many were lined on both sides by tall hedges, making it impossible to see around corners. But when the road opened up, Rory was struck by the most beautiful scenery she'd ever seen, the Vineyard with castles and a deeper color palette.

There were fields of green bisected by moss-black stone walls, dark hedges, and deep woods. Although signs pointed toward Cork City and Cobh, Dar drove southwest onto the N71. Rory knew they were headed for Skibbereen.

Rory read from a guidebook. "'Skibbereen means "little boat harbor." It was one of the towns hardest hit by the famine of 1848. Ten thousand famine victims are buried in the Famine Burial Pits of Abbeystrowry Cemetery. The River Ilen courses through the town.'"

"I wonder how many of our ancestors died of starvation."

"I can't explain why," Rory said. "But it helps me understand Dad more. Trying so hard to get what he felt was coming to him. Insurance against another famine."

"Always smoking his cigarettes, staring out to sea, as if he could see Ireland. Doesn't it make sense about him and Grandmother, too? She came from such privilege. Even in England, they had a house in London and a country estate in Kent. He must have looked at her as if she was from another world."

"The Kent place had a name," Rory said. "What was it? I wonder why she never took us there."

"It was called Chichester," Dar said. "I think it went to her brother, and they didn't get along. But she grew up riding horses and fly-fishing for salmon and dressing for dinner."

"That never changed," Rory said. She thought of her father, whose people had suffered and died because their potato crop had failed, watching his wife and mother-in-law, and sometimes even his daughters, dressing up for regular Vineyard meals.

Nearing Skibbereen they drove toward the River Ilen, rushing toward the Celtic Sea. Even the salt air smelled like the Vineyard, Rory thought. When they reached the town, they parked the car in a public lot. Rory needed lunch, so they found a cozy pub in the center of town.

"Let's just have a nice lunch," Rory said, trying to soothe Dar's tension; she could see it in her eyes and the cords of her neck. "And then we'll search."

"Okay," Dar said.

They sat in a sunny booth by the large window. The menu was filled with good homey dishes, and when Rory saw Dar looking at the salads, she ordered for both of them: fish and chips, and shepherd's pie.

"We can share—they both sound good," Rory said. She ordered a Guinness for herself, and Dar ordered a Diet Coke.

"This fish is amazing!" Rory said. "As good as New England cod. I wonder what it is. And the batter—wow. Try it!"

"I did, it's good," Dar said. "So's the shepherd's pie."

Feeling thrilled to not have to worry about staying perfectly svelte in case Jonathan stopped by to say he'd made the mistake of his life, Rory dug into both dishes and felt wonderful.

They paid up and asked the white-haired proprietor for directions to the local bookshop. Turned out there were two—the more famous one on Main Street and a smaller, used bookstore just out of town, near Abbeystrowry.

"Do you know which one is the McCarthy Bookshop?" Dar asked.

"The one out of town," he said. "But I'm not sure it's run by a McCarthy anymore. Times do change, and that name is worth its weight in gold, believe me. Let me write out the directions."

"Why is it worth its weight in gold?"

"Well, it's a fine name," he said.

"You don't happen to know Michael McCarthy?" she asked. "He would be around seventy-five."

"Oh dear," the proprietor laughed, looking up from his desk. "Are you aware that the most common name in Skibbereen and most of Cork is McCarthy? I probably know ten Mikes by that name. Do you have something else to go on?"

"He lived in the States about thirty years ago," Dar said. "He was tall with dark hair and sailed to Ireland on a boat he built."

"Well, a quarter of Ireland has lived in the States at one time or other. But sailing over and the dark hair would make him stand out. Most McCarthys are redheads like myself. Gone gray, of course, just like your Michael McCarthy would've. Who is he, may I ask?"

"Our father," Dar said.

"Ah. Well, I wish you luck finding him. He's an ijit if he's hiding from you."

"Thank you," Dar said, shaking his hand. She smiled. "If you see him, tell him we're looking for him."

"That I will. What're your names?"

"Dar McCarthy and Rory Chase."

"Lovely to meet you. I'm Frank Donovan." He grinned. "Let me know if I can be of further service."

"We'll do that," Rory said.

. . .

Dar drove back to the N71 and followed it a couple of kilometers to Abbeystrowry. The countryside was lush and verdant. Using Frank's directions, she found the bookstore in a weathered-silver barn at the edge of a spreading, deep green field surrounded by massive stone walls. She used her iPhone to take pictures of them to send to Andy. Then one of the bookshop, for Delia.

In the distance she saw a ruined abbey overgrown with vines, with the peak of one wall left standing. She felt pulled to walk there; wasn't that where so many famine victims lay buried? How many McCarthy's would she find?

"Are you ready to go inside?" Rory asked. "Or are you too nervous? My stomach is flipping like crazy."

"Now that we know how common the name is, do you realize how unlikely it is that this will prove anything? What an idiot I was to assume McCarthy's Bookshop was such a great lead. We're the Smiths of Ireland."

"You're an ijit all right," Rory said, laughing.

The two sisters composed themselves and walked into the vast barn. It was filled with stacks of books everywhere—along every outside wall, and toppling over on the tall bookcases that lined every aisle. Rory and Dar strolled slowly through one section, noticing that many books dealt with the famine. Another section dealt with genealogy, and another seemed filled with countless copies of the Cork Census going back a hundred years.

When they reached the back, they found a young man sitting at a high desk, smoking and engrossed in a book. He was skinny, with red hair and black-rimmed glasses.

"Excuse me," Dar said.

"Oh, I didn't hear you come in," he said. "Is it something special you're after?"

"Information, actually," Dar said. "Are you by any chance a McCarthy?"

"My mother is," he said. "I'm a Collins. Jimmy Collins."

Dar introduced herself and Rory. She gave the basics on their reason for being in Ireland. "I know it's crazy now, considering it's such a common name, but do you know a Michael McCarthy, about seventy-five?"

"He had dark hair, came here from the States," Rory said.

"Oh, I don't know," Jimmy said. "You could ask my mother when she comes in, which isn't often. She and her boyfriend have a caravan, and they're always camping up in Kerry and Connemara."

"How old is she, if you don't mind my asking?" Rory asked.

"Rory!" Dar said.

"Oh, that's all right. She's too old to be running around with that young jerk. Can you believe he was a year ahead of me in school? Her being forty-five and all."

"Okay, thanks."

"You might come back with more information, such as his birthdate and parish, his parents' names, his trade, the likes of that," Jimmy said.

"His birthday was, is, March 21st," Dar said. "And he's a boatbuilder. So were his father and grandfather."

"Lots of them in Cobh and Kinsale," Jimmy said. "But if you find out his parish, you're sure to get everything you need from the priest. As long as the records weren't burned, as they were in Dublin."

The sisters thanked him, bought a few books. They walked outside, breathing fresh air, glad to escape the mustiness. Dar reflected how little she actually knew about their father's background. He'd left when she was so young; surely if they'd had more time together, she'd have asked him a million more pertinent questions.

"We should tell people he sailed solo across the Atlantic," Rory said. "That might jog some memories."

"You're right," Dar said.

Without even consulting each other, they crossed the wide field toward the ruined abbey and entered the Abbeystrowry Cemetery. The sisters walked into the churchyard. They spotted a sign leaning against a stone wall:

Famine Committee Skibbereen
Area for Memorial Slabs
For deceased relatives
And friends
Contact Committee
028-21704 or 028-21466

"What does that mean?" Rory asked Dar.

Dar shrugged, reading the next sign, directing the way to the Skibbereen Heritage Center.

"Love, what it means," said an old woman dressed in black with a black lace shawl covering her head, "is that the dead are buried here in mass graves. There were so many who died, the cemetery couldn't keep up. They just poured limestone over the poor bodies and just kept shoveling them in."

"So how would you find a family member's grave?"

"You can't," she said. "If you have reason to believe you lost someone in the famine, you can call the committee, and they'll give you permission to set your own stone or marker."

"Thank you," Dar said, shocked. The sisters wandered around, noticing how many of the stones marked people named McCarthy. They found a Michael, who had died in 1847, the granite slab left by his "loving great-grandchildren." The carving was old, its edges softened by time and weather; there was no way of knowing when the stone had been left.

Clouds scudded in from the sea. The first raindrops started to fall, and Dar and Rory hurried to their car, back at the bookshop. They found a note on the windshield.

My mother called and said if she can be of any help locating your father, please contact her when she returns. Sorry to say, God alone knows when that will be. Jimmy.

"Wonder when she'll return," Rory said, climbing into the car just as the rain became a downpour. "Jimmy seems to think she and her sweet young lover are tearing up the countryside with their trailer."

"Let's call Delia once we find a hotel," Dar said. "And tell her what's going on. Maybe she'll know more than we do about Dad's parish."

"Right," Rory said. "She is the religious one."

"Amen," Dar said.

CHAPTER ELEVEN

Delia nearly collapsed when she answered the phone. She'd jumped every time it rang, waiting for Pete, not even expecting to hear from Dar and Rory so soon. In fact, holding the receiver, she let herself flop backwards onto her bed. Her sisters were on extension cords in their hotel room overlooking Kinsale Harbor.

"Kinsale is beautiful" Dar said. "And full of fancy restaurants. Much different than what I'd expected."

"It's the gourmet capital of Ireland," Delia said.

"How do you know?" Rory asked.

"I read cookbooks and watch cooking shows, and of course any time they mention Ireland . . ."

"How's Pete?" Dar asked. "Did he make it home okay?"

Delia closed her eyes as tight as she could. She couldn't bear to tell her sisters. She heard Jim yelling from downstairs.

"Who's calling at this hour?" he asked.

"It's Dar and Rory," Delia yelled back, covering the receiver.

"Delia? Is everything okay?" Dar asked.

Delia had been holding it inside for so long—days and days now. She'd put on a brave face for Jim, to avoid making it worse for both of them. She pulled her pillow over her face and bit hard, to avoid screaming.

She forced herself to control her voice, couldn't quite answer the question. "How are things going on your end? Any clues yet?"

"Actually, we need Dad's parish. And his middle name. And the names of his parents. And . . ." Rory said.

"His parish was Cobh, the diocese was Cloyne, and his family went to mass at St. Colman's Cathedral," Delia said. "His parents were James and Margaret Mahoney McCarthy, and he was baptized by the archbishop as Michael Francis McCarthy."

"How do you know all that?" Rory asked.

"I found his missal," Delia said. "When I was little. And Mom let me keep it after he left. All the information was written in the inside cover, in such a delicate, loving hand; it had to be his mother's." Oh, here it came, charging through her, the love of a mother, the sorrow of being left, of losing the one you love. Her eyes flooded and, since she was lying on her back, the tears ran into her ears.

"Delia?" Dar asked again, her voice incredibly gentle.

Delia held a bed pillow and rocked back and forth. She clamped it to her belly, pressing as hard as she could just to keep herself together.

"Pete," Delia began, hardly able to get the words out. "Didn't come home."

"Oh, Delia," Dar said.

"Honey," Rory said, "I'm so sorry. But isn't it possible he's still on his way? He just hasn't gotten there yet?"

"Jim doesn't think so. He says Pete just wanted the money we sent him. It was all a trick to get us to pay for his truck. Only Jim thinks . . . he thinks Pete wanted the money for drugs!"

"Would he do that?" Rory asked.

"Rory!" Delia said.

"No, I mean, of course not drugs. But maybe for something else?"

"He called us from Denver, and we haven't heard since. He could have crashed, something terrible might have happened to him, and how would we know?"

"He's on his way home," Rory said. "Worrying won't help. Just get on a plane and come over."

"Delia, you don't have to," Dar said. "If you need to stay there and wait . . ."

"I don't know what to do," Delia said. "He doesn't answer his phone—we just get a message that the service is off. He must not have had the money to pay his bill. Jim and I are fighting all the time. Instead of pulling together, he accuses me of being too soft on Pete, and I tell him he's treating Pete like a criminal before we know the whole story."

"Have you called the Denver police?" Dar asked.

"Yes, and there's nothing. I called the garage where he said he was having his truck fixed, and he didn't use the money for that. They had no idea of who he was! Nearly a week's gone by, and no word."

"Maybe because of his phone," Dar said.

"You think so?"

"Yes."

"I want to believe that," Delia said. "Maybe I should go meet you. It's awful here right now.

"He'll find a way to call my cell if he wants to—or yours, Dar. With you gone, I've been getting calls from Morgan Ludlow, asking me every kind of question. How deep is our well, was it dug or drilled, how far from the septic field, had we ever considered putting a swimming pool between the main house and the Hideaway . . ."

"Does that mean they're going to keep—"

"No," Delia said. "Tearing everything down. She just wanted to know if we'd ever hired someone to draw up swimming pool plans they could get in the bargain."

"Come over," Dar said, wiping Morgan Ludlow and the Littles from her mind. "We'll pick you up at the Cork airport the morning after tomorrow."

"Jim won't want me to go. The money—"

"I'm paying," Dar said. "The ticket will be in your name. Just type in 'Delia Monaghan' on Aer Lingus's site, and that's that. Just give your passport info."

"The only reason I even have a passport was that cut-rate cruise we took to the Caribbean three years ago. Can I ask you a favor?" Delia asked, standing up, looking at her full, tear-streaked face in the mirror.

"Anything."

"Will you stay in Kinsale? I don't want to miss it. My first chance at a culinary capital of the world. Not counting New York."

"We'll find the best restaurant in town for you," Dar said.

. . .

Dar had taken notes on what Delia had said about their father's parish. But reading a genealogy book she'd bought at the book barn, she realized that there was a difference between a Catholic parish and a civil parish. Cobh was a seaport in the civil parishes of both Clonmel and Templerobin. Which was most important in terms of finding someone in Ireland?

She buried herself in research to avoid thinking about Pete, Delia, and the house buyers. Rory went out to explore Kinsale, while Dar sat at the desk in their large room overlooking the harbor. She stared at the yachts, all of them so much bigger than her father's *Irish Darling*. But then she found herself pulling on a sweater, heading down to the waterfront.

She walked up and down the docks. Part of her thought she would recognize that beautiful white sloop, and see her father—older and weathered—sitting on deck. He had told her so often they'd sail to Kinsale together. What if he'd made it here from West Kerry, left his boat in a slip, gone to Cobh in search of what he'd come for?

An evening breeze picked up, and the boats began to rock gently. The air was cooling off; she felt glad she'd brought her sweater. If she closed her eyes, she could almost believe she was walking among the boats at Edgartown or Vineyard Haven. The sea breeze felt and smelled exactly the same. When she opened her eyes, she caught a glimpse of a boat several docks away: white, about twenty-eight feet long, with the same distinctive gleaming brightwork as the *Irish Darling*'s mast, boom, and rails.

She hurried in that direction, but the sun had shifted, slipped behind town buildings, and the boat she'd been looking for had disappeared into the falling dusk. Her eyes stung; she hadn't slept since the plane, and jet lag was really upon her. Evening clouds began to gather; they seemed dark and dangerous, or was it just her mood? She took one last look up and down the dock, but suddenly the sloops all looked alike. So she walked back to the hotel.

Meeting Rory in the lobby, they strolled through the narrow, winding streets, in search of the restaurant Rory had found. It was called Toledo, and specialized in seafood and Spanish cuisine. The front was stucco, with black shutters and window boxes of red geraniums. The host showed them into a dining room lit by candlelight, and they sat at a table by the window in straight-backed red velvet chairs. Rory ordered a Spanish sherry, and they decided to split paella.

"Maybe our ancestors started out here," Rory said, reading from the guidebook. "They called it the Siege of Kinsale, in the 1590s. It was a bloody, horrible battle, part of the Nine Years' War. But four thousand Spanish troops came ashore here to join with the Irish and fight Lord Mountjoy and the British. They held England off as long as they could. Irish and Spanish fell in love and had children, the so-called Black Irish."

"Us," Dar said.

"Exactly."

Dar looked out the window at the town. It twinkled with streetlamps and house lights, flower gardens everywhere.

Then the paella came in a copper pot, and they began to spoon out yellow rice, tiny clams, chorizo, and Dublin Bay prawns. It smelled delicious, like something she and her sisters would want to re-create this coming summer at the Vineyard. Don't think back and don't think forward, Dar told herself. Just be right here with Rory and eat the good food.

When Dar woke up the next morning, cool dawn light was just starting to come through the windows. She glanced across the room at her sister fast asleep. She felt a pang of love.

She, Rory, and Delia had had their own rooms growing up in Noank, decorated in different colors, but with the same layout: twin beds, bookcase, and desk. They'd often sleep in each other's rooms, in the other twin bed. They'd talk and laugh until they fell asleep—mainly they'd just wanted to be together.

Dar dressed in jeans and a sweater and silently let herself out of the room. She bypassed the hotel's breakfast room and walked straight outside. Deep blue morning clouds were stacked up on the horizon, but already they were starting to disperse, revealing a bright blue sky. There were pots of coral pink flowers along the path to the docks, and she watched emerald hummingbirds dart in and out.

She found a low rock just off the path and tried to meditate. The harbor spread before her, smooth as glass, glistening with early sunlight. A large, beautiful ketch left the dock, its engine barely audible, its hull scratching a white wake in the blue water. She found herself stirred up, and although she remained seated for twenty minutes, thoughts of what she'd seen last night raced through her mind.

Getting up, she walked straight to the docks; they were shaped in a U, with four finger piers extending out from each of the main arms. Last night darkness had obscured the boats, but today she felt determined to find the twenty-eight-footer with the shining wooden brightwork.

Water lapped under the sturdy wooden dock, splashing against the pilings. She loved the sound as she walked along, gazing at each boat, scanning the piers for a varnished wooden mast.

Hearing footsteps behind her, she turned around. A tall man came toward her, dressed in a blue uniform and carrying a lunch bag and thermos. He had weathered cheeks and white hair, yet he didn't seem old.

"Good morning to you," he said.

"Good morning," Dar replied, letting him pass. She'd already assumed he was the dockmaster as she watched him walk to the end of the dock and unlock the small shingled building beside the gas pumps. Giving him a few minutes to settle in, she walked out and glanced into the open door. He sat at a desk, going over some paperwork.

"Excuse me," she said.

"Hello again," he said, putting down his pen.

"I was just wondering," she said, "about a boat I saw here last night."

"Which one would she be?"

"I don't know," Dar said. "But she was a wooden sloop, twenty-eight feet, white hull, with beautiful woodwork."

He narrowed his eyes as if trying to bring such a sailboat to mind, then checked his roster for boats at his pier. Then he climbed off his stool and stood at the door beside Dar. "Nothing like that sounds familiar," he said. "And I don't have her down in my ledger. Can you show me where you saw her?"

"That's just it," Dar said. "I barely glimpsed her just before dark and haven't seen her since."

"Maybe she's a ghost ship," he said, his eyes twinkling.

"No, really," she said, half smiling, but feeling chilled. "Do you keep a description for every boat that docks here?"

"I do, and I have nothing like you're describing. That's why I say she might be a ghost ship."

Dar stared at him. "A real ghost ship?"

"Well. Believe what you want, but we honor a vessel whose captain and crew were lost at sea by welcoming her spirits. We've had many ghosts of the Spanish Armada pass through this harbor. Those ships would be much larger, however. And the *Lusitania* sank off Kinsale Head in 1915. We're haunted by that liner and many of her passengers."

Dar took it in. She thought of her father's call, of how the *Irish Darling* had carried him across the Atlantic, made landfall safely. But had he sailed safely around the peninsulas to Cork?

"You don't believe in such things? Ghosts or fairies?" he asked. "They can be tricky. Just because you don't believe doesn't mean they're not there."

"I trust what you're saying," she said. She knew Dulse would.

"Does the boat you saw mean something to you?" he asked.

"It reminds me of the one my father built," she said. "He sailed solo across the Atlantic and made it safely to Kerry. I know he loved Kinsale, though, and believe he would have tried to make it here afterwards."

"Solo," the dock master said. "On a wooden twenty-eight-footer? A boat that size would be just right for inshore sailing, but small for fighting those ocean waves. Your father must have been dauntless. You don't hear stories like that very often."

"Have you ever heard one?" she asked, her neck prickling.

He nodded. "A long time ago. I was twenty-two at the time, and everyone in Cork and West Cork was talking about it."

"Do you remember the name of the sailor, or of the boat?"

"McCarthy, I believe," he said. "That's why all Cork was so entranced and proud. He was one of our own."

"That was my father," she said, her heart racing. "The boat was the *Irish Darling*."

"Named for someone he loved," the dockmaster said.

Dar nodded. "So you see," she said, "my father's boat couldn't be a ghost ship. He made it here safely. Do you know where he is now?"

"I never heard anything beyond the story of his crossing. I seem to remember he sailed into Cobh and took a job at the seaport there. People talked for a while, but in Ireland, so many true tales fall into legend. It was many years ago. My mind could be playing tricks on me, and I could be wrong. How long ago would it have been?"

"Twenty-eight years ago," Dar said.

"Ah," the dockmaster said. "Plenty of time for the account to become local lore."

A glistening fifty-foot white fiberglass fishing boat pulled up to the gas dock, and the dockmaster gave Dar a look of regret. "I'm sorry we can't continue this conversation. I'm honored to meet you—McCarthy's daughter, imagine that. I'll be telling everyone, you can be sure."

"Thank you for talking with me," she said.

"It's my pleasure, and I wish you luck," he said as he walked toward the pumps. "Perhaps the spirit sloop appeared just for you, to inspire you. Keep your eyes open—you might see it again."

"I will," she said as he took the fishing boat captain's credit card and began pumping gas.

She began to walk, and then to run, down the dock. She had to get Rory up, and they needed to go to Cobh right away.

CHAPTER TWELVE

Rory held on to her seat as her sister drove like a mad-woman. They'd barely had time for tea and a scone before Dar insisted they check out and hit the road. Rory's pro-testations that Delia would be crushed if she didn't get to experi-ence the culinary wonders of Kinsale were met by a promise they would return once they found their father in Cobh.

That's when Rory knew she and Dar were on separate pages. Deep down, Rory believed this trip fell into the category of tilt-ing at windmills as well as a chance to forget about losing the Vineyard. The letters were one thing, but finding their father was another. Too much time had passed. He could have moved or died. And besides, what would they really want with a father who had so clearly abandoned them?

But Dar seemed wild, a little out of control, like the teenager she'd been during the years after their father had left. She focused on the road with ferocious concentration, punching the shift into high gear when they reached the highway heading east.

Rory hadn't slept well, but she'd stayed in bed until Dar had come to get her up. She wondered if Dar felt as moved as she, to be sharing a room again after all these years. And oddly, this crazed side of Dar felt familiar, took Rory back to their childhoods, when they'd all gone a bit mad, losing their father.

"Do you think you can trust the dockmaster?" Rory asked.

"What?" Dar said, already far ahead in her mind, strategizing their next moves.

"I mean, he didn't actually know, or even see, Dad. It could be one of those legends he told you about."

"He seemed sure of his own memory," Dar said.

"Okay. But I mean, how did he know Dad was working at the seaport? We're leaving that lovely town to go to Cobh, which makes me nervous, and I don't know why. It doesn't even sound the way it's spelled. I just liked it where we were. It felt like a good home base."

"We can always go back."

"I guess," Rory said, staring out the window at more lovely green scenery. She found herself wondering about Jonathan. She'd called before school to check on the kids, had a good talk with each of them. They missed her, but sounded so happy to be with their dad. They'd put him on the line.

Speaking to him had unleashed the demon. Even as they drove through the stunning and quiet countryside, she found herself dissecting their conversation. He'd said that although Alys wasn't staying with them, he wanted to spend a day with her that weekend.

Dar had spotted the turnoff for Cobh, and had her turn signal on a good minute too soon. The city came into view, a crescent of impeccably restored Georgian houses, then, a level below, colorful row houses in the shadow of a sprawling steel-gray cathedral with a skyscraping steeple.

"Too bad Delia wasn't here to see that," Rory said. "You know how much she loves cathedrals."

"She'll be here tomorrow. That must be St. Colman's, where Dad was baptized. She'll want to visit."

"That might even make up for missing out on Kinsale."

Holding the wheel, leaning forward, working the left-hand shift, Dar drove down the hill to the docks. Rory saw a boat launch ramp, fishnets drying on a steel fence, a shabby—compared to Kinsale—fleet of sailboats, fishing boats, work boats. She opened her guidebook and read.

"Hmm," she said. "'During the past two centuries, the port city of Cobh was the staging spot for people on their way to North America. Famous transatlantic liners called in at this harbor, transporting the masses to the United States and Canada. The *Lusitania* memorial may be found on the quayside. Victims of the tragedy are buried at Cobh's Old Church cemetery.'" She paused, glancing at Dar. "The famine tragedy cemetery, the *Lusitania*-sinking tragedy cemetery . . ."

As they drove along the dockside, Dar seemed to stare into every face, examine every boat—and there were hundreds of each. Rory's talk with Jonathan had left her feeling upset and insecure; she spied an Internet café and knew she had to log on.

"Hey," she said, trying to sound normal. "Why don't I jump out here, get us a couple of coffees. I need a break from tea. You can park the car, and we'll start asking around."

"Good plan," Dar said.

"I'll find you," Rory said.

So they parted, and Dar drove away. Rory watched her round the corner, then hurried inside and paid the attendant for twenty minutes on the Internet. She breathed more deeply just to be sitting at a computer.

She logged on, used *keithfarm* to open his Gmail account, and read. She steeled herself for e-mails to Alys. They missed each other; he reassured her that he loved her, thanked her for understanding about the kids. Alys had written a bitchy reply about Rory being unreasonable, and Jonathan hadn't disagreed. But there were other, sweet e-mails—to friends on the Vineyard, lamenting the sale of Rory's family's house. She read them over and over.

There was one to Andy Mayhew. Rory would never have expected Andy to have a computer. She thought he was firmly rooted in the pre–e-mail world.

> *I think they have to return to the Vineyard by closing. It's been pushed back to the first week of May. You have that long. Let me know how I can help.*
>
> *Jonathan*

And Andy's reply:

> *She'll be gone a long time, a trip she had to make. I'd have gone with her, but this is my busy season. She has Rory with her instead. You know what a jerk you are to let her go. Alice is like cotton candy. Pretty and tasty, but that's all there is. With the McCarthy sisters you get a lifetime of complications and depth. Think about it, man. Midlife crisis.*

Jonathan:

*She spells her name "Alys." She loves me and that counts.
Rory and I will always love each other, but we stopped
wanting the same things. She's so wrapped up with the
kids and her family; it was a long time in hell while her
mom was dying. And you know I loved Tilly too.
Something broke when she passed. The glue that had
held us all together. All that Vineyard joy was suddenly
replaced by sadness. I can't live that way. Life is too short.*

Andy:

Sorry for the misspelling. And sorry for butting in.

Jonathan's final reply:

*Rory and her sisters get back out here early May. That
doesn't give you much time. I'll be out there this weekend
visiting my parents with the kids. See you Friday night or
Saturday morning. Make sure Harrison's around. We all
want to see him, too.*

Rory felt immensely gratified by Andy's skepticism and expe-
rienced true respect for him. She had assumed that all men had
their heads turned by beautiful younger women. Both loving and
hating her husband was exhausting. She felt confused by that, and
by whatever Jonathan had agreed to help Andy with.

She was just about to get the coffees when Dar walked in and
found her at the computer station.

"Busted," Rory said.

"Don't worry about it."

"You might like to know our guys were e-mailing about us."

"Our guys?"

"Jonathan and Andy. Andy spoke up for me about Alys, and he made a really sweet comment about you and me."

Dar nodded in a way that let Rory know she didn't want to talk about it.

"Don't you want to know what he said?"

"No," Dar said. "Come on, let's get going here. I've got the coffees."

"Why don't you want to know?"

"Because if Andy wanted me to, he'd tell me himself."

"Fine," Rory said, letting the fringe of her short dark hair fall across her eyes so Dar wouldn't see how hurt she was.

"It's not good for you," Dar said. "That's what I care about. Let this thing with Jonathan and the girl play itself out. Then see how *you* feel—not how he does. Come on now, let's go."

Rory could have argued with her but chose not to. She was struck by how similar Dar's view was to Andy's. Rory gazed at her sister, wondering if she realized how rare that was.

Dar walked the docks without knowing what she was looking for. Rory was with her but seemed distracted by shops and flowers and people-watching. Dar had to admit it was frustrating to not be on the same wavelength regarding their search; it felt to her Rory might be afraid of what they might find—especially if they actually found their father.

As they strolled along, they drifted apart. Rory had her digital camera out and was snapping shots of typical Irish storefronts—doors framed and painted with glossy, deep, rich colors. Above the doorway the proprietor's or shop's name was stenciled in gold. She turned to the pots of flowers and small garden plots that seemed ubiquitous throughout the parts of Cork they'd seen.

Dar spent her time speaking to boat captains, showing them her father's picture, asking if they knew or remembered Michael McCarthy, if they'd heard the story of his solo crossing aboard the *Irish Darling*. But most of the captains she encountered were young. Some thought they'd heard a tale about some Irish guy sailing the Atlantic in a tiny dory; he'd supposedly made it here to Cobh only to disappear. It was like a fairy tale, some of them said.

"I heard he worked in the seaport," Dar said.

"Well, you're looking at the seaport," one captain said, waving his hand around.

"What was his trade?"

"Carpentry. Boatbuilding."

"You might try the sheds and loft up and down that wharf over there." He pointed. "He'd make a good living doing the carpentry. Everyone needs things fixed and repaired. He'd be an old guy by now?"

"Yes," Dar said.

"Well, good luck in your search."

Dar thanked him and headed toward the wharf. Rory hung back, taking pictures, while Dar turned toward the boatbuilding sheds and barns. Once again she showed her father's picture, went through the story. After the first few blank stares, and another few shakes of the head, it seemed to her that everyone in the Cobh marine industry was too young and uninterested in anything beyond their day's work to help her.

And then she came upon a large wharf building with a curved

arched sign over the double-wide doors leading straight to iron tracks down to the water, a heavy-duty boat launch. The sign, in gold, said *McCarthy Manufacturing.* Dar stared at it for a long time. The listing Delia had found on Google. They'd dismissed it then, but what they manufactured was obvious—through the open doors, Dar spotted several boats in various stages of production. She walked inside.

Again, she saw nothing but young men and some women— fiberglassing one cabin top, sanding a long, wide wooden hull, transporting a lead keel by forklift to the back of the loft. Dar followed it. The forklift reached a dead end, lowering the keel carefully to the floor.

Dar looked up. A pulley system was in place, attached to thick-hewn rafters, and above them a window overlooking the workplace. She found wooden stairs, the treads worn away in the middle, leading upstairs. She headed up quickly, holding the smooth, round handrail.

She emerged at the top into a single room that ran the width of the building. The space seemed to be out of the nineteenth century: wooden file cabinets along one wall, a grandfather's clock, a brass barometer marked *McCarthy's* behind the dials, one large oak partners desk with only one person seated there.

He appeared to be slightly older than Dar, with short salt-and-pepper hair and wearing an impeccable white shirt and jeans. He was bent over the only modern equipment in the room: a seventeen-inch MacBook Pro just like Dar's, referring to the screen while jotting down notes on an order pad.

"I saw you come in," he said, without looking up. "What's your business?"

"No business," she said.

"You're not a tourist, are you? Because this shop isn't on the tour. You could get hurt in here, all the equipment moving around. Or if a boat went off the rails, you'd be in heaven before you'd know what hit you."

"I'm not a tourist," she said.

He looked up with piercing blue eyes, waiting for an explanation.

Dar took a breath. "The sign says 'McCarthy's,'" she said. "Is that your name?"

He nodded. "Been in the family two hundred years. We fought the British in boats we built."

"My name's McCarthy, too," she said. "Darrah McCarthy."

"So you're an American tracing your roots," he said. "You'd be better off up the hill, at the cathedral. Ask Monsignor if you can go through the records. There are plenty of parish records for all the searching you want."

"I'm not tracing my roots. I'm looking for this man," she said, showing him the photo. "It was taken a very long time ago."

He stared at the picture a long time. "What do you want with him?" he asked.

"You *know* him?" Dar asked.

"I didn't say that. I'm just curious."

"He sailed his boat transatlantic, a twenty-eight-footer called *Irish Darling*, from Massachusetts to Cobh. He did it solo-handed."

"You sure he made it here?" the man asked.

Dar nodded. "He called home from Kerry, but someone in Kinsale told me he'd sailed on to Cobh."

"Home?"

It took her a moment, but she got the words out. "He was my father."

The man continued frowning at the picture, tapping it with his finger. Then he looked up—not at Dar, but somewhere in the middle distance. This went on for several minutes.

"You must have heard of him," she said, "even if you never met him. People talked about what he did. The dockmaster at Kinsale knew the story. He told me my father worked at the seaport here."

Silence as the man stared into space.

"What's your name?" she asked, partly to see if he was still awake.

"Tim," he said.

"Who do you share the partners desk with?"

"No one," he said. "Used to be my father and uncle, but they're long gone. I run the place myself."

He glanced up at her, seemed to make up his mind about something. "Michael McCarthy was an intrepid soul."

"You *did* know him!"

"Knew of what he'd done. It was all the family talked about for a while. Come here," he said, rising. They walked to the far end of the office. The rough-wood walls were papered with architectural renderings of sailboats, fishing boats, freighters. Tim pointed out the original drawings of the two ships they'd built to fight the British.

There were figureheads of saints and angels, their faces holy, their paint peeling, their wings and scepters worm-eaten; beneath them were wooden transom signs made to hang the width of the sterns of boats, stating the vessel's name and home port, some scrolled, others plain, the boat names deeply scored into the wood, painted gold.

Dar looked up and down the rows, knowing she'd see her father's there. She remembered when he'd worked on the sign himself, as elaborate and fancy as any here, and told her why he was naming the sloop after her. But his transom board wasn't among the others, and she felt her shoulders hunch forward.

"Here," Tim said, pointing at a four-by-twelve-inch rectangle of oak hanging at the very end of the row.

Dar leaned forward to look. The block was carved in bas-relief: scrolls on either end, curved like a banner, in lettering that read *Irish Darling*. Seeing the words made something come alive inside her, and tears pooled in her eyes.

"You did this?" she asked.

"When I was seventeen," he said. "I was as enamored as everyone else over your father's feat. When I learned he'd built the boat himself, that sealed it. Suddenly I knew what I had to do. A few spare boards from my grandfather's lumber shed, a hammer and screwdriver, and a few brass fittings from my own tool belt."

"My father would have been proud to know he'd inspired you," Dar said.

Tim stared at the block of wood he'd carved. "I'd forgotten this was here until you came in." He took it down. "I want you to have it."

Dar held it, looked up at him. "Please, keep it here. It will mean more to me somehow. Did you ever meet him?"

"I apprenticed beside him. When your dockmaster friend said he worked at the seaport, this is what he meant."

"What was he like? Did he say anything about his family?"

"I was seventeen. All I cared about was boats, making them and sailing them."

"Is he—is it possible? That he's still alive?"

Tim shrugged. The frown was back, the moment was over. He hung the board back on the wall, but Dar got the feeling he was doing it only to placate her. Perhaps she'd offended him by not accepting the gift.

"I've changed my mind," she said. "Your carving would mean the world to me. I'd like to take it if you'll let me, so I can show my sisters."

"Your sisters," he said.

"I have two. Rory and Delia. They're here with me now. Well, Rory is, and Delia's landing tomorrow morning."

"Enjoy Ireland," he said.

"We will, it's beautiful, but . . ."

"Don't just stay in Cork. Visit Kerry and Connemara. Sligo if you make it that far. You driving?"

"Yes."

"Hard with the left-hand shift, I bet. I had hell trying to drive on the right in America."

"Where did you visit there?"

"It's yours," he said, ignoring her and once again removing the carved sign from the hook on the wall. "Now, you'll have to excuse me. I have work to do."

"Isn't there anything more you can tell me? What happened after he stopped working here? Did he live in town? Did he stay in the area? Did you ever find out if you were related?"

"Different McCarthy," Tim said. "An entirely separate branch of the clan."

"But what about the rest? Where he lived, and if—"

"Look," he said sharply. "There's one person who might know, if she's willing to see you. It's doubtful, I'll be honest. She lives in a nursing home a short ways north, in the Blackwater Valley." He wrote down the address and directions.

"Who is she?" Dar asked.

"My mother," Tim said. "Who loved him."

CHAPTER THIRTEEN

Rory and Dar stood stone-faced at the arrivals gate at Cork Airport, waiting for Delia to clear customs. They'd argued last night, with Dar wanting to go to the nursing home right away, and Rory saying they had to wait for Delia.

Dar accused Rory of wanting to spend the night cyber-stalking her ex, and Rory snapped that Dar was obsessed with a dream that had stopped existing the day their father sailed away. Dar had shown her the board and told her what Tim had said about their father, and for a moment Rory felt speechless. Then she came back strong.

"He wasn't some other woman's to love," Rory had said. "He and Mom never got divorced."

"I agree with you."

"Who is this guy, anyway?" Rory had asked. Arms folded across her chest, stalwart, deep blue eyes suddenly coal black. "He doesn't know us, and I'll bet he never met Dad."

"He seemed so convincing, and did carve that sign . . ."

"Well, it's a pretty name for a boat. He could have come up with it on his own."

"It didn't sound that way," Dar said. "Why would he lie? I can't believe Dad came here and had a love affair."

"Think about it, Dar. He was a selfish asshole. He left us for a ridiculous reason. Who cares anymore? Why are we finding it hard to believe he'd get involved with someone else?"

Dar left her alone. They had checked into a harbor guesthouse, seedier than Rory would have liked and nothing like the charming hotel in Kinsale, but with a direct line of sight to McCarthy Manu-facturing—obviously so Dar could keep her eye on the place. This time the sisters had adjoining rooms. It was just as well; Rory was losing patience fast.

The flight from Boston was in, and they saw Delia lugging her suitcase behind her. No wheels, no extendable grip, an old Sam-sonite with a patched handle that looked about ready to give out. Once she came through the gate, Dar and Rory surrounded her in a welcoming hug.

Dar hefted the suitcase. Rory took Delia's shoulder bag. They started off down the hall. Rory kept silent, just waiting for Dar to find the words to start filling Delia in. But to her shock, Delia was the one stammering, trying to get something out. Her face was beet red and her eyes bloodshot, as if she'd been crying or drinking or both all through the flight.

"What is it?" Dar asked, stopping short.

Delia shook her head. "Not here," she said in a strangled voice.

Now they were really hurrying, hauling ass out the door, down the sidewalk, into the Opel.

Rory handed her a bottle of water. Delia guzzled it down, then clutched the near-empty bottle to her chest.

"Tell us what's going on," Dar said as they climbed into the car. Silence until she started it up, drove out of the parking lot, and then the floodgates broke.

"Jim and I are separated," Delia said, her voice still strained, her red face cracking into wrinkles as the tears began to pour down.

"Deel, what happened?" Rory asked.

"I'm so sorry," Dar said.

"We kept fighting about Pete, and Jim said he's given up on him. He said Pete's acting like an addict! And he accused me of never being home anymore, first the Vineyard, now Ireland, and I tried to tell him this isn't a vacation, it's us trying to find our father, and he just sat there planted in front of *CSI*. Watching someone with tweezers pull broken glass from a dead person's eyelids, and I just lost it. And then he said, '*Go* to Ireland then! But don't expect to see me when you get back!'" She put her hands over her face.

Rory and Dar were silent. Just for that moment, Rory didn't hate Dar. She knew they had to come together for Delia.

"Words spoken in anger, right?" Dar said.

"Definitely," Rory said.

"But he's never like this. We might fight, but we always make up."

"Maybe he's taking it out on you because he's so frustrated with Pete," Rory said.

"That's like saying you're on Jim's side," Delia said.

"I'm not at all," Rory said.

No one spoke for a while. Rory held the map in her lap, but Dar wasn't asking directions. She seemed to know exactly where she was going.

"At least Jim didn't say 'divorce,'" Rory said after a few minutes. "I don't believe in it for our family. *At all.*"

"Jim says Pete's not in our family anymore. He said he took the money we sent him to buy drugs. That he's a druggie!"

"He's not a druggie," Rory said.

"Jim said he inherited our 'family problem.' He was referring to you, Dar. Being an alcoholic."

"He could be right," Dar said. "Sometimes it's genetic. But at least I'm sober, and last I heard Pete was, too."

"The way I feel right now, I could join the party," Delia said. "Let's stop for a pint. We can drink to Jim."

"It's nine in the morning," Rory reminded her.

Delia shrugged, the hurt back in her face. "I wasn't being serious."

"I didn't really think you were," Rory said, reaching back to pat her on the knee. They exchanged smiles.

"Oh, one good bit of news regarding the broker and buyers," Delia said.

"Tell us," Dar said.

"Their title search did come back iffy. Morgan called to tell me because apparently she couldn't reach you on your cell. I also gave her Rory's e-mail address."

"Iffy?" Dar asked, giving Rory a small smile.

"Let's not get our hopes up yet," Rory said.

"It's supposed to be pretty straightforward. The land's been in our family since the 1600s. It started off on Grandfather's side of the family, and that never changed until he died and left it all to Grandmother. And then to Mom and the three of us."

"And you and Mom never found anything else when you went to Town Hall?"

"No," Dar said. "But maybe they dug deeper."

"You did say that their expensive team would turn up Dad's land grant if it really existed," Delia said.

"Now I don't want to get ahead of ourselves. But I'm wondering . . . is it possible that this could be a deal breaker?" Rory asked.

"I'm thinking the same thing," Dar said.

"You have been all along," Rory said, jabbing her arm. "It means we were right to come here, find out what Dad was after."

Rory nodded, and Delia tried to hold back a yawn. "It's so exciting," she said. "Takes my mind off Jim and Pete. . . . I want to talk more, but I think jet lag's hitting me . . ."

"Have a good nap," Dar said.

Time passed. Delia curled up in the small back seat. They drove another half hour, reaching a narrow, slate-colored river, the Awbeg, a tributary of the Blackwater.

"She's just in after a long flight; exhausted," Dar said in a near whisper to Rory. "I don't want to tell her till she's ready . . ."

"Tell me what?" Delia asked. "I'm just resting my eyes."

Dar took a deep breath and reached into the door pocket. She removed the wood carving, handed it back to Delia.

"Oh my God," Delia said, sitting upright, tracing the deeply scored letters in *Irish Darling*. "Did you find him? Is he actually here?"

Dar filled Delia in about the Kinsale harbormaster, McCarthy Manufacturing, and what Tim McCarthy had said.

"What Dar hasn't told you is that we're on our way to see someone."

"Who?" Delia asked, beaming. "You found him?"

"We're going to see a woman," Rory said.

"Who?"

"Tim McCarthy's mother," Dar said.

"What does she have to do with us?"

"Tim told Dar she loved Dad," Rory said.

"Whoever she is, she's expecting us," Dar said. "I called ahead. And we're almost there."

Dar felt the tension surrounding her and her sisters, but even more, curiosity. For once she didn't need Dulse to live her adventures for her. She knew she was on her father's trail, closer to him than she'd been since she was twelve.

The Blackwater Valley reminded her of inland parts of the Vineyard: farms, woods, glades, stone walls. With the car windows open, she smelled gorse, holly, and a distant hint of salt from the sea. The Blackwater and its tributaries wove a braid of bright water, and Dar let the peace and beauty of the region calm her heart.

She followed Tim's directions to Kanturk: the market town at the confluence of the Allua and Dalua rivers in the heart of Duhallow in northwest county Cork. The road just outside town tunneled through thick and ancient overarching beech trees, both lovely and menacing. There was a ruined castle, dominating the hill with sorrowful beauty.

Parking the car a distance from the nursing home, she and her sisters got out. No one spoke. She knew they needed time to decompress before going in. A small bakery drew them with smells of fresh bread and sweet rolls.

A bell tinkled when Dar opened the door. A young red-haired woman stood behind the gleaming counter.

"May I help you?" she asked.

"Yes, please," Dar said. "We'd like to take something to a resident at St. Anne's."

"What does she like? Chocolate or a nice fruit tart? Or perhaps a savory?"

"Well, I don't know," Dar said. "I've never met her."

The young woman nodded, as if that happened all the time. She watched Dar gaze up and down the case. Dar thought of her mother and grandmother, tried to think of what they would have liked.

"It's a kind thing you're doing," she said. "Visiting the old people. Imagine, a stranger bringing you a treat. May I make a suggestion?"

"Please," Dar said.

"Don't get her anything too gooey and sweet—she might have diabetes. And nothing too salty—she might have high blood pressure. Now, you can't get away with plain bread; it has to be sweet but not so much so their sugar acts up. Get her a nice flaky roll. It has a dusting of powdered sugar, and I'll put some butter and jam in the bag, too. I always say, go the middle way."

Dar smiled, thankful.

"Do you own this bakery?" Dar asked.

"Oh, no," the young woman said. "My aunt does. So this is your first time in Kanturk? Well, there's so much to see."

"I'm afraid we don't have enough time to see the sights."

"If nothing else, go see the Dalua Bridge, and read the inscription engraved upon stones set into the northern parapet. You might find something that will put you at ease. We have three lovely bridges here, as well as the River Allua, but I think that is the one you most need."

"How can you tell?" Dar asked.

Dar would have asked more, but the bell tinkled and another customer came in. The shopkeeper winked, and Dar paid and left. Outside, her sisters were sitting on a bench, taking in the watery beauty. The town was all gray stone and rushing water, the twin rivers flowing beneath three arched bridges.

She glanced at Tim's directions, and she and her sisters headed across a four-arch cut-stone pedestrian bridge. She felt a chill, hearing the water rush below. Slowing down, she glanced at the ironwork. No carving, wrong bridge. The clear water flowed over stones and sand. Her sisters had been moving in single file behind her, but she stopped them.

"The nursing home is just there," she said, pointing to a long, low white building immediately across the bridge, bordering the town park. "I'm glad we're together to do this."

"So am I," Delia said.

"It just feels so strange to me," Rory said. "We're about to meet a woman who supposedly saw Dad long after we did."

Something had shifted. It happened so often with her sisters, a magical switch being thrown, lifting the tension and making them okay.

They approached the white stucco building and rang the bell beside the bright red door. An elderly nun dressed in a starched white habit and veil answered the ring and greeted them smiling.

"Hello," Dar said. "Are you Sister Theresa? I'm Dar McCarthy; we spoke earlier?"

"Yes, welcome. And you must be Rory and Delia," she said. "Please come in. Mrs. McCarthy is looking forward to your visit."

"Mrs. McCarthy?" Delia whispered as they walked down a sterile white hallway. "Did he *marry* her?"

"Everyone in Cork is named McCarthy," Rory said.

"That's true," Sister Theresa said. "A lot of them are. Now, she has her good days and her bad days. It can change like the weather. She can be quite articulate, even poetic. But don't be upset if she strikes out or falls asleep in the middle of a sentence. She had a stroke, and has made excellent progress. Emotions are difficult for her. Mention something that bothers her and she will either wax elegiac or change the subject, as if the question had never been asked."

"Does a man ever come to visit her?" Dar asked.

"That is for her to tell you," Sister Theresa said. "The truth is, I'm not completely up to speed on her file. Just a fortnight ago I was transferred from a larger home in Cork City." She grinned. "They're putting me out to pasture, and I love it. Now, let me just check what's in the bag, and I'll take you to her."

CHAPTER FOURTEEN

Their heels clicked on the white tile floors. Every surface gleamed, but nothing could disguise the smells of old people dying. It took Dar straight back home, to the wicker hampers lined with plastic to hold her mother's diapers at the end.

Sister Theresa took them to the last door on the left and said loudly, "Hello, we're here, Cathleen. With a sweet for you."

"Come in," Cathleen called in a soft brogue.

Cathleen was dressed in her finest: a navy blue silk dress, pearls at her throat. She sat in a wheelchair, tied to the chair with a red sash around her waist so she wouldn't slip out. She was tiny, with skinny veined wrists. Her spine curved so acutely, she had to arch her neck to view her visitors. Her white hair was neatly brushed, tied with a piece of green yarn. Only her blue eyes—curious, warm—made her seem young.

"We brought this for you," Dar said, handing her the pastry bag.

Cathleen looked inside as if it were Christmas morning. She reached inside, pulled the roll out, and began to eat.

"It's very good," she said with her mouth full. "Thank you."

"Would you like it with butter and jam?" Dar asked.

Cathleen shook her head. "It's good . . . like this." Her lips and the fine hairs around her mouth were covered with powdered sugar and flaky pastry. She ate slowly, making sure she got every crumb. Rory and Delia watched her eat. Dar glanced around the room for photos, letters, anything that would indicate her father had ever been here.

"Do you have someone in your life?" Rory asked. "Someone to bring you treats and visit with you?"

"My son," she said, concentrating on the roll. "Sometimes. I worry that he is angry with me."

"Why?" Rory asked.

"I wish he'd come more often, but he's busy."

Cathleen bowed her head, as if blocking her company out, as if all that existed in her world were the remaining quarter of her sweet roll. After a long time she finished eating and looked up.

"Three sisters," she said.

"Yes," Delia said, surprising Dar by the way she went straight to Cathleen and knelt by the chair. "How can you tell?"

"You look just like him," she said.

"Like who?" Dar asked.

"Sisters are good," Cathleen said. "I had sons."

"Who do we look like?" Dar asked again.

"Dar, don't push her!" Delia whispered, as Cathleen's head tilted forward, chin resting on her chest, perhaps falling asleep.

"Nothing is fair," Cathleen said.

Cathleen stayed quiet a long time. Dar couldn't look at her sisters; she felt so afraid and so hopeful. She thought of herself at twelve, sitting on the stone wall, looking up at the stars with her father. She gazed down at the tiny old woman and hoped stories would pour out, details about him that Dar had been wishing to hear for so long.

"It's not fair when boats are lost at sea," Cathleen said, tears pooling in her blue eyes. "And it's not fair when you love someone and he goes away."

Now Dar knelt beside her. "Who went away?"

Cathleen delicately removed a white tissue from her left sleeve and blew her nose.

"You're so sad," Delia said.

"Not for me," Cathleen said. "For my son. And for his daughters."

"Your son?" Delia asked. "Tim . . ."

"He was so good to Tim," Cathleen said. "Almost like a father. I wanted that for my son . . . a good father like Michael. Such a fine man."

"We're Michael's daughters," Dar said, taking her hand.

"Did he talk about us?" Delia whispered.

Cathleen did the best she could to nod her head. "Darrrrrr," she said, stretching out the name, closing her eyes, seemingly exhausted.

"And Delia and Rory, too?" Delia pressed.

"Three girls," Cathleen said. "His three . . ."

More tears spilled over, and she began to moan, rocking in her chair.

"Where is he?" Dar asked. "Does he visit?"

"'*Hence Bluepool's waving groves delight*

Amuse the fancy, please the sight,
And give such joy as may arise
From sylvan scenes and azure skies,'" Cathleen quoted, choking back tears.

"Cathleen . . ." Dar began.

"The famine was great here. Go to Elbow Street and see where the starving people lived, twelve to a cabin, until they died. Your father . . . was so moved."

"He came here?"

"Of course. For the castle, and to search . . ."

"He searched the castle?" Dar asked.

"The old fort, we call it. It belonged to our chieftain, but d'you know the English Privy Council judged it too grand for McDonough McCarthy, just because he was an Irish subject. The king took it away from him!"

"The chieftain was a McCarthy?" Rory asked.

"Directly in your father's line. We helped answer his questions, helped comfort him when he didn't prevail at first." The memory seemed to shake her, and she closed her eyes. Without opening them, she said in a trembling voice, "No matter how disappointed he was, he was kind to me and Tim."

"Please, Cathleen," Dar said as gently as she could, with her heart banging inside her rib cage. "Prevail how?"

"He was another McDonough McCarthy, my friend Michael was," she said, her language halting. "Hardheaded. There was . . . a violence. Never for me and Tim." She paused, staring into Dar's eyes. "Toward himself. A tortured soul."

"Why, Cathleen?"

"You see, he let his family down."

"Is he still alive? My father?"

"Oh, Michael. My poor friend Michael," she said, hands over her eyes, in such obvious distress Sister Theresa heard and came into the room. The nun put her arm around Cathleen, brushed the sugar from her mouth.

"It's not your fault," Sister Theresa said. "She can get like this. They all can, thinking of what's gone by. This part of life is full of terrible mystery. And then, all of a sudden, profound joy. Please don't worry. But I think it would be best for her to rest now."

The three sisters stood still, not wanting to leave. One by one they bent over to kiss Cathleen's cheek.

Still she wouldn't look up or stop whispering "Michael, Michael . . ."

Dar, Rory, and Delia left the room, walked down the gleaming hall, and stepped out the front door.

Dar couldn't shake the sound of Cathleen saying her father's name. She breathed in the fresh, flower-scented air.

Slowly she and her sisters began to walk through town. There were signs, and Dar followed them to the Dalua Bridge. She thought of the woman in the pastry shop and looked for the carvings.

Engraved in six stones on the northern parapet was a poem in eighteenth-century rhyming couplets. The words were in Irish, but an English translation was provided on a plaque beside the last stone. The three sisters read.

"Look, there's Bluepool," Rory said, touching the stone. "The verse Cathleen quoted."

Dar read to the end:

The weary here in safe repose

Forgetting life's attendant woes
May sit secure, serene and still
And view with joy yon famed hill.

The sisters read the words, Dar trying to make out what any of it meant. They were all tired, and began walking slowly toward their little car, and Dar thought security, serenity, and joy a long way off.

"She sounded so sad," Delia said.

"I can't figure anything out," Rory said. "Where is he? And what does some romantic poem carved into a seven-arched bridge have to do with him? I feel we're more in the dark than before."

"Dad sought her out because she was a McCarthy," Dar said. "And she said he didn't prevail at first . . . but did he at all?"

"She must have meant the land grant," Delia asked. "But from what she said about the castle, it sounds as if the king would have been more likely to take land from Irishmen than to give it to them."

"Is it worth searching more?" Dar asked. "She sounded so sincere."

"She might not know everything," Delia said.

"Dad kept some things secret," Dar agreed.

"I miss my kids. I want to go home. Oh, Dar," Rory said. "Let's leave."

"But we're still missing something here," Dar said.

"I want to call the airline," Rory said. "Change our tickets and leave tomorrow."

"You know what's crazy?" Delia asked. "We thought life was one way, and then we came here and now it's another way. We wanted to find a place to say good-bye to Dad. But that seems even less possible than before. Where did he go from here? Why didn't he come home?"

"Because he didn't 'get what he was owed,'" Rory said. "Just like he said in the letter. He was too proud to return to us. I think we have to accept that."

"I don't want to," Dar said.

"Neither do I," Delia said. "But isn't it time to stop all this and let him be in peace? We've already learned so much more than we knew before."

"It's not enough," Dar said.

"Maybe not, but will anything be? Anything short of finding him alive? Cathleen saying 'my poor friend Michael.' He's dead, Dar. Can't we help each other try to face it?"

Dar closed her eyes tight because, no, she couldn't yet.

"I'm not staying!" Rory said. "If you want to keep searching for him, I guess I can't stop you. But we're not getting anywhere, just more upset."

"I agree with Rory. I just got here, and I'm jet-lagged," Delia said, putting a conciliatory arm around Dar's shoulders. "Too much time has passed. Everything is buried too deep."

"Dar, we mourned Dad before he was dead. He never even called us to tell us he was okay, or that he was on his way back to us. I don't know how to think about any of this!" Rory said.

"I know," Dar said. "You're right, Rory. But in his own way he's brought us here, and we have to see it through!"

"Look, we're all upset. Just get us back to that fleabag we so fondly know as our hotel," Rory said. "I need to lie down."

"Me too," Delia said.

So Dar drove them back to the guesthouse on the busy, noisy, boatbuilding quay of Cobh seaport, the sign *McCarthy Manufacturing* towering over it all, the dark reflection of the stone building and the sign's letters shimmering in the deep blue harbor.

CHAPTER FIFTEEN

The sisters napped in their separate rooms, each of which had barely enough space for a single bed, a bureau, and a crucifix on the wall. Dar fell into hard, instant sleep. She dreamed that she was trying to draw a straight line; with pencil first, then fountain pen, and then outdoors with a shovel and a pickax. She couldn't keep the line straight, but her determination was fierce. Rocks just below the surface made her zigzag back and forth until she felt herself rocking and tilting, first walking with a crowd of others on a collapsing mountain road, then on the deck of a passenger liner pitching on high seas. She had drawn herself into this danger, created it with her pencil, and it had come to life around her.

Her scream woke the other two up. They both knocked on her door, found her sitting on her bed rubbing her head.

"Are you okay?" Rory asked.

"I had an awful dream," Dar said.

They all sat still, letting it come back to her. "I felt I was going to fall off earth's surface, or that the boat was about to sink. The worst part was, I was taking other people with me."

"Who?"

"I couldn't see their faces; I just felt them nearby. The strange thing was, it had started with me drawing lines, as if starting a new Dulse. Except instead of her, it was me." She glanced at her sisters. "And maybe you. It feels as if we were together."

"On the deck of a sinking ship," Rory said.

"But why now? Just when we've found out for sure that Dad made it here, didn't drown?"

Rory kissed her and stood up. "Let's go down for tea. Oh—I checked messages, and Morgan is trying to get hold of us. Should we call?"

"I'll try her," Dar said. But the hotel had terrible cell reception, so the call didn't go through.

"Tea time," Delia said.

The three sisters went downstairs. No frills, just an electric kettle and a plate of soda bread. They sat in peace, not talking. Dar let the shock waves from her dream ripple away. She put on her green fleece and stepped outside to call Morgan.

"Hi, Morgan," Dar said. "Sorry to not call sooner, but reception is sketchy over here."

"That's okay. I'm just relieved to have you on the phone," Morgan said. "The title is a mess. I had asked you very clearly about rights of ownership, and you told me your mother sold it to you for a penny and loving kindness."

"She did," Dar said. "Her mother did the same before that."

"And what about before *that*?" Morgan asked. "The buyers'

attorney is very thorough; he investigated records on the Vineyard, but because the property has been in your family for so long, he needed to trace it back to the very beginning. So he went to the State House in Boston."

"What did he find?" Dar asked, her heart kicking over.

"Well, it's confusing. Please listen to this list and tell me who's who. Archibald Daggett, Jr."

"My maternal grandfather."

"Archibald Daggett would be his father, then."

"Yes."

"Percival Daggett."

"Great-great-grandfather," Dar said.

"John Daggett, I assume, would be your great-great-great-grandfather."

"Yes," Dar said.

"Well, there's a lien on the property dating back to 1625. There is no information whatsoever on precisely who placed it there, but there's a seal stamped into the record. The lawyer is having the image analyzed. Does any of this make sense to you?"

"I'm not sure," Dar said, staring across the harbor.

"Dar, you are not taking this seriously enough. The Littles are about to walk away from the contract. Because of this title problem, we'll have to refund their deposit. Their architect has flown over from London twice, and he's lined up a construction crew that's ready to go the instant we solve this."

"What happens if we don't?" Dar asked.

"Then the Littles will sue you for breach of contract. They are already in this for the cost of their architect and his first-class travel and the plans he's drawn up."

"They shouldn't have jumped the gun," Dar said quietly.

"The Littles may try litigation, but they'll be one step behind the IRS, who will padlock your doors and post signs around your property. They'll seize it and sell it at auction."

"So far we're not behind on taxes," Dar reminded her.

"No, but in June you will be. That's when the reassessments will translate into tax bills. You'll be sunk. You need this sale to go through now. Please do what you can to help me on it."

"Okay, Morgan," Dar said. "I'll see what I can find out."

Dar hung up, staring out the window.

The sun began to set. Its reflection blazed orange in the windows of McCarthy Manufacturing. Dar heard the whistle blow, watched ten or fifteen men walk out the side door and head for their cars. She walked along the cobbled quay, entered the manufacturing building just as the last man was leaving.

Glancing up, she saw that lights were still on in the office. She climbed the stairs quietly, stood standing at the top until Tim McCarthy turned and saw her.

"Did you have a good visit?" he asked.

"I'm sure Sister Theresa called you the minute we left," Dar said. "Didn't she?"

"She keeps me informed about my mother's visitors," he said.

"Your mother is lovely," she said.

"Thank you," he said.

Dar breathed slowly, looking into his eyes.

"She told me my father was good to you."

Tim nodded. "He was."

"I can't figure out why you sent us to see your mother instead of telling me yourself. I'm worried that we upset her."

Tim shook his head. "She's fine. They tell me she's been more restful since your visit than she's been in a long time. I'll go see for myself tonight."

"She seemed the opposite of restful while my sisters and I were there."

"Well, it was a huge deal to her, meeting Michael's daughters. I sent you there because I couldn't have let you leave without having you visit. You see, for many years, she was obsessed with getting in touch with you."

"Why didn't she?"

"Because he never told us where he lived in the States. There are more McCarthys over there than in Ireland."

"Can you tell me what happened? How it started and how it ended?"

Tim pulled out a heavy mahogany chair, worn and burnished, and held it for her. They sat across his desk from each other. He offered her a cigarette; she shook her head, so he lit one for himself.

"He was drawn by the name, of course. His own parents were dead, and his relatives spread around. His grandfather's boat shed was just down the quay from our building. We'd always been here, and he remembered."

"So he came here to ask questions?"

"Initially I guess. But he became our lodger. His sloop needed refitting after her long voyage, and he couldn't stay aboard. My mother let him move into our guest room."

"For how long?" Dar asked.

"A couple of months? Maybe three," Tim said. "He was very occupied with business at the church, and then in Cork City, after something that seemed very valuable to him. My mother would drive him, or let him use our car."

"Did either of them ever tell you what he was looking for?"

"Not really," Tim said. "I just knew it was incredibly important to him. My mother really tried to help him."

"She called him her friend today."

"Well, yes. He was that to her." He paused, gauging Dar's reaction. "More, in fact. My father was dead, so after a while, one thing led to another. She wanted marriage, badly, and for him to be a dad to me. And he was fatherly. I remember that. He was very good to me. But he wouldn't marry her. He said he still had a family in the States."

"The other day, when you said we were from separate branches of the clan . . ."

"That is the truth," Tim said.

"He left us when I was twelve, Rory ten, and Delia seven and a half." Dar felt dizzy, just thinking of it all. "He spoke of being poor, but I know how much he missed his life in Ireland."

"Everyone who lost grandparents, ancestors in the famine, thought they were poor. We'd always had the Manufacturing in our family. Enough for all. One thing my mother told me was that he said he was going to take care of his daughters. That you'd be set for life without your grandmother's money."

"He came out to our island looking for something that belonged to him," Dar said. "That's how he met my mother. We loved him the way he was."

"He was proud," Tim said. "We could all see that. He felt guilty for leaning on my mother, when he had no intention of staying."

"What are you talking about?"

"Well, he always planned his return to the States. To all of you. Once he'd accomplished what he'd set out to do."

"But he never did come back!" Dar said. "Did he change his mind? Did he get so attached to your mother that he couldn't leave? She said he didn't 'prevail at first,' but she didn't say he succeeded, either. Does that mean he didn't find what he was looking for, couldn't bear to return to us without it?"

The large room was dim. One green-shaded lamp glowed on Tim's desk. He pushed back his chair, walked over to Dar. He stood so close, she could smell him: sawdust, machine oil, tobacco. He touched her hair tenderly. For a minute she thought he was going to kiss her.

"That's not what happened, Dar . . . Come with me."

Tim led her downstairs, through the main boatbuilding shed, outdoors, down to a smaller shed with iron tracks running down to the water. Dar's heart beat so hard she could barely breathe.

Could her father be living here? Was it possible? She thought of Harrison on the Vineyard, living in a storage unit. Her father loved the sea; did he live aboard one of the boats in the cavernous loft? Or in a dock slip outside? Or inside this smaller shed?

"Are you ready?" Tim asked. His face was full of grief. Dar knew but didn't want to know. She wavered, and he steadied her. He kept his arm around her waist as he unlocked the brass lock, and eased her inside.

The space was dark, about thirty by forty feet large. It smelled of must, shellfish, and salt water. Tim turned on the light, and Dar spotted green crabs scuttling out of the glare and into the iron-brown water sloshing under the door. Blue-black mussels grew in colonies against the submerged iron rails.

"Look," Tim said.

Dar sensed the bulk behind her, but couldn't make herself turn. She felt Tim's hands on her shoulders, easing her around. She kept her eyes shut so she wouldn't have to see.

"No," she said, trying to push away from him.

"But you know already, don't you? He tried to sail home to you and your family—it was all he wanted. He left from here, this very dock, to attempt a second solo crossing."

Dar opened her eyes. She eased away from Tim, and walked over to the *Irish Darling*, up on a cradle. She looked just the same as Dar remembered her, except her white paint and brightwork were peeling and covered with algae, and there was a deep gash in the front quarter of the starboard side.

"She's been here for twenty-eight years," Tim said. "He sank just a mile off Kinsale Head. The weather was fine; he'd left on the outgoing tide of a full moon night. We'd stood at the end of the quay, watching him go."

Dar closed her eyes, trying to imagine that moment, wondering how her father had felt to be leaving, to be sailing home.

"We can only imagine that he hit a shoal, something uncharted. He never had time to radio for help. She must have filled fast, and he went down with her. My mother tried so hard to reach your family, but he'd never given her your mother's name, or where she lived. He must have wanted to spare her."

"Was he trapped inside?" Dar asked.

"No," Tim said. "We never found his body. He'd taken off his boots, belt, anything that could weigh him down. Maybe he'd tried to swim for shore once he was sure there was no hope for the *Irish Darling*. We found his belongings in the hold when we salvaged her."

"Would you mind if I went on board?" Dar asked. "Just to see?"

"If you want. But the old clothes are gone. We took them off. There's nothing of him left in there."

Even so, Dar climbed the ladder. She stepped over the rail, pitted with salt and mildew. She was standing in her father's grave. She touched each surface tenderly, whispering his name. She squeezed her eyes shut as hard as she could, tried to bring up his face. But she couldn't—it was gone. She had to reach into her pocket and take out the black-and-white photo.

There he was, her beloved dad. He had wanted to return home to her family. Sinking onto a bare wood settee, she held the photo and smiled at him. She loved him more than ever. If she closed her eyes, she could imagine him sitting right behind her. The Kinsale dockmaster had been right: she'd seen a ghost ship.

She stood up, began to move through the cabin. Time fell away, and she swore she was exploring the boat with her father, just like the first time. She looked at the bookcases he'd built because she and her sisters loved to read so much, the galley now stripped of its compact stove and refrigerator box. Algae had marred every surface. She scratched her name on a porthole; the dry green organism felt like dust and stuck under her fingernail.

Even the deck was covered with the stuff, in spite of the many people who must have tromped through over the years. She stared at the beautiful deck; her father had been so pleased with the teak and holly pattern he'd installed. And then she remembered: the tiny secret spot in the main saloon. She held her breath. Was it real? Had she dreamed up the hidden compartment for Dulse, for a story? She went straight to it—forward of the folding table, port side.

Crouching down, Dar pressed a square the size of a Scrabble piece. It released a mechanism, and a foot-square section of the teak and holly flooring lifted out. She gazed into the watertight compartment, but it was too dark to see. Feeling around inside, she felt squeamish. There could be crabs or something worse hiding there. Her hand found something: a pouch. She pulled it out slowly, carefully.

Made of rubber, wrapped in a plastic bag. Dar didn't want to take the time to learn what it held. Tim had had the *Irish Darling* all these years. He could have searched and found it; but now it was Dar's, and she slid it into the inside pocket of her jacket.

When she climbed down, she caught the compassionate look on Tim's face. "I'm sorry I didn't tell you right away, when you first came."

"Why didn't you?"

"Ah, it's shitty. I hated you for years—not just you, but his whole family. I wanted you to meet my mother—not only for her, but so you could see she was real. We existed."

"You mattered to him," Dar said.

Tim shrugged. "He'd been with us barely a few months, but he took a big slice of us when he left. He raised our hopes, that's how I think of it now. It was good to have him with us. But it hurt my mother to see him walk out to the end of the rock jetty, looking west every single night. As if he could see you, all he'd left behind."

"Hurt you, too," Dar said.

"Maybe," Tim said. Dar looked down, not wanting to cry.

"We'll stay in touch," she said, suddenly needing to get out of there, reaching into her pocket, giving him her card.

"Yes," he said, glancing at the bold charcoal print of a dark-eyed girl swimming among the strands of a kelp forest. "What's this?"

"That's Dulse," Dar said. "She's the main character in a series of graphic novels I do."

"Wow. My new friend's super talented," he said.

She glanced at her watch, knowing Rory and Delia were probably packing, waiting for her to get back for dinner.

"I want my sisters to see the boat," she said. "I know it's getting late, and you probably want to leave."

He shook his head. "I'll wait here till you get back."

So Dar hurried down the quay, into the small bed-and-breakfast, found her sisters standing in the lobby, looking at menus for local restaurants.

"Dar!" Delia said. "We exchanged our tickets, and we're all set. I'm going to the Vineyard with you instead of back home right away. Is that okay?"

"Where did you go?" Rory asked. "We were getting worried."

"I was at McCarthy Manufacturing," Dar said. "And I want you to come there, too. There's something you have to see."

The two of them stared at her, and she knew they could see the truth in her eyes, the smell of algae and the sea pouring off her. Her hands were dirty from touching their father's boat, but she used them to ease her sisters down, into creaking lobby chairs.

"I found out what happened to Dad," she said.

"What?" Rory asked, sounding afraid.

"Is he alive?" Delia asked, gripping Dar's hand.

"No," Dar said softly. She knelt down, her mouth dry. After so many years, all the hoping and wondering and giving up, she searched for the words. "He didn't make it . . ."

"He's dead?" Rory asked.

"He is," Dar said. "He died trying to sail home to us. It was a clear night, the tide was with him, there was no reason . . ." She broke down, picturing her father sinking just offshore, wondering what must have gone through his head. Her sisters held her.

"Did Tim tell you?" Delia asked after a while.

"Yes," Dar said. "He's waiting for us, so you can see the boat. They salvaged her, kept her all this time."

So the three of them headed out. The wind blew straight off the harbor, tasting of salt. Tim was waiting just outside the shed door; Dar saw his cigarette glowing in the dark. He spotted them coming, came forward.

"Hello," he said. "You must be Rory and Delia."

"Hi, Tim," Rory said.

Delia gave him a hug. "Dar just told us."

"I'm very sorry," Tim said. "Your father was a good man; we all knew how badly he wanted to get home to you . . ."

Dar watched her sisters take in his words. They nodded, tearing up. Tim turned to lead them into the damp boathouse, over to the wreck of the *Irish Darling*. Rory went straight to the hole in her side, cried out as she touched the ragged splintery edges.

Tim held the ladder so they could climb up. Again, he didn't follow, but let them be alone together. There was no surface untouched by salt water, and the hold smelled of seaweed and barnacles. Dar stood back, letting her sisters make their way around the small space, doing the same thing she had: touching everything he might have touched.

"He was on his way home," Rory said. "Even though he didn't get what he'd come for."

"Maybe he did," Dar said.

"But Cathleen made it seem he didn't," Delia said. "It's horrible, but that means even more to me, thinking he'd decided to sail home no matter what. I hated thinking of him basing everything on that land grant."

"I think Cathleen was wrong, or meant something else. I think Dad did find what he was looking for" Dar said, reaching under her fleece.

Her sisters gathered close, staring at the rubber pouch. The zipper had rusted out, so when Dar pulled on it, it ripped apart. She reached inside, pulled out a folded piece of parchment paper, the creases fragile and brown. They leaned over, gazing at impossibly fine writing, the black ink blotched and faded to almost nothing in spots. The pen's imprint had been strong, however, and there was a thick, cracked red wax seal beside the signature line.

"Is it?" Rory asked.

"I think so," Dar said.

"He was right, then," Rory said. "He was right all along . . ."

"I wish Mom could have known," Dar said. "She lived the rest of her life thinking he'd left her forever."

"Why couldn't he have called?" Delia asked. "Do you think he'd gotten more involved with Cathleen than Tim said? Maybe he was torn about coming home."

"I think he was involved with Cathleen," Dar said. "But I know he wasn't torn. He was always coming home. The things he was most confident about were sailing and the sea. He'd made it to Ireland in terrible weather; I'm sure it never occurred to him he wouldn't make it back to the Vineyard safely."

"He wanted to surprise her," Delia said.

"Or prove something to her," Rory said. "But he still could have called, told her he'd tracked down the deed. Or whatever it is."

"How *did* he track it down?" Delia asked.

Dar shook her head. She had no idea. They'd have lots of questions for their lawyer, Bart Packard, when they got home. But just then she and her sisters fell silent, thinking of their father, knowing they were in the place where he had died. The boat felt holy, just as the cemetery had when they'd surrounded their mother's grave.

Whatever their father had or hadn't accomplished had never made them love him more or less. Standing in the cold, dank saloon of the sloop he had built with such love, they felt his loss more than ever, and held hands with tears running down their cheeks.

PART IV

Water in all its phases is at its best on Martha's Vineyard.

NATHANIEL SOUTHGATE SHALER, 1894

CHAPTER SIXTEEN

The key was easy to find. It had always been hidden under the angel in the garden. During summer the chipped stone statue was covered by vines, surrounded by marsh grass, but in spring the grass was barely turning green and vines were a distant memory of summers gone by. Once Pete had asked Dar why they had an angel. No one was particularly religious. And she'd said, "Everyone needs a protector."

Pete thought of that now. When Granny got really sick, she allowed Dar to place a statue of the Buddha in the herb garden. But the angel predated the Buddha by a lot of years, and it had been keeper of the key all that time. He saw a small plastic doll sitting near the angel. A little girl had been around. His daughter.

Most of the time the house was left unlocked. But right now the three sisters were in Ireland, and the house was basically sold, and Pete guessed Dar didn't want any vultures entering without permission. She'd told him to go home to Maryland. He was a piece of shit who'd never even met his own kid, but he hoped his aunt would understand.

Everyone needs a protector.

Inserting the key into the lock, he thought of how ancient the metal seemed. Had the same lock been here since the house was built? He let himself in, and was instantly surrounded by Scup and the cats.

"Hey, guys," he said, petting them. "Good boy, Scup. Need to go out?" He opened the door and let the old Lab outside to do his business. Who was feeding the animals with Dar away? He saw almost-full bowls of kibble and water.

Pete smelled the salty, damp-dog mustiness that let him know he was home. Or was it his home anymore? He had fucked things up so badly he was now kicked out by his father. Pete had borrowed money from his parents one time too many. Dropping out of college—mid-semester, just past the limit for getting even a fraction of their money back—had been bad. Sleeping with a girl one night, her getting pregnant, never even meeting his own daughter, had sealed it.

Inside, he went to the refrigerator. He was starving, and found some smoked bluefish and horseradish cheese spread. A loaf of rye bread in the freezer made the meal, and he thawed the bread in the 1960s toaster oven, fixed a few sandwiches, and took them onto the porch to eat.

The temperature was about sixty, balmy compared to Alaska. Being here made him reflective, made him think about what had happened there. Staring past the pond out to sea, he scanned the horizon for a sailboat. He knew it was coming, he just didn't know when.

Up in Bristol Bay beginning of last summer, seining for salmon, he'd pulled a dumb move. First light, groggy, up in the bow and operating the hydraulic winch to haul anchor, he had slipped and fallen overboard.

The waves had swamped him, pulled him under the thirty-something-degree water. He was in particularly bad shape hang-overwise; his arms were too heavy and frozen to hold himself up. Trying to swim, he heard someone yell *"Man overboard!"* Some-one had seen him go over, and the captain of the salmon boat, *Helena Marie*, drove in circles looking for him.

Pete sank. His boots were dead weight, filling fast. Eyes open, he saw the peace of the underworld. Shimmering sun in the eupho-tic zone, that part of the sea where light penetrates. Off the west coast, the upwelling—the wave force that causes detritus to rise from the sea bottom—made the water murky and shrank the sunny part from two hundred meters to fifty.

Pete was as one with the phytoplankton, first link in the food chain, moving down into serious darkness where he would encounter apex predators, large sharks prowling the depths. His waterlogged boots sped him downward, his lungs bursting with the last breath he'd ever take.

Then, and here's where it got weird, he felt arms surrounding him. Big strong arms lifting him up. Pete was not a religious man, and he wasn't on hallucinogens. He wasn't crazy. He didn't think it was God.

But glancing down as they rose back up through the hazy water's light, he saw big hands gripping his chest, dark hair on forearms, a Claddagh ring facing in toward his savior's heart. The man could swim as if with jet propulsion. As they rose, he gave Pete air. Not with a regulator, and not mouth-to-mouth, but somehow magically he transferred H_2O to Pete's bloodstream.

When they broke the surface, Pete heard his shipmates shouting. "There he is!" "Hang on, Petey, we're coming for you!" They threw the grappling hook, and although Pete was too weak to grab the line, his savior did, and he wrapped it once around Pete's chest, hooking the line to hold it steady.

When Pete turned around, no one was there. The crew hauled him over to the *Helena Marie*, and by the time they got Pete on board, he was puking up seawater, trying to see over the transom.

"What're you looking for?" Hank McDuff asked.

"Nothing," Pete said, because it would have sounded insane.

Pete pulled himself up, stared into the bay. He saw a sailboat: small, pretty, white hull, gleaming brightwork. She shimmered like a mirage. He spit more seawater out of his lungs.

"You see her?" he asked, pointing.

"See what?" Catcher Langtry asked. "Come on, man, you gotta get off deck for a while."

Sailors and fishermen were superstitious about ghosts and their ships, and the notion of the sloop his grandfather had built, the *Irish Darling*—a legend to Pete, having been possessed by boats his whole life—filled his mind. He didn't tell anyone, and he signed on for every trip the rest of the summer. Come winter, he worked in the cannery. He'd stand at the end of the wharf, watching for that sailboat.

Now, finishing his lunch, he stared out at the calm blue sea off Squibnocket. After a few minutes he went inside, washed his dish, and headed upstairs. The house was rambling, with narrow hallways and unexpected wings and staircases. It unsettled him to see that most of the rooms were empty. Boxes were piled in corners, labeled *Dar, Rory*, and *Delia*—his mom.

Pete made his way down the long second-floor hall to the room that had been his grandmother's. She'd died last October; he hadn't made it to the funeral. Entering her room, he felt pangs of love and guilt. For some reason, this room was the last to be completely packed away. It still looked as he remembered it from childhood, coming out to the Vineyard every summer.

The white metal bed was no longer made up with her favorite linens from France. Her books had been taken down from the bookcase. But the brightly colored glass chandelier still hung overhead, catching the light. Her writing desk was still by the window. Beside it was the blue silk armchair he'd always loved because his grandmother would hold him on her lap while sitting in it, and they'd make up stories about the island, the sea, and a sailor who went wherever the wind took him.

Pete stood by the writing desk. His hands were trembling. He hadn't had a drink or drug in fourteen days, but he'd developed a real problem there, up in Alaska. After each trip, a lot of guys spent their shares in the bars. Pete had banked his for a while, but soon he found himself bellied up to the bar at the Cat's Catch, an old cathouse turned into a tavern, scoring crystal and drinking shots till the ups and downs flipped him over and he couldn't remember his own name.

Hand tremors took him back to drinking and drugging times, but right now he was filled with fear and emotion. Was his memory correct? Not about being rescued by a ghost, but about something his grandmother had shown him when he was six. She'd taken him into her room, locked the door behind her.

Pete remembered her short white hair and bright blue eyes. She always wore loose cotton dresses that went below her knees, bright colors she called coral, jade, periwinkle. The only jewelry she wore was a necklace with a silver knot pendant. She was strong, and she could walk fast, and she knew the batting averages of all the Red Sox. Smoking had given her a deep, gravelly voice, but to Pete it was also soft and full of love.

"You're my only grandson," she said, long before Obadiah was born. "And I have only daughters, no sons."

They stood before her ebony desk. She pulled down the slanted panel that provided the writing surface. Inside were several cubbyholes filled with her stationery, stamps, a letter opener. The center compartment looked empty, but she reached in, and all the way back was a green velvet box. She took it out and handed it to Pete.

"What is it?" he asked.

"A ring," she said. "It was given to me by my only love. And when you find your only love, I shall give it to you to give her."

She gestured for Pete to open the box. Inside was a gold ring with a strange symbol on it: two hands holding a heart. Pete liked it because it seemed like a story. Whose hands, and whose heart, and who would hold a heart anyway? He asked his grandmother these questions.

"The person holding the heart is you. Or me, or anyone. If you are alone, hoping for love, you wear it on your third finger with the heart facing out. But if you have found love, you wear the heart toward your own heart—facing in."

"Why don't you wear it?" he had asked her.

Her silence lasted a long time, and was full of sadness. "Because your grandfather sailed away from me."

Pete's hands stopped shaking. He stood by the writing desk, reached into the center compartment. It was empty. What would he have done if he'd found the ring?

His father was right; he was a druggie. He'd gotten into some bad stuff up in Dillingham, developed a meth habit, and sold his truck to pay for it. He'd asked his parents for money to repair a vehicle he no longer possessed—he'd sold it in Denver for booze and meth. Hitchhiked all the way home from Alaska, to cop along the way.

Fourteen days without drinking or drugs—a huge accomplishment for him—and right now staring into the compartment where that ring had been, he knew he'd half hoped he could take it into Oak Bluffs, find a guy, trade the ring, and get high. He wouldn't have done it, though. He swore to himself he wouldn't have thrown away his new sobriety to hock his grandmother's ring.

Pete was tired, skinny, covered with sores, jonesing for something to get him right. But thinking about that ring, he remembered how he'd nearly drowned. The arms around him, the hand wearing a ring to match the one he'd been looking for: heart facing inward. He wished his grandmother were alive so he could tell her about it.

He was sure his grandfather had saved his life.

Pete was tired. He lay down on his grandmother's bed. He must have fallen asleep in the sun pouring through her window. Too exhausted for dreams, he just crashed.

However much time passed, he suddenly heard footsteps. Heavy boots on the stairs.

"Hello?" came the deep voice. "Who's there?"

Pete struggled out of sleep. He tried to sit up, act as if he just happened to be sitting on the bed. A man stepped into the room, tall and rugged like the fishermen in Alaska. But Pete recognized him—one of his aunt's friends.

"Hey," Pete said.

"Who the fuck are you?"

"Pete Monaghan. I'm Dar's nephew."

"Pete! Holy shit, I didn't recognize you. I'm Andy Mayhew, remember me?"

"Sure do, man," Pete said.

Andy crossed the room to shake Pete's hand. His gaze took in Pete's sallow coloring, the open sores on his face, his cheeks sunken from missing back teeth. Pete felt tense, standing by his grandmother's open desk.

"It's not what you think," Pete said.

"It better not be," Andy said.

"My grandmother showed me something once," Pete said. "She said it would be mine when I fell in love."

"Are you in love?"

"No."

"That's because no one but another meth head would want to hook up with you. What are you doing here?"

"I needed to come home," Pete said, his voice shaking. "To get clean. It's fourteen days now."

"Okay," Andy said. "That's a good start. But you can't stay here."

"Man," Pete said, his eyes flooding, "I've got nowhere else to go."

"Yes, you do," Andy said. "I'll take you there. And listen. You can't just let Scup out and leave him. I found him halfway down South Road."

"Sorry, Andy."

"It's okay, Pete. Close the desk now."

Pete went to the writing desk. In spite of the fact that Andy seemed to be in charge here, Pete felt protective of the place his grandmother had kept her ring. He turned to check; Andy was watching him like a hawk. Then he closed the slanted wood front.

"Did you ever know my grandfather?" Pete asked.

"I sure did," Andy said.

"Just wondered," Pete said, still staring at his grandmother's desk.

Andy checked on the cats, then locked up the house. He let Scup ride in the back of his truck and Pete in the passenger seat. Pete asked to run back inside to get his backpack, but Andy said no. No telling what Pete might have hiding in there. Driving past the cemetery, he saw Pete straining his neck to see.

"Your grandmother's buried back there, on the hillside."

"I should have been here for the funeral."

Andy didn't reply.

They drove to Alley's Store, and Andy bought two coffees. He drank his black, but he guessed Pete would take his with milk and sugar. Returning to the truck, he caught Pete's glance of appreciation. They drove out of the parking lot, and Andy checked his watch.

"Am I holding you up?" Pete asked. "I don't want to. If it's too much trouble . . ."

"It's not too much trouble."

"But you have somewhere you have to be."

"Work, Pete. I'm my own boss, so I can take an hour to get you settled."

"What does 'settled' mean?" Pete asked, sounding nervous.

Andy didn't answer him right away. He knew that fourteen days clean and sober would keep Pete out of detox, but it didn't mean he was ready for the world. They drove down the pine-lined road, and Andy opened the window so Pete could smell the island. They passed Andy's small house and Harrison's storage park.

"Why are you doing this?" Pete said.

"I'm doing it for Dar, and for your mother," Andy said. "And because I remember the first day you surfed, really surfed, one April vacation when you were up here visiting your grandmother— I let you have my old wetsuit, and you got up on your board with hardly any help from Dar and me and rode the wave straight in to Lucy Vincent Beach."

Pete turned toward the open window, let the wind blow his hair straight back. Andy knew Pete was remembering what it felt like to go into the water in spring, wearing a wetsuit, paddle out past the break, and wait for the right wave.

They drove toward Oak Bluffs, past the hospital, and turned onto Peony Lane. It was a dead end, and the last house was a newly painted green Victorian needing some repair work on the porch—broken spandrels, ornate corbels hanging from the beams, a missing ceiling medallion. But the stairs and banisters were new, with a fresh coat of white paint.

"What's this?" Pete asked.

"A sober house," Andy said.

"You mean like a halfway house?" Pete said.

"Yeah. Got a problem with that? Or would you rather hock

something from your family's house, keep up your junkie ways right in your own backyard? You came home for a reason, Pete. I doubt it was for that."

Pete glared at the house. "Broken-down piece-of-crap place," he said looking at the broken lacework.

"For broken-down addicts," Andy said. "You stay here and go to meetings, and you won't have to face your family looking the way you do now."

"How do you know about this place anyway?" Pete asked.

"I came here when I wasn't much older than you," Andy said. "Saved my life."

Together they walked inside. Andy had always liked the way the light seemed so clean in here, washed by the old lead glass windows. A stained-glass fanlight threw pale colors onto the wide-board oak floors.

The current proprietor, Al Venner, came out of his office, grinned, and shook Andy's hand.

"How you doing, Andy?" Al asked.

"Doing fine," Andy said. "Busy with work, but that's good. Al, I want you to meet someone. Pete Monaghan. He needs a room."

Al and Pete shook hands, and Al looked him over.

"Do you have insurance, Pete?" Al asked.

"Uh, no. I was on my parents', but that stopped when I left college. And I had some up in Alaska, when I was fishing, but they cut me off when I left the boat."

"So, how are you going to pay to stay here?" Al asked.

Pete stared at his feet. Andy could almost read his mind: why should he pay for a place he didn't want to be, full of rules he didn't want to follow?

"He'll be working with me," Andy said. "Half his wages will go directly to you. I know you used to have 'scholarships,' do you still?"

"Depends on how willing he is."

"Willing?" Pete asked.

"To admit you're powerless over alcohol and drugs, and that your life has become unmanageable," Al said in an old-school-AA, boot-camp tone of voice.

"Can't deny that," Pete said.

"Well, we'll give you a two-week test period. Then reassess. The rules are on that board over there. Break one and you're out. No chance of getting back in. You get breakfast and dinner. Lunch, you're on your own. You have to hit a meeting every day for the first ninety days. And curfew starts forty-five minutes after the last meeting on the island closes."

"I don't have a car," Pete said.

"Then you can walk to meetings or get a ride with one of the other guys."

"And I'll pick you up for work tomorrow morning," Andy said. "Seven sharp."

"Okay," Pete said.

"Just 'okay'?" Al asked, his stern tone that of the drill sergeant he once had been, before getting addicted to heroin thirty years ago. He'd been an island kid, a few years older than Andy, gotten sober, and ended up running this place, "the Captain's House."

"No, good," Pete said. "It's good. I'll be ready."

CHAPTER SEVENTEEN

Dar, Rory, and Delia passed through customs at Boston's Logan Airport and got straight into a cab. Dar directed the driver to a building on Rowes Wharf. Before leaving Ireland, she'd called Bart Packard, her family's lawyer in Edgartown, and tried to explain what she thought she had in her possession.

He had listened carefully, growing excited, and suggested she and her sisters stop at Fitzgerald & Fitzgerald, LLC, a Boston law office specializing in land title issues. Bart often worked with Raymond Fitzgerald, and he made arrangements for the meeting, which he would also attend.

Now, stepping out of the cab, Rory paid the driver while Dar held the hard case they'd bought to contain the parchment. A sharp breeze blew off Boston Harbor, and Dar turned to feel it in her face.

"Should we go up to the office?" Delia asked.

"I guess," Dar said, but she didn't want to lose the feeling of the sea wind, her connection to the ocean and their father.

They entered a gray and white marble lobby, and took the elevator to the top floor. Walking through large glass doors stenciled with *Fitzgerald & Fitzgerald,* they approached an imposing chest-high curved walnut reception desk. They gave their names, and the young woman said that Mr. Fitzgerald would be right with them.

They took three seats in a sitting area overlooking the city of Boston. Elegant prints in dark frames revealed street scenes in Boston, Dublin, and Cork. One showed St. Colman's Cathedral, causing the sisters to exchange glances.

"So does that print remind you of where you just came from?" asked a man standing behind them—short, white-haired, dressed in an impeccably tailored pinstripe suit, speaking in a familiar Irish brogue. It reminded Dar of Tim McCarthy's.

"It's where our father was baptized," Dar said, standing to shake his hand. "I'm Dar McCarthy, and these are my sisters, Rory Chase and Delia Monaghan."

"Raymond Fitzgerald," he said. "Our mother was from Cork; Cobh is a beautiful place. That cathedral is magnificent. Shall we go into the conference room?"

"Sure," Dar said.

"Did you bring the document?" Raymond asked. "Your local attorney has told us about it, and we're quite excited at the prospect of examining it."

"It's right here," Dar said, patting the hard plastic case.

The sisters followed Raymond down a wide hallway. He led them into a windowless room lit by ambient light diffused through fine marble slabs on an outside wall. Raymond pushed a button, and overhead recessed lighting began to glow with a blue aura.

"We are frequently called on to defend old and rare documents," he said, showing them in. "Nothing harms old parchment faster than moisture or harsh light. We borrowed the document-examination technology of blue light from friends in the intelligence community, and of light-porous marble from the Beinecke Library at Yale University.

"They have one of the original Gutenberg bibles, as well as an early copy of the Book of Kells," said a man who looked and sounded just like Raymond.

"This is my twin brother, Jack Fitzgerald," Raymond said.

"Identical twins," Delia commented.

"Exactly," Raymond said. "Our mother said she was blessed twice over."

"Now, let's see this document," Jack said.

Raymond opened the plastic case and used forceps to remove what he called "the instrument." He explained that he was placing it on a non-alkaline blotter, and both he and Jack donned headgear that resembled miners' helmets, but with lamps that gave off the same pale blue light as that from overhead. They examined the document carefully, exchanging murmurs as they worked.

Meanwhile, Dar, Rory, and Delia sat in chairs along the wall, watching.

Jack produced a book from a bookcase, and he and Raymond pored over it, comparing the parchment and the volume. After forty-five minutes, the three sisters felt lulled by the dim light and the brothers' melodic Irish voices, when suddenly Raymond stood up straight.

"Now," he said, "if you will permit us to lock the document in our safe, and then accompany us to our office, we will explain to you what we have learned."

Dar looked at Rory and Delia. "Is it okay with you if the document stays here?"

Her sisters nodded.

As she and her sisters watched, Jack entered a combination into a vault in the room's corner. Raymond placed the parchment in a special lacquer tray, slid it into the safe. While Jack relocked it, Raymond handed Dar the plastic container.

The sisters accompanied the lawyers into one of the most spectacular offices they had ever seen. A Waterford crystal chandelier hung from the twelve-foot ceiling, and a wall of windows faced Boston Harbor, the gray-blue outer islands, and the white-capped ocean beyond. Aside from bookcases lining the opposite wall, the only furniture was a partners desk, two matching chairs, and a three-cushion sofa with a long, low table in front.

The brothers sat facing each other at the desk, while Dar, Rory, and Delia sat together on the sofa.

"Now," Raymond said, "Bart Packard has retained us on your behalf. Therefore, we are your attorneys. We will keep the parchment in our safe as long as need be, meanwhile having it authenticated by colleagues from Harvard and MIT."

Dar and her sisters exchanged looks. "Thank you," she said.

"Additionally, we will represent you before the Supreme Court of Massachusetts if it comes to that," Jack said, "in terms of fighting any onslaught from your buyers and their brokers."

Dar nodded.

An assistant walked in bearing a tea service and a plate of

sugar cookies. She poured tea into Belleek china cups, and served everyone. Jack passed the cookies around, serving himself and Raymond last.

"Nothing like teatime," Raymond said.

Dar sipped her tea, thinking the Fitzgerald & Fitzgerald experience was both comforting and surreal.

"Having learned definitively of your father's death, it is natural you would find yourselves overcome with grief and sorrow," Jack said.

All three sisters nodded.

Raymond gazed at them with a glint in his blue eyes. "There is perhaps one ray of sunshine in all of this."

"Two," Jack said, "if you count the fact that your father did an extraordinary job of protecting the parchment—it's miraculous that it has survived intact, considering the time it must have spent under seawater."

"He put a sealed, waterproof compartment into the *Irish Darling*. I guess it worked," Dar said.

"Beautiful name for a yacht," Raymond said.

"So, what does all this mean?" Rory asked.

"Let's start with the fact your buyers' title agent and lawyers dug very deep, appropriately so, considering the length of time the land has been in your family. They needed to go back to the beginning, to learn whom your earliest ancestor bought it from, and that turned out to be Bartholemew Gosnold."

"The original English settler," Jack added.

"That's amazing," Rory said.

"However, a discrepancy was discovered. A narrow strip of that Gosnold property had been granted by the British Crown to one of its subjects. The seal that so mystified your broker belonged to King Charles I."

"That's who Dad always said it came from! But you're saying the land was given to one of the king's subjects—an Englishman?"

"Remember, by the time of Charles I, Ireland had been taken over by the British. So, tragically, even an Irishman was considered a subject of the Crown," Raymond said.

"This is making the buyers want to back out of the deal," Delia said. "And sue us for all the expenses they've incurred."

"Yes, Bart told us. Well, good luck to them, and good riddance. If you want to be done with them, this is the way. Let them believe the title is faulty, which at this point, legally, it is."

"You mentioned good news," Rory said.

"Your father must have gone to the county archives to find it, and then used parish records to prove his lineage, in order to receive it," Jack said. "That is how these claims are traced and made."

"But what is it?" Rory asked.

"It's a direct land grant," Raymond said. "From King Charles I to McDonough McCarthy."

"The man who built the castle in Kanturk!" Delia said.

"Never occupied by a McCarthy," Raymond said. "Because the English Privy Council thought this Irishman, regardless of the fact he owned the land and had built the castle himself, was above his station, thinking he could live in such a grand place."

"How do you know all this?" Dar asked.

"McDonough McCarthy is an Irish legend. He brought war against the English for occupying his castle."

"The parchment . . ."

"We must have it authenticated, but to us it appears to bestow a parcel of land to McDonough McCarthy right here in the Commonwealth of Massachusetts. On the island of Martha's Vineyard, Dukes County, town of Chilmark."

"Our father knew," Dar said.

"I can't believe it's real!" Rory said.

"What if a different ancestor comes forward and tries to make a claim?" Delia asked.

"It would be of no avail. Whichever McCarthy possesses the parchment had to have presented his credentials back in Ireland. Your father may have hired a barrister, or he might have been able to do it through the cardinal, right at St. Colman's. No way of telling. But I assure you this: it wouldn't have been easy."

"How will it affect what happens going forward?" Dar asked. "We still can't afford the taxes on our land."

"Not to mention estate inheritance tax," Raymond reminded them.

"Perhaps you could pay all of it," Jack said, "if you were to sell a portion of the land, retaining the rest. You might decide to sell the McCarthy section that, according to the title search, is the easternmost section of your family property, marked by four granite posts hidden by brush, and with an easement to the salt pond and beach."

"Or," Raymond said, "we could enter the document into the real estate records, certifying a copy, and you could sell the original to a collector or dealer—many of whom we know directly—possibly for more money than you could get for the land itself."

"That paper is worth more than oceanfront property?" Rory asked. "It's barely legible."

Raymond nodded. "That wouldn't matter to a collector. Of course, as we said before, we'll call experts to take a look, but I am positive it's the real thing."

Dar and her sisters exchanged glances.

"Well, the three of you have a lot to think about and talk over with your families, and then we'll have some decisions to make. Meanwhile, Jack and I will investigate the buyers—the Littles, I believe Bart told us was their name—and assess how litigious they might actually be."

"We can't afford high legal fees," Delia said. "We don't have the means, which is how we've gotten into this in the first place."

"Understood," Raymond said. "Certain concessions will be made out of respect for your father's determination and the pride he brings on Ireland and Cork, and also for the honor of your leaving such a rare and important document in our vault."

"That's not to say there won't be a charge," Jack said. "But as Raymond says, concessions will be made."

"Thank you," Dar said. She and her sisters rose, shook the Fitzgerald brothers' hands. Then they left the office, went down the elevator to the gray and white marble lobby, out the doors to Rowes Wharf, where they again stood holding hands, facing out to sea with the wind in their hair, toward Ireland.

It wasn't until they had all returned to Logan Airport, heading off in three separate directions, that the reality hit them.

"We might actually be able to keep the house," Delia said. "Can you believe it? All of us spending the summer together again."

"That would be the best part," Dar said. "I'm already imagining all the spring garden things we usually do. The post-winter repairs I've let slide. The family together for the summer."

They grinned to think of it, hugging and kissing. Rory headed to the parking lot for her car, and Dar and Delia walked slowly toward the sitting area for Cape Air. While they waited for their flight, Dar called Andy to tell him they were on the way.

"That's the best news ever," he said. "I can't wait to see you."

"Neither can I," Dar said. "He did it, Andy."

"What?"

"My father. He made it to Cork and found what he was searching for."

"Dar," Andy said, his voice filled with emotion, "I know what it means to you."

"You do," she whispered. "We'll be there in an hour."

She hung up, and she and Delia sat silently, Dar thinking of those four granite posts hidden by brush and how she and her father had looked for them so long ago.

CHAPTER EIGHTEEN

Martha's Vineyard welcomed them home. As the plane banked for landing, Dar could see the salt ponds stretching all along the south shore. She remembered her grandmother telling her that in winter the ponds would freeze, and they would skate all the way from Chilmark to Katama. But for now they were brilliant blue, rippled by a sea wind.

From the air she saw that the island had turned green while they were gone; the brown grasses of winter had come back to life. Tips of the tree branches were pink in the late-afternoon light. A green island in the middle of the blue sea.

The plane landed smoothly, and when they got out, Andy was waiting just outside the terminal. His crooked smile grew wide as Dar got closer, and they hugged hard and long, as if no one else were there. Delia went inside the long, low terminal building, claiming her bag and Dar's as they came off the plane, wheeled in on metal carts.

They all climbed into the front seat of Andy's truck and drove home with the windows open. The air had a slight chill, but it smelled spicy, with all the springtime changes: soft earth, new grass, daffodils and jonquils blooming in the moors. She stared down ravines leading to the ponds, the barrier beach, and the ocean beyond.

Andy drove past their driveway to Beetlebung Corner, and they all went into the Chilmark Store to stock up on food and supplies. Andy held the basket while the sisters filled it with fresh bread, apples, baby spinach, milk, cheddar cheese, potatoes, a steak.

Driving home, Dar felt peace overtaking her. The hills of Chilmark were lifelong landmarks—Alice's Hill, Abel's Hill, Mosher's Hill, Whale Hill, Peaked Hill. She thought of all the times she and her sisters and best friends had ridden their bikes up the steep slopes, wanting to see their island from every perspective.

She thought of McDonough McCarthy, his fighting and rebellion. She wondered if her chieftain ancestor had ever set foot on the Vineyard, ever lived on the land given him by the king.

Andy pulled into the farmhouse driveway, and they all jumped out of his truck. The yard was filled with yellow daffodils and white narcissus. The setting sun painted the white house butterscotch. Walking inside, Dar crouched down so all the animals could circle her. She rubbed noses with Scup, felt the cats walking all around against her legs.

"It's so good to be home," Delia said, in spite of the fact almost everything had been packed away. She found the box holding kitchenware, and unpacked three plates, three sets of silverware, a tarnished copper pan, and a cruet of virgin olive oil.

Andy fired up the Weber grill on the side porch, set about seasoning the steak with coarse sea salt and freshly ground pepper. It hit the fire with a satisfying sizzle.

"Steak always tastes better at the beach!" Delia called to him as she chopped garlic, sautéed it in the copper pan, then threw in the baby spinach leaves.

Dar wanted to be in the kitchen helping, but first she felt the need to run across the yard. Scup followed, wagging his tail, as she ran straight toward the easternmost edge. The brambles were thick, a hedge of abandoned wild roses and scrub yew. As she reached in, thorns scratched her hands. She heard a phone ringing in the distance, parted the branches, found nothing.

"Dar!" Delia called. "Telephone!"

"In a second!"

Dar tried to remember whether she and her father had ever looked in this exact spot. She thought they had—they'd covered pretty much every inch of the property, but Delia was calling again. Wiping her hands on her jeans, Dar tapped Scup on his back, making him turn and follow her back to the house.

"It's Raymond," Delia said, smiling as she handed Dar the phone.

"Hello?" she said.

"I've already told Delia, but I want to tell you as well," Raymond said. "We have our two best authenticators here—called them the minute you and your sisters left, and they came right to our office. Rafe Belladonna, a document specialist from MIT, and Susan Mallory, a conservator from Harvard. They were as excited as Jack and I by the prospects of what we have here . . ."

"What do they say?" Dar asked.

"With initial analysis, the ink and vellum are authentic to

the period. The parchment, signed by both King Charles and McDonough McCarthy, states that in return for land in the New World, McCarthy will leave Ireland forever. There is language indicating that as chieftain, he was devoted to fighting the English, and perhaps capable of driving them out of Ireland more efficiently than the Spanish Armada was able to do. There is not another document of its kind in the United States. You come from fighting stock, Ms. McCarthy!"

"What does it mean in terms of our land here?" she asked, staring at the beloved vista of yard, marsh, ponds, dunes, and sea.

"It most likely means that you will be able to pay back your buyers, fulfill your tax obligations, and keep your family home."

Dar was silent for a minute, taking that in. "How?" she asked.

"It may mean selling this document at auction. We often use Sotheby's, but we can discuss that later. One thing, it is sure to bring a very high price."

"Thank you so much, Raymond," Dar said, her voice breaking.

"We'll be in touch soon. And thank you. I can't remember the last time Jack and I were so emotionally engaged by a case."

Dar thanked him again and hung up. Dinner was ready, and they decided to eat at the table outside, on the porch facing the beach. They were hungry, glad to be home and together, eager to tell Andy the story in all its details.

Andy held her hand under the table. They listened to waves breaking on the sandbar, sand blowing all along the beach, the friction sounding like a bow playing a stringed instrument, music carried on the soft breeze, saying *welcome home, welcome home.*

. . .

That night Dar and Andy stayed in the Hideaway. Wrapped in each other's arms, they huddled under the quilt. When Dar thought of home, this was it. Andy kissed her gently, but their lovemaking was anything but.

"I missed you, Dar," he said when they were still again, covers untangled and tucked around them. "I have to tell you something."

She closed her eyes, wanting him to think she was asleep, but he knew her ways. He held her close, mouth against her ear. "Two things to tell you and show you," he said. "Not tonight."

"Not tonight," she whispered, turning on her side, feeling time speed backwards and forwards, lulled to sleep by Andy's closeness, the freshness of the air, the music of the sea.

Back home in Old Lyme, Rory waited for Jonathan to drop the children off at their white colonial on Lyme Street. She sat on the front steps, hearing crickets in the hedge. Connecticut was weeks ahead of Boston and the Vineyard in terms of spring. The daffodils had already come and gone. The oak leaves were the size of squirrels' ears, meaning that shad were already swimming upriver. Tall bushes of white-blossomed shadblow swayed in the warm breeze.

Closing her eyes, she heard Jonathan's car before she saw it. It was a habit—she'd memorized the sound of his engine and could tell when it was a half block away. He parked at the curb. The children piled out of his Jaguar, flying into her arms. She started to wave at him, sure he'd just drive away. But he didn't. He walked up the blue stone path right behind the kids.

"They're sure happy to have you home," he said.

She smiled, arms around all three of them—Sylvie, Obadiah,

and Jenny. Her throat ached. This was her home—but it was Jonathan's, too.

"I missed you," she said to the kids, but she meant him as well.

"Yeah," he answered. "We all missed you, too."

Tingles down her spine. What did he mean?

"Mom, can we go inside? I have to finish my homework," Sylvia said.

"Yeah, and can we watch TV? Just for half an hour?" Obadiah asked.

"No TV at Daddy's," Jenny said, shooting him a scolding look.

"Go on in," she said. "I'll be right there."

Jonathan sat beside her on the steps, so close their knees almost touched. They'd done this a thousand times. While the kids were inside, absorbed in their lives, Rory and Jonathan would sneak out for some air and time alone. This felt the same, but so different from all those times before. Her hands were shaking as she reached into her pocket for a cigarette. Jonathan took her lighter and lit it for her.

"So, how did the trip go?"

"How do I even start?" she asked, blowing a plume of smoke up toward the sky.

"Did you like Ireland?"

"I barely noticed it after the first night. Dar was right. Our father had gone there on a mission. He did it for us, and died trying to sail home."

"I'm so sorry," Jonathan said.

"Thank you," Rory said.

"I remember your father," Jonathan said. "He taught me and Harrison to sail."

"Harrison remembers that, too," Rory said. "He said my father never would have been lost at sea, he was too good a sailor."

"He was great," Jonathan said, and they sat silently for a while. "How are your sisters?"

"They're fine. We were all shaken up, but there's a happy ending. We might not have to sell the house."

"Really? That would be amazing."

Rory shrugged. "I don't know, and I can't explain this, but part of me doesn't care. It's hard for me to be on the Vineyard."

"Is that because of me?" Jonathan asked.

Rory gave him a long gaze. She'd always found him so beautiful, and still did. His long, graying brown hair curling behind his ears, his gray-green eyes, sharp cheekbones, wide mouth. She'd never, ever looked at his mouth without wanting to kiss it.

"Because of us. Do you know how hard it is to spend time in the place where we fell in love? Where every road, tree, beach, reminds me of you?" Rory asked.

"I do know," he said. "I took the kids out to see my parents. And to give Andy some advice on a house he's building for some art collectors."

Rory turned her head away so he wouldn't see her eyes. She had hoped this moment here on the steps would lead them back together. That's not how it sounded. He would go back to the Vineyard before long, showing Alys all the magical places.

"Are you saying you don't want to keep the property?" he asked.

"I don't know. It would have been different if we hadn't had to sell in the first place, if the taxes hadn't murdered us. I steeled myself back then. Packing made it real, and the trip to Ireland was something like a dream . . . it felt vivid while we were there, but it will fade away."

"What will your sisters say?" Jonathan asked.

"I don't want to tell them," Rory admitted. "They're both excited, and have hope that they can pull this off and hold on."

"Mom!" Jenny called from inside. "Come in and talk to me."

"She missed you," Jonathan said.

"Sylvie was okay?"

"Yes. She's wonderful."

"That shouldn't come as such a big discovery," Rory said. "For so long, you raised her as your own."

"I know it was just a few days, but she called her father while you were gone. He offered to come get her. Thought I should give you a heads-up."

Rory nodded. She stood, stepped toward the door. Her body ached for Jonathan to hold her again, to want to be a family again. He'd only moved a few miles up the Connecticut River. But to Rory it felt as absolute as her father sailing to Ireland. Leaving broke up the family; the distance didn't so much matter.

CHAPTER NINETEEN

They had begun to unpack boxes containing the items Dar and Delia needed most: kitchen goods, bedding, family pictures. They found several of their father; they had been tucked away in the back of their mother's bottom drawer. They had gone through them last night, but now Delia was alone while Dar did some yard work, and she took her time.

One photo showed him in work clothes, when he first got to the Vineyard, a cocky expression and big friendly grin on his face. Another, their wedding picture, showed him in a morning coat and their mother in the beautiful lace wedding dress and veil her mother, then Rory, then Delia, had worn. She paged through an album of snapshots from a time when they were a young family.

The photos were arranged by year, and Delia saw the happy young father in the first few albums give way to a man emotionally weighed down in later ones. When Dar came in, all dusty and muddy from digging in the hedge, Delia got her a tall glass of water.

"Did you find the posts?"

"Not yet."

"What if they're not there?"

"They have to be," Dar said. "You're looking through the pictures again?"

"Yes," Delia said. "I love seeing the ones where Mom and Dad look happy. I know they were separated when he left, but do you think they'd have gotten back together?"

"I do," Dar said. "I really want to believe it."

"So do I," Delia said, thinking of how complicated marriage was, how transformed it could be by events and feelings you never saw coming.

"Has Rory called back?" Dar asked. "I've left her two messages."

"No," Delia said. "What do you think is going on?"

Dar didn't reply. She just walked over to the porch rail, tested it with her right hand, to make sure it hadn't loosened in winter storms. Then she turned around, streaked her thumb across a first-floor window, coated with dust and salt. Delia heard a truck pull into the driveway. Probably Andy.

"It's almost lunchtime," Delia said. "I'll make some sandwiches."

"Wait here a minute," Dar said. "Andy said he's bringing a surprise."

"I'm not sure I can handle one more surprise," Delia said, only half kidding. "Do you know what this is?"

Dar shook her head. "He wouldn't tell me. He wanted you to find out at the same time."

The two men came around the corner of the house. They were about the same height, over six feet; Andy was rugged and muscular, and the other man was skinny, hunched over, head averted. From the side, Delia could see he had scabs on his cheeks. She heard herself gasp, recognizing him just as Dar said his name.

"Pete," Delia said, running straight to her son, standing on tiptoes to hug him tight.

"Mom," he said.

"Oh my God," Delia said. "Pete. Honey, it is so wonderful to see you. I can't believe it! You're here!"

"Wow, Pete," Dar said.

"Hi, Aunt Dar," he said as she came over to hug him, too.

"Pete and I brought lunch. Ham and cheese, roast beef, eggplant Parmesan, take your pick. All kinds of sodas."

"Sprite for me," Pete said.

"Worked up a thirst this morning," Andy said. "All that sawdust flying around."

"You're working with Andy?" Delia asked.

"It's a long story. I'll tell you all about it later, Mom."

"Have you called your father?" she asked.

"No," Pete said. "Not since I asked for money to fix my truck."

Delia felt tears burning her eyes. The more she loved Pete, the closer she felt to the edge of losing it completely. Her body ached, holding herself back from grabbing and shaking him. She wanted to explain everything so he would see it. Surely if she could get him to understand, he'd behave differently. She felt like screaming, but instead she bit her lip and turned away, keeping her tears to herself.

"Come on," Andy said, spreading the lunch on the porch table. Delia watched him put a fatherly hand on Pete's shoulder. "Let's eat."

After lunch, Dar and Andy walked into the yard, Scup bounding along beside them. The sun was warm, beating down on their shoulders. He put his arm around her.

"When did he arrive?" Dar asked.

"While you and your sisters were in Ireland."

"Why isn't he staying here?"

"He's in Al's sober house," Andy said.

"Really?" Dar asked. "Is that your doing?"

"I made the introduction. But he's staying on his own."

"That's great," Dar said.

They walked to the edge of the yard, and Dar showed him where she'd been looking for the markers.

"How could four granite posts be so hard to miss?" she asked.

"Well, you have to think like the guy who put them in," Andy said, peering along the property line. "I'd sink one by the pond, another by the road, and two in between. Easiest place to look might be the pond. The hedge isn't so thick there."

The sun shimmered on the sea, the pond, rocks hidden in the hedge. The light reflected blindingly bright-white, glinting on bits of crystal and mica in the rocks. Andy scanned the area while Dar crouched down, into the shade of the thornbushes.

She'd looked here before, but the sun's angle had been different. She'd hurried along, trying to cover too much ground, and Andy hadn't been with her. Midday sunlight penetrated the low, thick brush, and a flat stone caught her attention: four inches square, about an inch high.

"Andy . . ."

"You got it?" he asked.

She dug around the stone's edges; Scup nosed his way in, curious about what she'd found. He lunged at the strange square rock, scrabbling at one straight side with his claws, uncovering an inch or so of smooth granite beneath the ground's surface.

"It's granite," she said. "Some kind of a marker, but it doesn't look anything like a post."

"Sure it does," Andy said, sitting on his heels beside her, reaching in to scoop away more dirt. "Buried with almost four centuries of sand and soil. It probably goes down two feet."

"Let's dig and see!

"We'll excavate all four," Andy said. "That's a promise, Darrah. But first you've got to take a ride with me."

"But . . ."

"No. Come on. I've been waiting for weeks; I can't take it anymore."

Dar hesitated, but he pulled her to her feet. She followed him to his truck, and they climbed in.

He drove onto Middle Road, down the narrow valley where a month ago he'd shown her the millpond and old millstone. They parked in the same place, and she followed him down one side of a shady glade to the pond and brook. He held her hand to help her across, and she raced him up the sunny slope opposite, touching the millstone as she passed. When she got to the top, her heart sank.

A foundation had been dug and poured, and the first part of a house had been framed.

"I thought you said the owner wasn't going to build," she said.

"The old owner wasn't, but the new owner is," he said.

"Another part of the island being eaten up," she said, sitting down on the foundation. She looked around; they were above the tree line, and from here had a long view toward the sea.

"Don't hate me for this," Andy said. "But I'm the builder on this project. Got Pete helping me out."

"How could I hate you?" Dar asked. "Building's your job. I just have problems with new owners who have to take up every bit of land, when there are so many beautiful old houses for sale."

"I hear you on that one, darlin,'" Andy said. "Bunch of land-grabbing sons of bitches out here these days. But I'm refusing to work on any project that cuts down trees, or fills in millponds, or tears down existing structures."

"Well, you've got a point," Dar said. "No existing structures here. Will the house be huge and sprawling?"

"Nope. A pretty little cape with a nice front porch. And a room with tall north-facing windows."

"Really?"

"They like art," he said. "Jonathan consulted on that part."

"Pete's helping you out?" Dar asked.

"Yep. He's a good worker, in spite of everything."

"I can already tell," Dar said. "That he's been on drugs. He looks so yellow; was he sharing needles?"

"It didn't get that bad," Andy said. "He's been clean nearly three weeks, and he's been hitting meetings."

"That's great," Dar said.

"It is," Andy said.

"I wish I could turn my mind off," Dar said, lying back on the concrete foundation. "So much to think about—about my father, and Morgan and the buyers deciding what to do…"

"Doesn't the land grant take care of that?"

"Well, at least it held up the closing. But I'm not sure about what my sisters have in mind."

"You can stop thinking," Andy said, lying beside her. "Everything's going to work out."

"It will? How do you know?" Dar asked.

Andy didn't reply, just stroked her bare arms, turning her mind off as he kissed her in the sunlight.

Three weeks passed, and by the third Friday in May the cottage began to take shape. The woods smelled of new growth; there were leaves on the branches, patches of white dogwood showing through the oaks and cedars. Andy had been worried the leafing out would block the house's view, but it only framed it more beautifully.

"Hey now," Andy said, just as Pete was ready to pound nails into a wide-plank tiger maple floorboard. "Make sure that's level. These are old boards, and some of them are warped. You want to nail them in sets of three. Three nails making a triangle, see?"

Pete watched Andy show him how it was done.

"Where'd you get them?" Pete asked.

"From a beautiful old house someone tore down."

"Seems to be a thing out here," Pete said.

"Seems to be a thing anywhere there's nouveau riche," Harrison said, lying on his side in the mossy glade outdoors, smoking a cigarette. "You realize you're in the presence of a master, don't you?"

"Yeah," Pete said. "My aunt says there's no better carpenter on the island. Not since her father."

"That's high praise," Harrison said. "Captain McCarthy was a helluva boatbuilder. Right, Andy?"

"That's right," Andy said, using his miter box to angle another group of boards.

"But not a real sea captain, right?" Pete asked.

"Man, your grandfather sails transatlantic, I think he deserves to be called 'Captain,'" Harrison said. "Don't you, Andy?"

"I'm not so big on titles," Andy said. "But sure. The man made it to Ireland." He glanced up, looked at Pete. "I'm sorry he didn't make it back. That you never knew him."

"Yeah, me too."

"He was a tough guy," Harrison said. "He'd have kicked some sense into you. You're supposedly into meth, on the lam with your parents' money, right?"

"Hey, Harrison," Andy said harshly.

"No, it's true, I was," Pete said.

"'Was' being the operative word," Harrison said. "I can't seem to kick my little habits, but then, I don't want to. I've constructed a life where they don't matter to or bother anyone."

"You live in a fucking storage unit," Andy said. "Anyone driving within miles can smell the weed."

"I like to give pleasure to my neighbors," Harrison said. "This island's getting too prissy. Got to remind them of the days of smugglers, pirates, and ruffians. Right, Pete?"

"Sure, Harrison," Pete said, laughing. He checked his watch, and Andy saw and handed him the truck keys.

"What, you're letting him take the truck?"

"Yep," Andy said.

Harrison shook his head. "You're a brave man." Then, "Have a nice ride, kid."

"I will," Pete said.

Driving out to Chilmark, he felt as nervous as if he were taking someone out on a date. He pulled into the driveway, and his mother stepped out as if she'd been waiting and watching. She wore a blue dress and low black heels, a white cashmere shawl over her shoulders, and the dressiness of her outfit broke Pete's heart a little. He jumped out to help her into the cab, shut the door carefully behind her. Dar waved from the kitchen window, and his mother waved back.

They had a long drive, but he'd allowed for plenty of time. Knowing his mother, he expected her to talk the whole way, covering everything from his father to trouble with the farmhouse buyers and their lawyer to Pete's own troubles. She'd grilled him for days, wanting to know what he'd taken, whether he'd seen a doctor, whether he'd been tested for AIDS, when his drug-taking had started. He'd done his best to answer every question as patiently as possible.

Uncharacteristically, on the ride to Vineyard Haven, his mother didn't say a word. She stared at the dashboard clock, watching it tick toward noon. Pete began to feel nervous about the silence, so he turned on the radio. Andy had it tuned to the island station, and they were playing the Arctic Monkeys.

They finally reached Vineyard Haven, got into a little traffic heading toward the noon boat. His mother pulled the visor down, saw there wasn't a mirror, opened her purse to remove a compact and check her lipstick.

"Oh God, I'm sweating," she said.

"Here, Mom," Pete said, handing her some napkins from Andy's door pocket.

"I'm not sure I belong . . ." she said. "Are you sure you want me?"

"Yeah, I do," he said. "It's an open meeting."

He was afraid to look at her, to see how unsettled she seemed. But he looked, and she was, so he took her hand. It didn't matter that they'd talked about what to expect, that she'd asked a million questions, and he'd answered the best he could. They got a good parking spot on Woodland Avenue, just around the corner from Williams Street. She stayed in the truck, waiting for him to help her out. He could feel her jangling nerves, just as if they were his own.

It had always been so hard for his mother to see him as he was, as somebody much less than perfect. He'd grown up hearing his father yell, "You're not living up to what we expect!" His mother had gone the opposite way: praising him for the smallest, most insignificant things, always encouraging him. It had made him sad, seeing her get her hopes up, always knowing he was going to dash them.

Now, seeing the mess drugs had made of his teeth and face, she couldn't pretend nothing was happening.

"Honey," she said, as he came around to open her door. "Let me wait here for you. It's private, what you're doing here."

"Are you afraid someone will see us going in?" he asked.

"No, it's not that," she said quickly. But he saw her look around. He felt how ashamed she was of all this, and was ready to drop it, just drive her home. But then she smiled, gave a quick shake of her head, and jumped down from the truck's cab.

As they walked up the sidewalk, she held tight to his hand, just the way she'd done walking him to the first day of school. He wanted to tell her to look at the white and purple lilacs, blooming all around. But she kept her head down, still worried that someone would recognize her and her son going into the meeting. He remembered that feeling.

Grace Episcopal Church was old-school: weathered wood with a chimney on one roof and a cross atop a small white tower. Stained-glass windows caught the midday light.

"You know," she said, "when I was really young, Catholics weren't allowed to go into other faiths' churches. It was a sin we'd have to confess."

"Don't worry, Mom. You won't be sinning," Pete said, leading her around back to the Parish Hall. AA and NA meetings were held here, and he'd been careful to choose one that was open to anyone, not just alcoholics or addicts.

"Sweetheart," she said, stopping on the sidewalk.

"Are you okay?"

"Why do you want me here, Pete?"

"I don't know," he said. "I just do. I need you to see me in all this. I know you want me to be someone better, a different kind of son. I've put you through hell. I want you to see me trying for a change."

His mom gazed up into his eyes, and suddenly he knew she got it. She looked ferocious. He'd seen that look in the face of a

Kodiak bear. "You've put *yourself* through hell," she said. "And if this will help you come back from it, I'm with you. Come on. I'm ready."

Walking in, he recognized nearly everyone in the place, standing in clusters around the room. He took his mother to the coffee table, poured her a Styrofoam cup, and offered her an oatmeal cookie.

"Well," she said, sounding calm. "I know people here."

"They're here for the same reason I am," he said.

"That's good," she said.

The chairs were set up in a circle, and they found seats together. Pete heard his mother say, "Hello, Rose," and "Hello, Steve."

"Hey, Delia."

The group leader took her seat, asked someone to read "How It Works," someone else to read from "Daily Reflections." Pete stared at the window shades hung on the wall, noticed his mother reading the Steps intently, wondered whether they made any sense to her.

After the readings, Judy, the group leader, asked if anyone was celebrating an anniversary. There were three: Buddy with one year, Karen with fifteen years, and Roy with thirty-five. The room went wild.

"Is anyone counting days?" Judy asked next.

She called on everyone with their hands up; when she got to Pete, he said, "I'm Pete, alcoholic-addict, and I have twenty-one days."

The room erupted in applause, as it always did. Pete glanced at his mother, saw her clapping as loudly as anyone.

Judy glanced around the room, smiling.

"Do we have any visitors?" she asked.

Pete held his breath. Out of the corner of his eye, he saw his mother raise her hand. Judy gestured, calling on her.

"My name is Delia," Pete's mother said, her voice unsteady. "And I'm here to support my son Pete."

Everyone in the room clapped for her, and Pete saw the smile of love and pride begin to spread across her face.

CHAPTER TWENTY

Spring's peace and serenity on the Vineyard gave way to Memorial Day: festivities, crowds, and the unofficial start of summer. Dar had worked in the farmhouse garden every day, clearing the perennial beds, planting annuals, sprucing up the vegetable gardens with tomato, pepper, cucumber, and squash plants, creating a border of white ageratum around the herb garden, replanting the rosemary and sage plants they'd brought inside for the winter, as if keeping her hands in the earth could help her hold on to the family home she couldn't bear to let slip away.

A woman Delia had met at Pete's AA meeting had suggested Delia give Al-Anon, the group for friends and families of alcoholics, a try, so Dar had started going with her. They'd sit together, sipping their coffees, listening to people tell their stories, share about what was going on, hair-raising and agonizing stories about loving someone who couldn't stop drinking or drugging.

Delia was still shy, but she'd found an Al-Anon sponsor: Dana

Bickerton, a woman Dar respected for her kindness and strong sobriety. Sometimes Pete and Andy would meet them afterwards, and they'd all wind up going out for "the meeting after the meeting" at local cafés and ice cream shops.

Dana was kind and encouraged Delia to share her story with her. It wasn't easy, but Delia made a beginning; she knew this part of her journey meant facing her own demons, the guilt and grief she felt about having a son addicted to drugs and alcohol.

Andy wasn't spending as many nights with Dar as usual. She knew he was working hard to finish the millpond house, and she had her own work to do. The trip to Ireland and all its aftermath had caused her to be late on a deadline. So she'd stay up drawing half the night, windows open so the summery air could flow through.

As always, Dulse's life reflected hers. Having learned the truth about her father, Dulse understood that he had entered the afterworld, a place of ghosts and spirits separated from the living only by a veil finer than silk. They stayed close to this world and those they'd left behind. They lived in mirrors and shallow bodies of water, and could gaze through the glass or shimmering surface into the eyes of those they loved, letting them know that they were never far away.

Many of the farmhouse mirrors were antique, mottled with age. Dar would stare into her own eyes, hoping to get a glimpse of her father or mother. Sometimes she had to remind herself that Dulse's world was invented. But since it seemed to come from a place so deep down inside herself, couldn't it possibly be true?

The trip to Ireland had raised questions too large for Dar or even Dulse to answer. Frequently Dar found that her character was wiser and braver than her creator, as if in Dulse, Dar could travel through her family's psyche and return with spiritual truth.

But this time Dar felt exhausted, dragged down by all the uncertainty. After a flurry of connection with Raymond and Jack, they seemed to be holding back until the document and its provenance were legally authenticated.

Morgan called one morning; Dar saw her number on caller ID and hesitated a long moment before picking up.

"Hello?" she said.

"Dar, it's Morgan. Well, the Littles have officially backed out of the deal. He called me last night and said he's tired of being strung along. He wants their deposit back, so I'll write the check from escrow today."

"I'm sorry for all the trouble," Dar said. "I know you worked hard to put all this together."

"I'm not giving up!" Morgan said. "Property like yours comes on the market so rarely, I have a waiting list."

"Oh, Morgan," Dar said. She would have liked to tell her the property was no longer for sale. But there was still so much uncertainty; taxes would need to be paid soon.

"I know it's hard to jump right back in," Morgan said. "But I'm sure people will be making offers right away. You can slow it down, take your time before accepting anything."

"That's good to know," Dar said. "Thank you."

One day, uncovering the third post along the eastern boundary, Dar heard tires crunching up the clamshell and gravel driveway. She peered over her shoulder and saw Harrison park his blue panel truck. He came lumbering toward her.

"Hey," he said.

"Hey yourself!"

"What are you doing?" he asked.

"Uncovering these posts. Four hundred years old."

"Holy shit," he said. "Andy told me. Very cool." He gave the third post, excavated nearly a foot down into the ground, a long look. Then he tapped Dar's shoulder. "Got food?"

"You're hungry?"

"Totally," he said. "I had to deliver an antique Martin guitar to a big house in Aquinnah, and they were just sitting down to lunch, and do you think they'd invite me in? Looked really good, too—leftover roast beef."

"Well, I don't have that," Dar said. "But I could use lunch, too."

They walked the path from the farmhouse to the Hideaway. Scup had been lying in the shade, but he struggled up and followed them through the tall grass. Every so often one of the old cats would pounce at their feet, then retreat back into the grass forest, green and filled with wildflowers.

"So, what do you hear from Rory?" Harrison asked as they settled into rocking chairs facing the ocean and she served lemonade and tuna fish sandwiches.

"She's home in Connecticut, busy with the kids."

"Is she coming out soon?"

"Well, they have school, and activities on the weekend. It's not so easy for her."

Harrison wolfed down half his sandwich, chewing furiously as he stared out to sea. Dar sipped from her lemonade, gazing at him. Like Dulse, she saw people's essences more than their outsides. She could see how tender his heart was, as clearly as if it were beating outside his skin.

"Is she still fucked up over Jonathan?" Harrison asked.

"Yes," Dar said.

He ate the rest of his sandwich in two bites. She heard the porch floorboards creak beneath his rocker. "Why doesn't she get over him?" he asked. "He doesn't deserve her."

"I think she's working that out," Dar said.

"You mean getting over him?" Harrison asked, snapping his head to look at her.

"It's hard for her. They have children together. They've been together since they were so young."

"A lot of people have loved her since she was young," Harrison said.

Dar gazed at him, saw overwhelming love in his eyes. "I know you have," she said.

"I don't mean just me."

"Rory loves you," Dar said.

"She told you that?" he said quickly, his chair stopping mid-creak.

"Isn't it obvious? No one means more to her than you, Harrison. But I'm not sure she can ever really take her heart back from Jonathan. Or at least she's not ready yet."

He resumed rocking, gazing over the field with hooded eyes.

"She never saw me that way," he said. "She loves me, I know. The way you all do, like a big brother. She'd never even guess. Besides, I'm not like tall, dark, and handsome fucking Jonathan."

"You're better," Dar said. "Ten times better. And she would."

"Would what?"

"Guess," Dar said. "The way you feel."

"Shit," he said. "That's probably not good."

"Actually, it keeps her going. Couldn't you tell, when she was out here for that week? The times we got together with you made her the happiest. Part of her loves you the same way."

"She actually said it?"

"Yes," Dar said. "Not in words, but in deeper ways. Her eyes, her laughter, the way she is with you."

"God," Harrison said.

Dar watched him hold emotion inside. She wondered, and had all along, what he would do if she and her sisters left the island for good. If Rory did.

"Thanks for telling me," Harrison said.

"When's the last time we had a serious conversation?"

He laughed. "I do my best to avoid it."

Dar laughed, too. Then he leaned over, pointing.

"You going to eat that other half sandwich?" he asked.

"It's all yours," she said.

"You're my good friend," he said, shoving it into his mouth. In spite of the laughter, she saw weariness in his eyes.

"And you're mine," Dar said, reaching for his hand as they rocked and stared out at drifting clouds making shadow patterns on the blue salt pond and the sugary white dunes.

Delia and Pete stood at the ferry landing, waiting for the *Island Home* to pull in. Pete was silent, and Delia felt so anxious. The sky was brilliant, bright blue with no clouds. Jim used to call it "a brochure day"—the kind of weather tourist towns always wanted on their billboards and brochures.

"Are you okay?" she asked Pete.

"I think so. Are you?"

"Yes," she said. "Maybe even a little excited."

"I'm definitely not excited," he said.

She wanted to take his hand, remind him of the courage he'd shown by taking her to that AA meeting. It had led her to Al-Anon, where she was learning to take life one day at a time, and to respect herself in the process. From as far back as she could remember, she'd given her power and voice to others: her parents, her older sisters, Jim, even Pete at times.

Sometimes it felt as if she'd given up so much, bargained away chips of herself, just to make everyone else happy. She'd stayed busy, kept herself from seeing what was really going on, viewed only what she wanted to see, what she could handle. Now, being awake and alive every moment was sometimes so frightening and painful, so daunting; deep feelings were rising to the surface, making her face them head-on.

The cars rattled over the metal ramp onto the dock and into the parking lot. When Delia spotted the Ford, she nudged Pete and nodded. She raised her hand to wave, and Jim pointed up the hill, to a parking spot where he could stop.

"Safety first," Pete said, making Delia laugh.

"That's your father," she said.

She told herself that this had been arranged primarily for Pete. That she had no idea what would happen between Jim and her. But the sight of him driving their car, knowing he'd come to the Vineyard for the first time in years, touched a very sore place she hadn't let herself close to in weeks.

He parked the car, got out, and stretched. Now Delia did take Pete's hand. He'd brought Vanessa the doll he'd found in the yard, cleaned it up for her. They hurried up the hill together, came to a dead stop in front of the family car.

"Dad," Pete said.

"Pete," Jim said, gruff as ever. Then he reached out to shake Pete's hand, but instead pulled him into a hug. He was crying hard, shaking his head. "I thought I'd never see you again. I thought you were dead, that you'd never come home to us."

"I'm here," Pete said, stiff, but giving in to the hug.

Breaking away, Jim put his arm around Delia. He squeezed her tight, but didn't say anything. He seemed as emotional as she felt, and she knew he couldn't trust himself to speak yet. Instead, he let go of her, opened the back door. Delia watched him hunched over, fumbling with the seat belts.

When he turned, he had lifted Vanessa from her car seat.

"Gram!" she cried at the sight of Delia, but Jim handed her to Pete instead.

"Your daughter," Jim said.

They watched their son hold Vanessa, saw her frown and lean back as she studied his thin face and blue eyes.

"That's your daddy," Delia said.

"Hi, Vanessa," Pete said, giving her a little bounce. "I brought you your dolly."

"Gram!" she shrieked, and began to cry, reaching out her arms for Delia. Delia took her, looked up at Pete.

"It will get better," she said. "Just wait."

"It will," Jim said. "She's shy with guys. You should have heard how loud she'd howl any time I got near her. But now I'm 'Gramp,' and she can't wait to come over our house. Right, Deel?"

"Right, honey," she said. She gazed into her son's eyes to see whether he felt hurt or rejected, then stopped herself. Dana would tell her to stop feeling everyone else's feelings and feel her own. So she did; and because she was filled with joy, she smiled and said she wanted to take everyone out to lunch.

They went to the Black Dog, Jim's favorite, and got sandwiches and brownies to take out. They found a bench in the shade to eat, and they said very little, just looked out at the boats and smooth water. Afterwards they strolled through the Martha's Vineyard Camp Meeting Association in the center of town, looking at the Victorian gingerbread cottages painted in bright colors.

"Perfectly preserved," Jim said, said. "What's that style called again?"

"Carpenter Gothic," Delia said, remembering being taken on walks here with her own mother and grandmother. She watched Vanessa look from the beautiful cottages to Pete and back.

They cut over to Circuit Avenue, where all the clubs were, where Delia and her sisters had come to dance and drink and look for cute boys. Some of the club names had changed, but the super honky-tonk feeling was the same—even in bright sunlight you felt haunted by nights you could barely remember.

Delia glanced at Pete, wondering if it was triggering him. But he seemed focused on Vanessa, playing peekaboo with her as she half hid her eyes in her grandfather's shoulder and pretended to ignore him.

At the foot of Circuit Avenue, Pete tapped Vanessa's hand.

"Hey, Vanessa," he said. "Want to take a ride with me on that?" He pointed at the Flying Horses, the oldest carousel in the United States. He had loved it as a boy, just as Delia and her sisters couldn't get enough rides as girls.

"Gramp?" she asked.

"No, honey," Jim said. "Gramp is too big for that. He might break one of the pretty horses. Go with your dad. Gram and I will be right here watching."

"Gram?" she asked.

"That's right, sweetheart," Delia said. "We'll be right here. You'll see us wave when you go by!"

"Dolly?"

"Yes, she can ride, too," Pete said.

Mesmerized by the horses riding round and round, music and bells playing, Vanessa reluctantly let go of her grandfather's neck and let Pete take her in his arms as he put the doll in her hands.

He bought tickets, and when the ride stopped, he climbed onto the platform with Vanessa. They walked slowly around as he let her pick out the horse she wanted to ride: bright yellow. Pete buckled her on, and stood right beside her as the bell rang and the carousel began to move.

"Remember when we'd bring Pete here?" Jim asked.

"As if it were yesterday."

"He's doing all right?"

"We both are."

"Deel," Jim began, but he was choked up again. She held his hand to let him know it was okay.

"What you said to me hurt," she said. "But it was a wake-up call. I didn't want to lose you, our marriage."

"Neither did I," he said.

They waved at Pete and Vanessa each time they passed, but neither glanced over. Vanessa gripped the pole, her doll pressed under her elbow, and seemed completely focused on her ride. Pete had his arm around her and never once looked up.

Delia took a deep breath. She was standing here with her large, somewhat overweight, graying, conservative, middle-manager Irish Catholic husband. They owned a medium-sized house on a small lot on the outskirts of Annapolis. The Vineyard had always been the magic in her life—the world of her English grandmother, mother, and sisters. She had just embarked on a deep, dark quest—not only the one to Ireland with Dar and Rory, but the one into her own self. She knew without doubt that life was full of treasure. Dar had found a very particular one in the hold of their father's boat. But standing here with Jim, she knew it was time for real life.

"It would be nice to be able to help Pete get back on his feet," Jim said.

"He's doing pretty well, working for Andy Mayhew. He seems to be saving all his money."

"Life's expensive," Jim said, waving again as Pete and Vanessa went around. "Kid doesn't even have a truck anymore."

"We can't help too much; he wants to do it on his own."

"Not that we're made of money, anyway," Jim said.

Delia stared at the carousel. The Flying Horses had been on the Vineyard since 1884. She had no doubt that her maternal grandfather had ridden them as a boy. So much on the island had brought her family delight and wonder.

She'd talked to Rory last night, and she thought of it now, lulled by the carousel. Since returning to Old Lyme, Rory had felt both safe and depressed. The trip to Ireland, learning the truth of their father's death, the parchment, the frantic need to fight off Realtors and developers—it had all worn her out and gotten her down.

"Jonathan and I have talked a few times," Rory had said.

"That's good, right?"

"Well, I guess so. He's thinking about breaking up with Alys. He said she was so bitchy about him taking the kids while I was gone. She wound up joining them for a hike to Gillette Castle, and he said she was so overbearing toward them, possessive of him . . ."

"So he's seeing the light! That's great."

"He's not coming home," Rory had said. "At least not in the near future. He told me he's been unhappy in our marriage for a while. It was hard for him to get it out and tell me."

"Hard for *him*! What a selfish bastard. Have you told Dar all this?"

"I'm not sure why," Rory had said, "but I can't talk to her right now. I'm really struggling, Delia, with what I want to happen."

"About the house?"

"And the land, and the deed, and the amazing, incredible Irish parchment. I almost wish she hadn't found it."

"Why?" Delia had asked, even though she sometimes felt the same way.

"Because it's made everything so complicated. We're having to fight so hard to keep what we'd always loved and taken for granted. When it was just our family place, it was so lovely and right. It wasn't about money, or value, or taxes. What a childish way to think, right?"

"That's how I've thought of it, too."

"Now, dealing with it as 'property' has changed everything."

"I know."

"I was happier, honestly, that week when the three of us got together to start packing, knowing we were going to lose the place by the end of May, than I am now—even with the 'hope' that if all goes well, we'll be able to keep it."

"Do you want out?" Delia had whispered.

"I think so. Do you?"

Rory's question had hung in the air.

Delia hadn't answered last night, but standing by the Flying Horses, watching as the ride ended and Pete lifted his daughter down, seeing Vanessa laughing in glee with her arms around her father's neck, her feelings soared.

Money from the sale would give Jim and her a nest egg, and then, in spite of what she'd said about Pete wanting to do it on his own, they could help him buy his own house in Maryland and play a role in raising Vanessa. Vanessa's mother was well meaning but unreliable, at eighteen nearly ready to give birth to her second baby, and Delia knew her granddaughter needed Pete in her life.

The thought brought hot tears to her eyes, but when Pete and Vanessa approached, everyone assumed they were tears of joy. Sentimental Delia so happy to see her son and his daughter together, to be with her husband again. They didn't realize her heart was on its way to breaking, for Dar, for Rory, for the gathering place they'd always so simply loved.

CHAPTER TWENTY-ONE

Morgan Ludlow called Dar, giving her fair notice of a second showing.

"These buyers really seem hot to trot," she said. "We survived the disaster of the Littles, and it would be great if we could manage to not screw this deal up."

"By 'we' you mean me, right?" Dar asked.

"Well, yes. But not that I blame you. Selling family property can be wrenching at best, and I will admit the Littles' plans were quite extreme. With all your acreage, they would have covered a great deal of it with their chateau or whatever it was. Based on something they saw in the Luberon—inside swimming pool, tennis court, and all."

"The town never would have given them a permit."

"Well, true. And that's why they didn't sue you for breach of contract. They've moved on—to Nantucket, thank God. But Dar.

These new people are lovely. John and Martha Riley. You would love them, and I hope you'll meet, but do me a favor and don't be there today. They need to 'feel' the house again."

"Feel the house?" Dar asked.

"Yes. Fingers crossed, but this doesn't seem to be a teardown situation. Anyway, can I count on you?"

"Sure," Dar said, feeling remarkably unsettled.

Morgan wanted to go over more details but Dar had a meeting in Edgartown, with Raymond and Jack, at Bart Packard's office. Locking up, she loaded Scup into the car and headed east.

Low clouds hung over the island, mist captured in the leaves and branches of the trees. It softened the contours of every building, of the road itself. This was Dulse weather; it always pulled Dar from real life into her imagined world. It had kept her safe and protected for all these years. Dar wished she could stop and draw Dulse and her sisters on State Road as it lifted from this earth and become a portal into a stormy dream.

By the time she reached Edgartown, a fog bank was rolling in over Chappaquiddick, into the harbor. She parked in the private lane behind Bart's law office, shook off the cobwebs of Dulse, and took a moment before entering. Her emotions had been churning since Morgan had mentioned showing the house again. She let Scup make a round of the alley.

She and Scup entered the old building and headed upstairs. It was as radically different from Fitzgerald & Fitzgerald as a place could be: on the second floor of a commercial building. A café and art gallery were downstairs, and the stairs and crooked hallway smelled like French roast.

Bart's name was stenciled on pebbled glass in the top half of his office door. Dar never came here without feeling she was about to encounter Sam Spade or a shady bookie. But Bart had done her grandmother's and mother's wills and trusts, and had helped Dar find a market for her original drawings, and was one of the kindest and most honest people she knew. She entered without knocking, knowing that both she and Scup were expected.

Bart, Raymond, and Jack were sitting around Bart's desk, telling stories and laughing, when she walked in. The office windows were open; harbor noises drifted in, and papers anchored by many paperweights riffled in the breeze. All three men stood to greet her. Scup went straight to Bart for a dog biscuit.

"Good boy," Bart said. "Hello, Dar."

"Lovely old fella," Raymond said. "What's his name?"

"Scup," Dar said.

"Like the fish! Wonderful!" Jack said.

"Won't you all be seated," Bart said. "Dar, take the armchair."

She did, as the lawyers pulled their chairs into a semicircle around her. Their expressions were neutral, neither positive nor negative. Her pulse began to race, sure they were going to give her bad news.

"What is it?" she asked Raymond. "I knew something important had happened when Bart said you were flying down."

"It's been a complicated month," Raymond said. "Dealing with all aspects of the instrument."

"By that he means 'document,'" Bart translated.

Dar nodded, listening.

"We've had it analyzed and dated; we've dealt with the authorities in Ireland, starting in Cork City, Cobh, St. Colman's, and proceeding to Dublin. We then had to communicate with England."

"With the Crown itself!" Jack said.

"They flew to London," Bart said. "That's on us."

"We had no choice. Listen," Jack said, "until you hear the outcome."

Raymond continued. "In order to get as far as the Court of St. James, we had to have positive dispositions in each of the primary steps along the way. In other words, the instrument was certified authentic, dated 1626, by our sources at MIT and Harvard; the Irish court confirmed that Michael McCarthy procured the document by hiring a barrister and going through the proper channels to prove his lineage and right to inherit. And the Court of St. James was unable to dispute the land grant, and thereby stands by King Charles I's gift."

Raymond grinned at Dar. "The land will be yours, free and clear. The lien upon the title will be lifted as of today, in the courthouse just up the street."

"Care to come?" Jack asked.

Dar smiled, nodding. She left Scup in Bart's office, and she and the lawyers walked up the street. The white-columned courthouse was imposing, even in pea soup fog. Dar followed the counselors inside to the court clerk's office. Liz Allen was Andy's cousin, and she smiled past the lawyers at Dar.

"Hello, Liz. Let me introduce you to my co-counsel, Raymond and Jack Fitzgerald. I'm sure you know Dar McCarthy," Bart said.

"I sure do. Good to see you, Dar," Liz said.

"You too," Dar said.

"We've come to file a document, clearing the title on Dar's family's property," Raymond said. "I believe my office called you to explain the unusual details . . ."

"Yes," Liz said.

"Excellent," Raymond said, reaching into his briefcase. "We'll keep the original and file these certified copies and self-proving affidavit."

Liz spread the papers out on her desk, read and examined each one. She nodded, impressed.

"Do you by chance have the original with you?" she asked.

"Yes," Jack said. "But it goes to Ms. McCarthy and her sisters."

"I realize that," Liz said. She grinned. "But do you know what it's like, sitting here every day dealing with the here and now, when all of a sudden a document dating back to the birth of Martha's Vineyard walks through the door?"

Raymond opened a different compartment, gingerly removed an archival folder, opened it for Liz to see. Dar could tell he appreciated her interest, and Dar herself couldn't help leaning closer to gaze at the water-stained parchment.

"Your dad went to Ireland for this," Liz said, glancing up at Dar. "I remember when he left. We didn't know what happened to him . . ."

"No one did," Dar said.

"Well, he did you all proud," Liz said, reaching into her desk for the court seal. Raymond put the original back in its folder, and Liz signed and sealed each copy of the land grant and accompanying documents.

"Consider this deed filed!" she said.

"Thank you," Dar said, and everyone shook hands all around.

She and the lawyers returned to Bart's office so she could get Scup. The three men buzzed with excitement about the case, about how it had all turned out. They slapped each other on the back, beaming. Then, turning solemn, Raymond reached into his briefcase, carefully removed the deed in its opaque container.

"This is yours."

"It's incredible," Dar said.

"Whatever you decide to do with it, keep it protected in that airtight folder. If you sell it, the auction house will know how to handle it. But if you keep it, go to the best framer possible, one who will use museum-quality, archival materials—UV-protected glass, acid-free mats, with an impenetrable seal."

"I will," she promised.

"Excellent," Raymond said. "Let us know; we'll be interested."

"Thank you all," Dar said. "For everything you have done for me and my sisters. It's been an honor to work with you."

"I know the best people to call," Bart said.

"You do," Dar said, kissing his cheek. She tried to shake Raymond's and Jack's hands, but they hugged her, too. She knew that none of them could tell she was levitating, feeling the nearness of her parents and grandmother. The lawyers couldn't see that she was shaking inside, and that it took all her effort to hold her feelings back.

"Come on, Scup," she said. Wagging his tail, he waited by the door, then preceded her down the stairs. She let him out into the back lane, let him explore once more, then opened the hatch for him to jump into the Subaru.

The fog was thicker than ever. She had to put the windshield wipers on. She placed the folder on the seat beside her. Her sisters were waiting for her to call and give them a progress report. Andy had asked her to stop at his millpond site on the way home, to let him know what happened.

Dar intended to do those things. But instead she drove straight back to Chilmark. She parked by the farmhouse, relieved to see that Morgan had come and gone.

There was a note on the kitchen table, but Dar ignored it. She walked straight up two flights of stairs into the attic. Scup stayed downstairs, curled up in his plaid bed. All five cats accompanied her, skulking up the narrow attic stairs, bursting into the dark space and again frightening all the bats out through the vents.

She opened the chimney cupboard where her mother had hidden her father's letters, as if this were the place Dar could feel most close to her parents. She held the deed's case to her heart.

"You did it, Dad," she said out loud. "You brought this home for us, and we're so thankful. You found what you'd set out for, and Rory, Delia, and I know it."

Closing her eyes, she listened and heard her voice echo in the deep and narrow brick chamber. She swore she heard her father speaking back to her. It might have been the sea wind, coming across the waves, whistling in the rafters. But she believed it had been sent by her father.

Later Andy brought scallop rolls for dinner, and both Rory and Delia phoned, wanting to know what had happened. Dar explained it three times. Her sisters listened carefully and, as if they'd already spoken to each other, said they'd be up over the weekend.

"To celebrate!" Dar told Andy. "None of us can quite believe what just happened."

"Your father was a brave man," Andy said quietly.

"And a smart one," Dar said. "Who could have imagined he could accomplish all this? He had a dream, that's for sure—and he made it come true. He thought he needed to prove himself, and he did."

The day was cold, the sea churning. At the foot of the beach, waves the color of rusty iron broke on top of each other. Dar and Andy stood in the farmhouse kitchen, woodstove crackling to drive out the fog's chill. Dar broke out a bottle of sparkling water, cut lemons and heated up the scallop rolls, spooned coleslaw onto plates. As they sat down to eat, Andy pointed at a white envelope.

"What's that?" he asked.

"Oh, I forgot to look," Dar said. "A note from Morgan."

"Want to get it over with?"

She nodded, slit open Morgan's embossed envelope, and pulled out a slip of her monogrammed stationery and an official-looking typed form and read them.

"Well?" Andy asked.

Dar smiled, wadding up the papers and tossing them into the woodstove, watching them blaze, then fizzle into ash. "An offer," she said. "From the Rileys. Guess we won't be needing it now."

She lifted her glass to clink with Andy.

"Here's to that," she said.

"Here's to it," he said, and drank. But he didn't look very happy. Dar felt like bubbling over, but gazing at Andy, she couldn't help wondering why he looked like this was the end of the world.

When they finished eating, he helped her clean up.

"What's wrong?" she asked.

"Shouldn't you tell your sisters about the offer?"

"Why? We're not going to accept it."

"You don't want to, but shouldn't they have a say?"

Drying dishes, she turned from him, started stacking plates in the cupboard. He'd spoken softly, but his words cut her. He sensed it, too. She felt his breath on her neck, his arms coming around her from behind.

"I'm on you're side, Darrah."

"There aren't even supposed to be sides," she said. "They're my sisters. We want the same thing."

"You probably do," he said. "But if it were me, I'd want to make my own choice. Have all the information."

"Fine, I'll tell them."

She felt him nod his head, his cheek brushing hers.

"We'd better stay here," she said. "Instead of going to the Hideaway. I don't want to leave with the stove still going . . ."

"Thanks," he said, "but I'd better get home. I'm behind on getting my invoices out, and I left all the paperwork on my desk."

"You're mad at me."

"Not at all," he said. "You know I hate paperwork, and I don't want to get behind. I need to get paid."

"Okay," Dar said, kissing him, confused, wishing he would want to stay. Standing at the kitchen door, she watched him disappear into the fog. His truck lights came on, illuminating swirls and gusts of mist blowing off the ocean. He backed out, and she called good night, but he didn't call back.

Needing to celebrate with someone who'd appreciate the moment, she tried Pete's cell phone. It had been turned off; she checked her watch and figured he was probably at a meeting. Then she called Harrison.

"Guess what?" she asked.

"Sweetie, I already know. Rory called to tell me."

Dar smiled, thinking of how happy that must have made Harrison. "She beat me to the punch! Isn't it amazing?"

"It truly is. Captain McCarthy, the great seafarer, has brought incredible riches to his daughters."

"He did," Dar said.

"Did Rory sound happy?" Dar asked.

"Mmmm," Harrison said. She could hear him taking a long drag on a joint.

"About getting to keep the house?"

"Mmmm," Harrison said, letting out a big lungful of smoke.

"Did you know she and Delia are coming back this weekend so we can celebrate?"

"I did know that. You know how much I love a good celebration."

"We'll have a party," Dar said. "Friday night, dinner, here at the farmhouse, as soon as they arrive. We'll get Pete, Andy . . ."

"Yes, the family."

Dar smiled, loving that he put himself in that category.

"Perfect," she said. "I'll plan something great for dinner."

"Maybe I'll bring Les Paul with me," Harrison said. "I have to deliver a sweet Gibson, signed by the master, to New York on Saturday. If I pick the guitar up in time, I'll have it join us for the soiree. I'll try to play 'Moon River.'"

"You can't play the guitar, Harrison."

"I'll fake it," he said, and they laughed.

She hung up, feeling warm inside. It was great to have such wonderful friends—another reason she could never leave the Vineyard. Her family—whether blood-related or not—belonged here.

Staring at the phone, she wanted to call Andy, just to make sure they were okay, and to tell him about Friday. But she decided to leave him alone, let him have his peace.

Instead she opened her laptop and logged on. It was too late to call Ireland, so she sent an e-mail instead to Tim McCarthy, telling him all about what had happened since she'd last seen him, since leaving Cobh.

And then she found herself writing another e-mail, addressing it to each of her sisters.

> *Dear R & D,*
>
> *I know it's beside the point, but we now have an offer from the Rileys. I took the liberty of burning it, considering there's no longer a reason to sell. I'm sitting in the house right now, feeling love pour off the walls, knowing it's all from our family. I love you, and can't wait to spend every single summer for the rest of our lives together, right here.*
>
> *XXOO Dar*

CHAPTER TWENTY-TWO

Friday dawned clear and fine, and the sky grew more blue and the breeze dropped as the day went on. Harrison came early to help Dar get ready. She sent him on errands—to Poole's in Menemsha for swordfish, the West Tisbury market for fingerling potatoes, mesclun greens, tiny yellow tomatoes, and small purple beets. She made a plum tart. When Harrison came back, she sent him into the wine cellar to choose whatever bottles he thought would go best with dinner.

Wines chosen, Harrison helped Dar pull the weathered teak table off the porch and onto the lawn. She covered it with one of her grandmother's French country tablecloths, bought on a trip to Avignon, set it with the best china, silver, and crystal. She and Harrison carried the Hitchcock dining room chairs outside, giving them a good dusting; they hadn't been used since her mother's epic parties.

Overhead, the low, wind-twisted pines and oaks were still.

There was barely a breath of breeze, making the morning hot, but assuring Dar that the evening would be warm and beautiful. She went into the basement, brought up strings of colorful paper lanterns.

Dar had made them with rice paper, painted them with pen and ink, in homage to the Camp Meeting's Illumination Night. She and Harrison strung them from the porch roof to two poles set in the ground by the table. When the time was right, she would light the tea lights set inside each one, making them all glow like beach jewels.

Harrison wasn't one for moving too far too fast, but Dar convinced him to walk down to the beach and collect shells with her.

"What do we need them for?" he asked.

"Table decorations," she said. "Party favors."

"Party favors?" he asked skeptically. "As in 'Oh goody, I got a clamshell'?"

"Well, or a pretty rock, or a fish jaw, or whatever interesting thing you might find. What's the matter? You used to love to walk on the beach."

"I've got to get back to it. Into shape and all."

Was he thinking of Rory? Dar took his hand as they walked along the hard sand. Harrison was tall and stolid, his hand powerful. She had the feeling he could have crushed her bones, but he'd always been a gentle soul.

"Rent's going up on the storage unit," he said.

"Can you afford to keep it?"

"As long as there are vintage instruments to be delivered."

"I think you're amazingly creative and resourceful. Finding a way to stay on the Vineyard. Luckily, there are lots of musicians here."

"I was saving the unit beside me for you," Harrison said. "Although Andy always had a fallback plan for you."

"What does that mean?"

"Ask him."

Andy. Dar hadn't seen him since the night she'd burned Morgan's letter and the Rileys' offer.

"He's been private lately," she said.

"Oh, you artistic lovebirds," Harrison said. "I hear it from him, I hear it from you. Two lonely souls who are too dumb to live together."

"Thanks," Dar said.

"Baby, I'm only stating the obvious. You're living on the most beautiful island in the world; you might as well do it together. You'd think you were both tortured."

"Maybe we are. It happens inside," Dar said, remembering all her years of pain and misbehavior, drinking to chase the demons away. Andy had his own; he never talked much about his childhood, but Dar remembered his father's drunken rages, the homemade moonshine he'd brewed from a recipe passed down from his Tennessee grandfather.

Dar and Harrison picked up a collection of shells and sea-smoothed shell fragments, small bits of driftwood, a few crab carapaces, a broken piece of blue and white crockery, a red gingham button.

When their hands and pockets were full, they headed across the boardwalk to the lawn. Harrison needed a Heineken, so he went into the cool kitchen while Dar arranged the beach treasures at each place setting.

Dar had chosen every plate, glass, and piece of silver carefully, wanting to remind her sisters of what they had here, the memories that would never die as long as they stayed, and what they stood to lose.

She had sharp radar for her sisters' emotional lives. Both Rory and Delia had been massively kind, yet deeply withholding on the phone each time Dar had called. They couldn't be thinking of selling. She told herself so, but the nagging thought kept returning. The traumas of this house, and what they'd just done to discover their father's truth, had been a lot to bear. For Dar as well. But she knew they would get through it, as they always had.

"Hey," Harrison said. "Is Pete coming?

"Yes, why?"

"Andy said he's taking a little time off from work."

That gave Dar a jolt, but she decided not to panic yet. She wondered why Andy hadn't called to tell her.

"Is Andy coming?" she asked.

"Yep," Harrison said, going to his truck and returning with a battered leather guitar case. "I brought the music."

"Excellent," Dar said as Harrison opened the case, revealing a custom wine-red vintage Gibson electric guitar, chrome gleaming. She used to feel nervous about his bringing such valuable instruments, but had given up.

At other times, he'd brought rosewood fiddles, a mandolin with ebony inlays, a double bass played by a musician at La Scala. Harrison always enjoyed sitting quietly with the instruments he transported, tilting them toward the beach so that, although he couldn't actually play them, the wind would strum across the strings, echo through the f-holes of violins or arch-topped guitars. He told Dar the music stayed in him, inspiring him as he drove the instruments long distances. The music got him through the miles.

Dar looked around the yard. Daggett's Way and the Hideaway had always been her inspiration. Dulse, Heath, and Finn had sprung from this rocky earth, surrounded by salt ponds and the ocean. Could she continue the series, such an important part of her existence, if she didn't have this place to come to?

That's why she had to be wrong about her sisters. They couldn't be thinking of giving it up, after all they'd been through. That's why dinner had to be perfect. She wanted to look across the table, into her sisters' eyes, and know that they were all together on this, still in love with their family home.

With twilight coming on, Rory and Delia rode the ferry. They had decided to come together—solidarity. They stood on deck, watching the island shimmer on the sea, a beautiful mirage.

"I'm nervous about seeing Dar," Delia said.

"Me too. I can't believe it," Rory said.

"Did you tell her we talked to Morgan?"

"I chickened out."

"She had to figure we'd want to know the details of the offer, right? She did send us that e-mail," Delia said.

"I'm not sure she thought we'd check," Rory said.

"I would never be feeling this way if the Littles were still in the picture," Delia said. "But it's not so hard to take, knowing the Rileys will keep the house and land the way it is."

Rory nodded. "I guess that's how I see it," she said.

"Can we put it in the agreement?" Delia asked. "That they can't destroy or alter the house in any major way?"

"We'll have to ask Bart," Rory said, staring into the water, seeming sad but relatively serene. No maniacal checking of her BlackBerry, no hacking into Jonathan's e-mail. Delia didn't understand. In less than an hour they would have to break the news to Dar, but Rory seemed calm.

"I notice you're not checking up on Jonathan," Delia said.

"I'm just so tired. Chasing him, hoping for him to come back. It's worn me down."

"I'm sorry," Delia said.

"I really believed we would last forever. He's left Alys, and once the kids are out of school, he'll take them to the Vineyard for two weeks."

"Maybe you'll see him!"

Rory closed her eyes. "It hurts to see him, Delia."

"Are you sad about the house? Deciding we want to sell it?"

"Of course," Rory said, almost harshly. "Aren't you?"

"I feel like someone in Shakespeare. Betraying Dar, trying to wash the blood off my hands."

"There's no blood," Rory said, as the ferry entered Vineyard Haven's harbor—the town and sky were painted with streaks of sunset orange and gold. It was time to go down to the cars.

Rory felt overwhelmed by the evening's beauty—blue sky fading to amber sunset, planets and a few stars already visible in the darkening sky. She supposed that one blessing would be that she wouldn't have to see all the familiar landmarks on the way home. It would be too dark to see the large, twisting oak, the row of cedars, Alley's Store, the vistas looking south toward salt ponds, dunes, and the Atlantic Ocean.

When they dipped down the hill in West Tisbury, Rory heard a quick siren burst. She instantly checked her speedometer. She'd been going fifty; had the speed trap gotten her, or was he after the car heading toward Edgartown?

"Shit, he got me," Rory said.

"Cops always hide here," Delia said.

It was pitch-black in this glade of thick trees, and the officer shone a bright flashlight on the license plate and all around the car. He stayed carefully back from the two front doors, and in the side-view mirror, Rory saw he had his hand on his holster.

"Can you believe it?" she asked Delia. "He's got his hand on his fucking gun. We're two middle-aged moms!"

After a while he stood right beside Rory's car, shining his light in her face, indicating for her to roll down her window.

"Any idea how fast you were traveling, ma'am?"

"Fifty," she said, hands on the wheel, staring straight ahead.

"That's right. The speed limit here is thirty. You were going twenty miles per hour over. License and registration, please."

Delia had gotten them ready; Rory passed them into the officer's waiting hand. He thanked her for them and went back to his patrol car, doubtless to call them in and make her wait and stew.

Little did he know Rory didn't care. She was turning to stone as she sat there. Numb couldn't begin to describe it. Being on the island brought Jonathan back to her in a way too wrenching to bear.

"He's writing you up," Delia said, looking over her shoulder.

In a much shorter time than Rory would have expected, the officer returned. She saw his smile, illuminated by the flashing lights.

"You're one of the McCarthys," he said. "My dispatcher told me when I gave her your information."

"Yeah," Rory said. "That was my maiden name."

"You're the daughter of the guy who sailed to Ireland and found some kind of paper that gives him and his kids right to land in Chilmark."

"Basically, yes," Rory said.

"Well, I still have to give you a ticket."

"Well, thank you," Rory said. "I appreciate it."

"Take it easy," the officer said. "Arrive alive."

"You bet," Rory said. She turned to Delia. "Thought maybe he'd let me off."

"Killed a little time for us, anyway," Delia said.

As Rory pulled slowly away, up the hill and bearing left toward home, she felt chills. They drove along South Road, and just before they got to their house, Rory paused—prolonging the moment before she'd see Dar—and gazed out to sea. A marsh hawk flew low over the grasslands.

Just beyond, Rory saw a white sailboat coming into view, sailing slowly along the coast. The sloop heeled into the wind, looking so beautiful and mysterious, barely illuminated by a rising moon. Rory stared at it for another moment, wondering where it was heading, whether it was leaving the Vineyard or just arriving.

CHAPTER TWENTY-THREE

The party had started. That is, Harrison had placed several bottles of champagne and a six-pack of Heineken in a battered tin washbasin filled with ice. Andy had lit the tea candles, making the paper lanterns glow above the table. Dar had gathered bunches of wheat and beach grass, placed them in old blue bottles. Coals were bright red on the grill; dinner was almost ready to cook, but Rory, Delia, and Pete hadn't arrived.

"What's taking them so long?" Harrison asked, drinking from his own bottle of champagne while lying in the grass beside the electric guitar, now back in its plush-lined leather case.

"Whose guitar is that anyway?" Andy asked. "Would you want your priceless freaking instrument to be sitting in someone's yard?"

"If it were the right someone's yard," Harrison said. "Yes. I would. So. Where's Pete?"

Andy shrugged and shook his head. He looked toward Dar, and she gave him a quizzical glance. He flushed and looked away.

"What's going on?" she asked. "You don't know where he is?"

"No, not exactly," Andy said.

"But isn't he working for you?"

"He asked for a little time off," Andy said.

"Just as his mother's coming out? Delia will be so disappointed."

"I think he spoke to her about it."

Dar was still, taking that in. She walked into the kitchen to check on the sautéed fingerling potatoes, chilled salad, and tiny purple beets. She checked the cooling plum tart—it looked pretty good, considering she never baked. Moving around, she kept her eye on the driveway, watching for headlights.

Pete. It wasn't a good sign that her nephew had asked for time off work and that he wasn't here at the family celebration. She knew that the odds of an addict's staying sober were much worse than those of his going back to using. In spite of Andy seeming calm about it, Dar worried.

She'd left Pete messages on his voice mail, inviting him to the party, telling him his mother and Rory would be here, too. It was out of character for him not to call her back. Just in case, she tried him again, with no answer.

The night lit up, and headlights came swinging toward the house. Dar stepped outside. She'd put on a long navy blue dress, fitted at the waist, then flaring to her bare feet. She wore silver hoop earrings and a collection of long silver chains. She'd hoped Andy would think she looked pretty, but he seemed lost in thought. Only Harrison seemed really ready to celebrate.

Dar thought of Tim McCarthy. He had answered her long e-mail with an even longer one of his own, asking if he could visit the Vineyard and see the famously rescued property as well as the parchment land grant at the end of the summer, when his busiest time was over. She had written back yes, she and her family would love to have him.

And here they came now: her family. Her two sisters approached the house. They each wore shorts and T-shirts; they weren't carrying luggage. Dar ran to them, and they all collided in a hug, their heads pressed together.

"You look beautiful," Delia said.

"It's a Daggett's Way summer party!"

"I'm so sorry. This is it," Rory said, gesturing at her cargo shorts and Mystic Aquarium shirt.

"We should have figured," Delia said.

"That's okay," Dar said, her arms around both of them. "We're together, that's what counts."

She and her sisters walked around the corner of the house, and Harrison let out a wolf whistle.

"But we're not even dressed up," Rory said.

"So what? You're still the hottest beach girls on this island."

Andy came over to say hi, kiss the sisters' cheeks, and they hugged him back.

Rory stared at the guitar, then closed her eyes to listen to the breeze drift across the strings. Harrison disrupted her reverie, reaching for her hand. She glanced down and smiled.

"Coming inside?" she asked.

"Of course," Harrison said, stubbing out his cigarette, shoving his bottle of champagne under his arm, letting Rory pull him up.

Dar saw Delia acting nervous, pacing around. She waited for her to ask about Pete. As Rory and Harrison carried the guitar into the house, the wind picked up. It sent the lanterns swaying on their wires, then blew the tea lights out all at once. The temperature suddenly dropped.

Glancing up at the sky, Dar saw her galaxy of stars obscured by scraps of cloud blowing in from the east. She'd checked the weather for tonight—nothing had been predicted, but this felt like a front moving through. The first raindrops fell, few and far between.

"Andy, will you help me move the table?" she asked, as Delia gathered up the place settings.

He grabbed one end, and she got the other. Together they carefully lifted the heavy teak table up the wide plank stairs, kept it level, and settled it on the house's leeside porch, as the wind yanked at the tablecloth. Andy went back for the chairs, and Dar and Delia grabbed one each.

The rain began to fall hard, driving sideways along the south shore. It slapped the house and made windows rattle. Scup ran inside, four ratty cats and the people right behind him.

Dar stood in the open doorway, scanning the yard for the fifth. "Here, kitty," she called. "Here, kitty kitty."

"Which one is missing?" Harrison asked.

"Number Five," Dar said. They'd been feral kittens, and her mother had never really named them, not wanting to get too attached to animals who might not stay. She'd called them "Untitled Number One," "Untitled Number Two," all the way to Five, trying to be as unsentimental as possible in case they ran off.

"Your mother killed me, naming them that," Harrison said. "She was so not a minimalist. Just check out her décor—I mean before you boxed most of it up. She had a needlepointed coaster on every mahogany surface, sterling-silver framed photos on the goddamn grand piano. That is not a woman who names her kittens 'Untitled.'"

"She had secret nicknames for them," Rory said. "After flowers . . . Dahlia, Tiger Lily, Daisy. That's all I can remember."

Delphinium and Holly, Dar thought.

"You know what's the worst thing about parents dying?" Harrison said. "It's all the questions you'll never get to ask them. Little things you thought you'd have forever to find out."

"It's true," Rory said, leaning into him.

Andy walked in. "Well, I think it's a nor'easter," he said, putting his arm around Dar. "The rain's completely doused the coals. We'll have to start over, or broil the fish in here."

"Fish," Harrison said, pretending to pound the table. "I should have put in my request for a nice steak."

Dar went to the refrigerator and pulled out something wrapped in butcher paper. "Just for you," she said.

"Thank you, sweetie," he said. "See, this is what's great about us. No deep dark secrets. No saying you can't have beef, it'll give you gout. No holding back on the champagne. Or, if you're off the sauce, good for you. We applaud you, and shall drink yours. Let's get our glasses," he said, rushing onto the protected porch, returning with the crystal.

Andy poured mineral water for Dar and himself; Harrison poured champagne for Delia and Rory, topped off his own glass and raised it.

"To our Vineyard family," Harrison said. "And to Michael McCarthy for keeping us together."

They clinked, and Dar, hesitant, met her sisters' eyes. Their expressions were dark and solemn.

"What is it?" she asked, knowing but not wanting to know. Her heart was in her throat and she couldn't speak or swallow.

"Dar, we love you," Delia said.

Rory took Dar's hand, held it in both of hers against her heart. "We had to come in person, we couldn't tell you on the phone."

"Who is it? What happened?" she asked.

"This has been incredibly hard," Rory said.

"It has," Delia said. "I've lost so much sleep thinking about it; I know Rory has, too."

"Just tell me!"

"We've decided we want to sell," Rory said.

"Sell?"

"Daggett's Way. The whole property, even Dad's land grant," Delia said.

"It's too much for me," Rory said, her eyes pooling with tears. "I'm so sorry, Dar. But this place is loaded, way more than I can take."

"Because of Jonathan?"

"And everything," Rory said. "Just what we all went through for so long. Thinking Dad was dead, never hearing from him. He never called to say that he'd made it safely to Cork."

"He never doubted he'd make it home," Dar whispered.

"But he *didn't* make it home," Rory said.

"Dar, Mom living here was one thing. But it would be so hard for us; none of us has the money to keep it up the way it should be."

"But if we auction off the deed . . ." Dar said.

"Did you hear what we're saying?" Rory asked. "Delia and I want out. We'd like us all to agree to accept this most recent offer. I spoke to Morgan, and she says it's all cash, and that the couple has no intention of tearing down the house. The opposite—they love it and want to keep it just the way it is."

Dar's heart and mind were numb. She turned from her sisters. Harrison and Andy were hanging back, waiting for the dust to settle. She hurried past them without a glance. At the French doors in the living room, she grabbed the flashlight her mother had always kept there, and walked outside.

Someone called her name, but she ignored it. She was Dulse, a water spirit, and no rain had ever bothered her. It soaked her long dress, made it drag through the mud and sand. Her bedraggled hair fell into her eyes. The wind was blowing so hard, she had to lean into its force; it tried to blow her back to the house, but she fought hard.

When she got to the boardwalk, she saw that it had been blown off the normally gentle creek into the yard. She waded through the surging torrent of the incoming tide, feeling crabs scuttle under and over her toes, minnows pecking at her skin. Stepping out on the other side, she climbed to the top of the dune.

She shone her flashlight out at the ocean. The beam caught one turbulent frothy white wave after another. She held the light steady, and just beyond the surf break she saw a white sloop heeled over, slicing through the sea. It sailed with such grace, even through this wild storm.

She took a step closer, into the tall dune grass, and felt something soft with her toes. Shining the light down, she cried out, knelt in the sand, picked up the small, ragged body. Its fur was knotted and tangled, covered with blood and sand. The marsh hawk had come down here to hunt, and had gotten Dahlia, the tiny fifth cat.

Holding the body, Dar began to cry. The storm covered her howls as she rocked back and forth. The wild cats had been part of her family forever, and now one was gone. Her parents were dead, and her sisters didn't want the house.

Dar felt arms encircling her.

"Dar," Rory whispered.

"We love you," Delia said.

Dar couldn't look into their eyes, couldn't stop sobbing. "The poor little cat," she wept.

"Come inside," Rory said, gently easing her toward the house.

"It won't be the same," Dar sobbed. "How can you do this? We'll fall apart. *We* won't be the same without this place . . ."

"We always will. You can come to us," Rory said. "We all have to heal from this spring, and everything that came with it. You already know this house has changed—for you, me, Delia. For all of us. Dar, please . . ."

But Dar drifted away. It was just like when she'd been twelve and she'd thought she'd never see her father again. The grief had wrapped around her like the ugliest vine. She felt it coming for her again, kneeling in the wet sand. It twisted through her, strangling her insides, wrapping her heart like a mummy. She couldn't fight it; she just buried the tiny old cat as deeply as possible in the sand and went away.

Dar never actually passed out or lost consciousness; she just went so deeply inside herself there were no words to be spoken, heard, no communication at all. She had locked herself in, yet she knew what she was doing as she moved along through the sludge.

Before she left the house, she signed the quitclaim deed Rory and Delia had provided. *Do you see this part?* they seemed to be asking her. *Are you sure?* She might have nodded. They thanked her, or at least she saw gratitude and worry in their eyes. She saw Andy's eyes glinting with fury, and she could almost imagine him telling them Dar wasn't in her right mind. She would have put her hand on his wrist, reassured him that she was.

She wasn't sure where she slept that night, but when she woke up in the morning, she was in her mother's bed, Rory and Delia on either side of her. Sunlight came through the window. When she got up she looked out. The sea was calm, as if last night's storm had never happened.

She had to leave. Seeing her sisters was too much—she felt she barely knew them, yet the sight of them filled her with despair. She would never have gone against them; she'd thought they were in this together, and it killed her to know that they weren't. She had always loved things too much, she told herself. This house and people and little wild cats.

Tears streamed down her cheeks; she knew that this was the moment when everything changed, yet again, forever. Losing her father had not prepared her for the many subsequent losses of life. A house was nothing but boards, shingles, bricks, mortar. A structure, inanimate and impermanent.

And she and her sisters: the threads that had held them together all their lives had just given way. The worst part was Dar knew that Rory and Delia had cut them.

PART V

I am thinking of a child's vow sworn in vain
Never to leave that valley his fathers called their home.

FROM "UNDER SATURN," BY WILLIAM BUTLER YEATS

CHAPTER TWENTY-FOUR

For Pete, everything about it sucked. His mother had called to break the news to him about the house and to tell him how hard it was going to be for Dar. His mother had asked him to make sure to be at the family dinner with her and Rory, but there was no way Pete was going to sit at a table watching them break Dar's heart.

He had told his mother no, asked Andy for a couple of days off work, given a guy at the sober house a hundred bucks to let him take his car, and headed to the ferry. By leaving he was blowing his chance with Al, and he knew he'd have to move out when he got back. But still, he couldn't stick around while his family did that to Dar.

Driving north with no real destination, he'd felt some old familiar twinges. Not drugs, he told himself. He needed to get away from this sandy coast, head up to Maine where the air would have a tangy chill and the pine trees would grow on rocky promontories like they did in Alaska.

Driving straight through, radio on, he'd made it to Portland in record time, just kept hugging the coast and heading northeast. When he got tired that first night, he pulled over in a rest stop and slept a few hours. By first light, he was back on the road.

Maine looked good to him. He'd gotten used to the rugged beauty and hardships of Alaska. The colder temperatures suited him. He liked the scenery, and the sight of real working harbors. Just past Damariscotta he stopped at a diner, had blueberry pancakes and a lot of coffee. The thought of finding a meeting crossed his mind. But he pushed it away and started driving again.

The roads were pretty empty this time of year. He passed a few dingy motels that reminded him of where he'd lived in Dillingham. Slowing down past one, he took a long look. Junk heaps in the parking lot, shades down in all the windows, looked really downbeat and familiar. The crazy thing was, seeing that kind of place kicked off his craving.

Once it started, it was like a fever creeping up. His skin began to crawl, almost as if the physical addiction was back on him. Pete tried to stay focused on the road. He forced himself to drive about the Vineyard, figured the party would be over now. Trail of destruction back there, and he was glad not to be part of it. He imagined Dar, cringed at how she must be feeling. That thought made him want to use even more.

He stopped for gas across the bridge in Bucksport. Standing at the pump, he saw some guys in a pickup truck at the next island— commercial fisherman. The driver looked sort of like Andy, and he had lobster traps in the truck bed, so Pete walked over.

"Hey," he said, nodding toward the traps. "How's it going?"

"Going okay," the driver said. "After a lousy winter."

"Yeah?" Pete asked.

"You fish?"

"I used to," Pete said. "In Alaska."

"Going after what?"

"Salmon."

"You do okay at that?"

"Made my fair share," Pete said. He noticed both guys were drinking coffee. They looked strong and healthy, about as far from drugs as Andy was. Talking to them made him feel grounded. The sleazy motel seemed very far away.

"Well," the driver said when he'd finished pumping gas. "Nice talking to you. Have a good day."

"You too," Pete said. He went inside the convenience store, feeling ten times better. He bought himself a large coffee with lots of milk and sugar, then got back into the car.

The sky was bright blue, very clear. He had the idea that he would drive all the way to the Canadian border near Machias, then turn around and head home to the Vineyard. That would give Dar the chance to recover a little, so he wouldn't have to dread facing her so much.

Thinking of Dar, and how much he loved her, made him start to feel like crap again. He'd looked up to her when he was a kid; she'd been so good to him, always taking him places, twice even drawing him into her graphic novels. She'd given him two cameos, not even changing his name. His friends had said the character looked just like him.

Of all the people he'd let down, other than his parents, Dar was the one that he most regretted. She'd even stayed close when he was at his worst, as if she had faith in him that he couldn't begin to understand. All that, and here he was, the craving creeping back, covering him like spiderwebs.

Maybe driving to the border was a little too ambitious. He started thinking of that motel back along the road. He'd passed plenty of bars, too, some of them definitely seedy enough for what he had in mind. He had a nose for meth, and the kind of places he could get it.

Suddenly he was back in the "should I, shouldn't I?" world of craving. It had always been the same thing: he'd make a promise to last a day, or an hour, or another ten minutes. But he'd break out in a sweat, just like he was right now, and all his promises would fly out the window.

He found himself pulling over, waiting for the chance to make a U-turn and head south, back the way he'd come. That motel might be the right place. He could get a room; he could use a decent rest. He didn't have to go looking for meth, but if it happened to be there, then he could make his decision.

The miles sped by so fast, he couldn't believe it when he saw the neon motel sign, all but two letters burned out. This time, instead of just slowing down, he turned into the parking lot. The motel was one story high, about twelve units. The roof was sagging, a couple of windows boarded up with plywood. The office had red curtains pulled across the windows.

One of the junkier cars was up on concrete blocks; they'd probably sold the wheels. Another had left since he'd first driven past, but as he sat there he watched it pull in behind him—a dented blue Chevy, one flat tire, heavy plastic duct-taped over the broken rear window. The car limped down to the last spot in the row. A woman got out, giving him a shifty look as if she thought he might be a cop.

Pete didn't indicate anything one way or the other. He'd seen that woman before, and a hundred just like her. She was rail skinny, greasy hair, animal eyes. She had two little kids in the back seat, and he knew that when they got out of the car they'd be lucky if she fed them or changed their diapers.

She stared at him, then slunk into the last unit. The older kid, about four, had to open the back door and help his brother, maybe two, out of his car seat. They walked to the door and it opened a crack and shut again.

Pete's hands shook. He held his cell phone, staring at it, wondering why he hadn't charged it before leaving. The battery was low, but he had enough to make a call. He punched in Andy's number.

"Hello?" Andy said.

"It's Pete."

"Where are you?"

"Maine."

Andy took a deep breath. "Okay. Are you all right?"

"Yes, but about not to be."

"Tell me what's going on, Pete."

"I want to pick up," Pete said.

"Have you yet?"

"No."

"Then you still have a choice," Andy said.

"I fucked up. I left Al's, and he won't let me back in."

"You going to let that be your excuse?"

Pete was silent. He saw the curtain in the last unit move. He wondered about those little boys. It had made him sick in Dillingham, to watch how meth heads treated their kids. What if he just stormed the place, took those boys away, brought them to the police station?

He thought of Vanessa. The kind of father he'd been to her so far, since she was born. He'd finally met her on the Vineyard; he'd held her, she'd called him Daddy. Again he glanced at that last unit, knew that was the loser life he'd have to offer her if he used again.

He thought of how he'd made this escape from the Vineyard to avoid seeing Dar be hurt. And he thought of himself, how hard it had been to stay clean for this many days. The idea of going back to this made his head hurt more than the craving.

"You there?" Andy asked.

"Yeah. My phone's about to die."

"Then listen fast. Here's what you do. Drive away from wherever you are while you have me on the phone."

Pete had his hand on the gearshift. It took everything he had to put the car into reverse, back around, pull out onto Route 1.

"Okay," he said. "I'm driving."

"Have you eaten? Have you slept?"

"I could use both," Pete said.

"So head to the next decent-sized town. Find a meeting first thing. You know how to make the call, so make it. Be sure you put your hand up, let people know you're having a tough time. Stick around afterwards, see if they're going to the diner. Okay? Have something to eat. Then take a power nap, and get back here."

"But," Pete began.

"You start back down that old path," Andy said, "and I'm afraid we'll never see you again. You know what you have to do, Pete."

"Okay," Pete said.

"I need you back here," Andy said. "We still have work to do, to finish up."

"How's Dar?"

Andy was silent. Then, "She'll be okay."

Perfect timing: Pete's phone quit. By the time he got to Camden, the sun was going down behind Mount Battie. He pulled into a gas station with a phone booth outside. The thing ate money, so he had to buy some gum and get change. He clanked in two quarters, dialed information.

"Can I have the number for Alcoholics Anonymous in Camden?" he asked.

The operator said yes, and the computer voice gave it to him. Pete's finger was shaking as he pressed the buttons. How many times had he done this before? Usually his cell service would have been long cut off, he'd be sicker than a dog, drinking and drugs taking him to his knees, the local pay phone his only way out.

"Hello," a woman said.

"I'm looking for a meeting in the Camden area," he said.

"There are two tonight," she said. "One in Camden, one in Rockland."

"Which one starts soonest?"

"There's a Step meeting at six-thirty, St. Thomas's Church in Camden. It's at 33 Chestnut Street."

"Thanks," Pete said, and ten minutes later he was parking his car, saying hi to people, following them into the meeting. There was coffee, cookies, meeting lists. He took a list, stuck it in his pocket. Fixing himself a coffee, he said hi to two older bearded guys, looked like fishermen, old-school alcoholics, probably never took drugs in their lives, standing at the end of the table.

"How you doing?" one of them asked.

"I'm good," Pete said. "How about you?"

"Good," he said. "I'm Joe. This is Turner."

"I'm Pete."

"You new to the area?"

"Just passing through." Pete paused. "I haven't been clean long, and I feel like using. Meth."

The two fishermen clapped him on the back.

"I'm glad you told us," Joe said.

"Come on, sit with us," Turner said.

The meeting was about to start, and they walked him up to the table, sat on either side of him. Pete felt his shoulders sink down, the weight of something terrible starting to slide away.

The Hideaway was well named. Dar knew her grandparents had built it as a beach cottage, the name meant to be whimsical. But to Dar right now it was dead serious. She closed the door behind her, hid away from the world. She turned her phone off, disabled her Internet connection. She thought about hanging a sign on her door: *No Contact.* It killed her to realize that the sign would be aimed at her sisters.

The movement of air hurt her skin. Every sound seemed magnified, startling her. The earth had shifted, and she was afraid that if she moved, she might slide off the edge and never stop falling.

Andy approached her gently. She lay on the bed, facing the wall. She felt him standing over her, saw his shadow on the pillow.

"You have to eat," he said.

"I'm not hungry.

"I'll make you toast."

"Andy . . ."

"Darrah, it's all going to be okay."

What would be okay? She felt she had lost her place, not just on the island, but in her family. So much love falling away, trailing off, impossible to hold on to. She trembled, so tired of tears.

"Please eat, Dar," he said.

"I don't want to. I know how much you want to help, I do . . . I can't stand myself like this." She rolled over to face him. "Just let me get through it, and I'll be fine. I promise."

"You will be fine, but I'm not going to leave and 'let you get through it,' " he said. "Don't you get it?"

"I do. I know you mean . . ."

Andy shook his head. He touched her tenderly, but his expression was stubborn. "I don't mean well. Is that what you were going to say?"

"Yes."

"Well, you're wrong. I don't mean well at all. I'm not doing a good deed."

"I'm fucking miserable, and I'm bringing you down."

He actually laughed. "You're ridiculous. Bring me down? I love you and want you and am not leaving till you eat toast."

She heard herself laugh.

He smiled, stroking her hair. "That's a little better."

"Yeah," she said. "Can I ask you, I don't actually want to hear but I have to know, have my sisters told you when this whole thing will be final?"

"I have no idea," he said. "I'm too busy trying to make you eat."

She watched him cross the small space, walk into the sunny kitchen. He opened a brown paper bag, took out a loaf of bread. She saw him pop two pieces into the stainless steel toaster, find butter and jelly in the refrigerator. When the toast was ready, he carefully fixed it for her, cutting the bread into triangles and arranging it on a plate.

"There," he said, handing it to her. She propped herself up on one elbow and took a bite.

"Thank you," she said. "I feel bad, taking you away from work in the middle of the day."

"You know, don't you?" Andy asked.

"Know what?"

"The place I've been working on, with Pete," he said. "That cottage by the millpond."

"The new owners cracking the whip?" she asked.

He shook his head. "There's no new owner," he said. "It's me. And I built the house for you."

"Andy!"

"For us," he said.

Dar took it in. She closed her eyes, remembering their first visit to the site, when the brown field and gray river stones were covered with frost. He'd held her hand, shown her the meadow and millstone. Right now, lying on her bed, she could almost feel the chilly April breeze as he'd stood beside her.

"Will you move in with me?" he asked.

She knocked the toast over as she hugged him, shocked by his love and generosity. What if she couldn't live up to it? What if she had too much of her father's blood in her, and took off one day to prove something unprovable to Andy or herself? But as they faced each other across the spilled toast, she felt her heart settle down.

"Is that a 'yes'?" he asked, smiling nervously.

"Yes," she said.

He looked so relieved, they both started laughing. "You had me for a minute there, Darrah. But this is right. I know it is."

"So do I." She paused. "You kept it such a secret," she said.

"Well," he said. "I'm not the only one . . ."

She waited for him to explain, but he didn't. He hugged her hard.

"I'd better get back," he said. "If you're okay alone."

She nodded, pushing the covers back, gathering up the plate and toast. "I'm getting up."

"Good. See you tonight?"

"I'll be here."

Andy kissed her softly on the mouth. She watched him leave, heard his truck start up. She walked over to her desk, and almost immediately Dulse's story filled her mind.

Sitting at her drafting table, she pushed her drawing tablet aside. She began to sketch in a simpler and more basic way, on a blank page of paper: Dulse on a train across the sea.

Dulse was the only passenger aboard the train, and when she made her way through many empty cars to the engine, she realized no one was at the controls. Instead of being afraid, she stationed herself in the engineer's seat and waited to see where the train would take her.

Dar took her time inking in those first panels, using her smallest-gauge Micron pens to capture the fragility of train tracks on the ocean's surface, the delicacy of the train, thirty cars long, gannets and puffins perched on the roofs, octopi entwined with the metal links between cars, barnacles and starfish attached to the tracks, long tendrils of kelp trailing from the rails.

Up above, a ring around the moon, layers of reddish space particles. Instead of predicting rain, the moon's ring itself began to drizzle, sending space dust down to earth. Sitting in the engine, Dulse saw the air fill with rust-red snow, making it impossible to see where the train was taking her.

Dar went back, erased the pencil lines, added color to the sea and red dust, Prismacolor pens for the train and sea creatures, a softer effect using watercolors and a fine sable brush for the moon's ring, a wide, flat brush to color the deep green-blue sea.

Scup interrupted her, scratching at the door. Dar leaned over, let him in. Someone had tied a blue ribbon around his neck, a small white paper attached; Dar untied it and read the note in Rory's handwriting: *Dar, we love you.*

Dar placed the card on her desk, slid it under the small pewter dory her father had carried with him from his grandfather's boat shed in Cobh. She made herself a cup of tea.

Opening to a new page, she made three quick sketches: the train pulling into the Atlantic port town of Arcachon, thousands of oysters attached to the pilings of the train pier; on a map, Arcachon's harbor appearing as if a sea monster had taken a large bite out of France's southern Atlantic coast; a dune as tall as a mountain, the largest sand dune in the world.

La Pyla, the name of the dune, appeared in a bubble over its rounded peak, high above sea level. Trailing green seaweed and salt water, minnows falling from her pockets and being snatched up by seagulls, Dulse strode through Arcachon's wind-twisted pines, looking up at the great dune. The moon's ring-dust had fallen here, covering the white sand with a layer of garnet red.

Dulse began to climb. She produced a leather sack, crouched down, used a hard, amber-colored piece of whale baleen to sift the topmost layer, the red moondust, into her pouch. A great wind picked up, swirling the red particles around, sending them into the air and harbor, mixing them deeply within the dune. But by then, Dulse had all she needed.

Dar inked over the pencil sketch, then began to paint, delicate watercolors to suggest the fleeting nature of space dust. And what did red moondust mean to Dulse? Dar didn't try to figure it out; she merely painted, then crosshatched fine circular shadows to indicate the wind's power.

When she was finished, she opened her door—the first time since she'd shut herself in two days earlier. She blinked into the blindingly blue sky. Scup ran out ahead of her, down the sandy path toward the beach. Dar put on a windbreaker and followed him, barefoot.

They crossed the boardwalk, passed the little cat's grave, stepped onto the sand. These dunes were low and long; the path between them was wide. Dar watched Scup run down to the water's edge, sniffing along the tide line, spending quality time with a dead skate caught in clumps of seaweed.

She sat high up on the beach, the dune just behind her, in the sun-hot sand. Letting it run through her fingers, she saw twinkling black mica stick to her skin. She wished she had a baleen comb like Dulse, to separate out the sparkles.

Once, when they were young, Harrison had brought her and her sisters to Mink Meadows, his father's favorite golf course over in Vineyard Haven; they'd taken magnets into a sand trap, dragged them across, come up with long trails of iron ore, nearly microscopic bits magnetized to each other.

Was that the inspiration for Dulse's latest adventure? Dar wasn't sure. She only knew that her ideas came from deep down, experiences and emotions of her own.

Sitting there, she barely heard them coming. But she sensed them even before she saw their shadows. Rory and Delia had walked down from the big house, sat on either side of her.

"We saw you," Rory said.

"I'm here," Dar said.

"Do you still want to be alone?" Delia asked.

Dar didn't reply. She just kept remembering that day with the magnets, all the iron ore they'd collected. They had collected it in a leather golf club cover Harrison had filched from his father's custom 5-wood.

"Why was there iron in the sand trap?" she asked.

"The sand trap?" Delia asked.

"With Harrison!" Rory said. "That day with the magnets."

"There's iron in all sand, even here at the beach." Dar said. "But nothing like that day."

"I guess I thought it came from the golf clubs," Delia said. "All that metal banging around at the ball. I figured little bits got chipped away over the years, mixing in with the sand."

Dar nodded. That made sense.

"Dar," Rory said. "I'm sorry."

"So am I," Delia said.

"I know," Dar said. "It's all right."

"That sounds so contained," Rory said, sounding sad. "I'd almost rather have you yell at us."

"But why?" Dar asked. "What good would that do?"

"You're hurt, but we are, too," Rory said. "We don't want it to be this way. Dar, we can't afford to keep the house the way we've known and loved it all these years. How long before we'll need another new roof? What about the rattling windows? Even without taxes, what about repairs?"

"We love it too much to let it go that way," Delia said.

A steady breeze carried the sound of the bell buoy tolling off Nomans Land to the beach. Dar heard it, and a memory flooded back. When she was very young and her family was waiting for the ferry, her father had walked her past all the Woods Hole Oceanographic buildings, showing her the buoy lab where four-story-high scientific research buoys—fresh from their positions throughout the Atlantic Ocean—lay on the wharf waiting for repair or for their data to be recovered.

"What's data?" Dar had asked.

"Information," her father had answered.

"What kind?"

"Well, these big buoys are set out in the middle of the sea, and they measure wind, tides, wave heights, and the space between one wave and the next. Wind creates waves, and these buoys record wave anomalies."

"Anom . . . ?"

"Variations. Strange happenings, rogue waves. The ocean never stays still; the wind won't let it," he'd said. "A good sailor knows everything is always changing."

And it was. And so was life. Dar listened to the distant clanging, brought to her by the wind.

"I signed the paper," Dar said, staring at the mica on her hands. "Did the sale go through?"

"Yes," Rory said.

"The inheritance tax has been paid, and there's a lot left over. Bart wrote three checks, one for each of us," Delia said.

Scup came running back, a bone in his mouth. Dar pried it loose: the size of a tennis ball, it had to be a whale's vertebra. The whole moment felt unreal, and all she wanted was to go back home and draw more Dulse before packing up.

"Will you come with us?" Rory asked.

"Not right now," Dar said.

"Please," Delia said. "The sale isn't straightforward. We need you to see something."

"Have you talked with Andy? Did he tell you about the house he's building for us?" Dar asked.

"Yes," Delia said.

"Come with us," Rory said, standing, offering a hand to pull Dar up. Dar let her, and there was no way to express her reluctance to follow. If the house wasn't theirs anymore, she wasn't sure she could ever set foot inside it again.

"Can't you just tell me here?" Dar asked.

But they wouldn't, and so she walked along with them. Crossing the yard, she saw Harrison's van parked behind her sisters' cars. He was lying on a towel in the sun, but when he saw them coming, he grunted himself up and opened his arms for Dar.

"Hi, sweetie," he said. "Been a shitty couple of days, hasn't it?"

"Yeah," she said.

"I'm here for you. You know that. Even if Andy wasn't working double time on the house and your sisters hadn't come up with their brilliant plan, I'd have made room in my place for you. I'd have given you the bed. Or maybe we'd have shared it. Either way."

"Thank you, Harrison," she said.

The house should have looked the same as ever, but it didn't to Dar. Dar's gaze swept the gracious exterior, every shingle, shutter, porch rail, windowpane untouched, and wondered what was missing. Now it was just a big waterfront house, no longer her family home.

"That's okay," Delia said.

"I'll get it," Rory said, running into the house.

Dar watched the four old cats skulk in a pack along the bramble hedge; did they miss Dahlia? She had the feeling they did, that they were looking for her. She wanted to gather them up, take them with her, keep them safe. Andy wouldn't mind; she was positive of that.

A minute later she heard the screen door brush shut, saw Rory coming toward her with an envelope. The check, Dar thought. Her share of the sale.

Rory and Delia smiled.

"We told them they couldn't have it," Rory said.

"At first they said no, because it's such a charming part of Daggett's Way," Delia said. "But then they agreed to trade."

"Trade what?"

"Open this," Rory said, thrusting the envelope at her. Dar reached in with mica-covered hands, leaving black sparkles on the paper.

"It's a deed," she said, reading. Before she could digest the words, Delia spoke up.

"We traded them the strip of land grant property for the Hideaway."

"It's almost exactly the same square footage," Rory said.

"The deed is yours," Delia said.

Dar stared at the paper.

Her sisters' smiles quavered, hesitant, wanting to make sure Dar was really okay, that she was happy, that they'd done right by her.

"The Hideaway belongs to you," Rory said. "It could never go to anyone else."

"Thank you," Dar said, stunned.

"One thing," Harrison said. "You'd break Andy's heart if you didn't move into that house he's building . . . Jonathan even came up to show him the best place to situate your studio. Big windows facing north over the meadow."

Dar reached out to hug her sisters. They stood in a tight knot, heads together, not wanting to let go.

"What about the parchment?" she asked finally. "Did you have to hand it over with the actual land?"

"No. Bart and the Fitzgeralds saw to that," Rory said.

"We should give it to a museum," Dar said. "That's been in the back of my mind. What if we sent it to Ireland, on loan, to Kanturk Castle? We could make it in memory of Dad."

"I like that," Rory said.

"I do, too," Delia said.

Dar thought about calling Tim, asking him to help make the offer. She could write an account of their father's story, send it to the castle along with the deed.

"Listen," Rory said. "We're going to have to get going soon. We couldn't leave before we cleared all this with you. But . . ."

"You have to get home. I understand."

"If we get going, we can catch a late ferry. Let's just walk through one more time," Rory said.

"Come on, Dar," Delia said. "Please?"

Dar started to say no, but changed her mind. She and her sisters walked into the big house, and this time she knew it was really good-bye. Standing in the kitchen, she realized it still smelled like home and probably always would.

Moving into the living room, they looked out the seaward windows. A snowy egret flew overhead, yellow legs trailing behind, making its slow, elegant way to the salt pond. Reeds along the beach walkway rustled, and there were the four great hunters, their little tiger faces with amber eyes staring from the camouflage of tawny marsh grass.

Dar turned, took in the big room where her family had come for so long. She let her gaze take in the stone fireplace, granite mantel, window seats, burnished wide oak floorboards, brass sconces. She thought of all the music, conversations, celebrations, and sorrows this room had held. She touched the mantel, and then she was ready.

"We'll stop by as soon as we pack up the car," Rory said.

Dar nodded. She kissed her sisters and walked out the door. The sun was setting; Harrison had made himself a cocktail; she saw him watching the clouds fill with pink light. Scup lay on the porch beside him, so Dar didn't disturb them and hurried past the old well, cellar hole, ancient apple trees, and lilac grove.

Andy was home from work, his truck parked in the drive. She walked inside, found him looking out the window.

"I wondered where you were," he said.

"With my sisters. They held on to it. The Hideaway."

"I know," he said.

"That was the other secret?" she asked.

He gazed at her with sharp green eyes. "I should have told you right away. But I was afraid you'd say no to moving in with me. You still might, now that you know."

"When will our house be ready?" she asked.

"I'm aiming for us to be in by October. Before it gets too cold."

Dar stepped toward him, pulling him close. They held each other, not speaking for a long time. She could imagine her sisters coming here over the years. It would always be their connection to the beach, the sea, each other.

She'd been afraid everything would feel wrong, surreal, with Daggett's Way, the center of her childhood universe, sold. But instead she felt lighter. She felt deep certainty that her father had set off on his final voyage filled with love for his family. Dar's chin rested on Andy's shoulder, and she looked down at her desk. Sunlight hit the surface at an angle.

It bathed her pens, brushes, pencils, and drawings, everything on the desk, in luminous light. Her eyes caught the edge of her sisters' card, *Dar, we love you*, sticking out from beneath the tiny pewter dory.

Dar heard Rory and Delia coming to say good-bye, their cars pulling into her driveway, their voices happy as they climbed out. She stayed in Andy's arms, hearing laughter outside, transfixed by what she saw on her desk.

Just a corner of the white card, a fragment her sister's hand-writing, jutting out from beneath the dory. The sunlight's alchemy had transformed the dull pewter into shining sterling—the single object her father had carried with him to America from his grandfather's workplace, a little silver boat keeping safe his daughters' words of love, and holding the memories of the long journey they'd made to bring him home.

Read on for the first chapter of
Luanne Rice's thirtieth novel,
Little Night,
coming in June 2012
from Pamela Dorman Books/Viking.

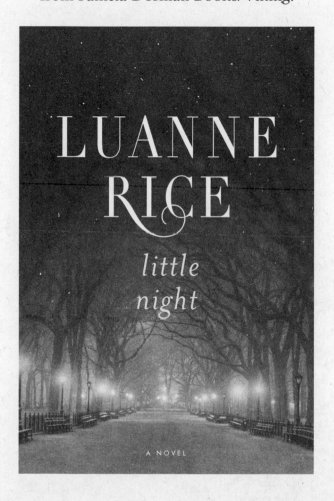

CHAPTER ONE

November 8, 2011

The letter arrived the second Tuesday in November. Standing in the narrow vestibule of her West Chelsea brownstone, Clare Burke unlocked the creaky brass door to her mailbox and reached inside. There, among a pile of bills and flyers, was a single ivory envelope.

She stepped into her parlor floor apartment, slung her messenger bag off her shoulder. Still holding the mail, she removed her notebook and camera and placed them on the kitchen table. Three cats—Blackburn, Olive, and Chat, all named for passerines they would most certainly kill if they had the chance—darted around her feet as she opened the refrigerator door and filled their bowls.

Setting the bills aside, Clare turned to the envelope. In a world of e-mail it stood out for being personal, an actual letter—people didn't write each other anymore, and she felt instantly curious. She saw the name in the return address, and her breath caught.

Rasmussen was written in a tiny, sharp hand, above the address: P.O. Box 1041, Millinocket, ME. The handwriting was not her sister's. Clare turned over the envelope and saw the Burke crest stamped in blue sealing wax. Their parents had given the sisters family crest rings on their twentieth birthdays, and the seal had been imprinted with Anne's.

Clare walked into the living room; trying to keep her hands steady, she opened the letter and started to read:

Dear Aunt Clare,

We don't know each other really, but I'm planning a trip to New York and wondered if we could meet. I'll be doing research for a project. I read your Institute for Avian Studies blog and look at your photos—I especially love the one of the snowy owl. I didn't know they wintered on city beaches.

This letter must seem really out of the blue. It is for me, too. I didn't plan on writing it, but then this opportunity came up, and I thought who do I know in the city? This is not a trick to get revenge for my father or something. Please do not be worried about that.

Just so you know I'm a serious person, I'm in my senior year at Emerson College in the Documentary Production program. I am inspired by nature, and am working on a project that combines sculpture and film. I have something under way, and I want to visit New York to film a certain habitat.

I know you spend a lot of time in the parks and at the beach, and are very busy. From your blog, it seems you watch birds all over the city. I'm sure you know the place I'm interested in, and I'd love to tell you about it when I see you.

It's funny, I haven't been to New York City since I was in third grade. My father had an exhibit and we drove in and stayed for a few days. While he was setting up the show, my mother took Gilly and me to the Met. She showed us lots of her favorite paintings, but there was one in particular she said you and she used to love. It was by Winslow Homer, and there was moonlight. I remember she looked happy and sad, staring at it, both at the same time.

This might seem presumptuous, but I was wondering if I could stay with you a few days while I work on my project. I know the address, of course, from family history. Your number is unlisted, so I can't call; I plan to show up at 495 West 22nd St. and hope for the best.

Love,
Grit

The letter felt real in her hands, but nothing else did. The day's last light spilled through French doors, burnishing the oak floor and washing the books that filled the tall bookcases with gold. In the small park across Twenty-second Street, bright yellow ginkgo leaves glinted on dark branches. She hadn't had contact with anyone in her family for nearly two decades. Clare felt as though she were dreaming.

Bowls rattled in the kitchen, the cats finishing their dinner. Old radiators clinked and hissed as Clare turned on a lamp and sat on the couch. "Love, Grit." Clare had assumed Gillis and Grit had been raised to hate her. The part about not wanting revenge: did that mean forgiveness? "Love": what a peculiar way to sign a first letter, or maybe it was not strange at all. Clare seemed to have lost all perspective.

Somewhere in the apartment, probably in a box at the back of her closet, Clare had the picture she'd taken the day she'd attacked Frederik. Anne, Gillis, and Grit huddled together by the dying fire, all looking shell-shocked. Clare's lawyer had offered the photo at trial—an exhibit to show Clare's state of mind (immediate concern for her sister's life) and Anne's affect (beaten down, fearful), hoping to convince the jury that Anne was being abused, and that Clare had attacked Frederik to defend her.

Eighteen years had passed, two of them in prison. Now Grit was twenty-one, a college senior. Any moment the doorbell would ring, and a young woman would be standing there. She would be just five years younger than Anne when she'd married Frederik and estranged herself from her family.

Clare had a sudden, crazy desire to talk to Anne. In spite of everything, even in prison, the need for her sister had never gone away. She remembered their old pre-Frederik ease, the way they'd check in constantly no matter where they were, just to talk, remind each other to watch for the full moon, tell each other what they were having for dinner. In spite of not being cooks they loved food. They fought, but they always laughed.

Before and during the trial, Clare had been barred contact with Anne. After the verdict Frederik sold the Montauk house and moved the family away. Clare couldn't stop herself from hoping Anne would write, or even visit. But it never happened.

Sarah had heard from Anne during the first couple of years after Clare's conviction, and told her they were living in Newburyport, Massachusetts. But then the family moved to Denmark, and Sarah never heard from Anne again.

After closing arguments, the jury had been instructed to consider charges of attempted murder as well as the lesser charges of various degrees of felony assault.

Six hours later they returned with a verdict for assault.

Although the first police officer on the scene hadn't insisted Anne take off the scarf she wore to hide Frederik's handprints on her neck, one forensic technician had taken a picture of Anne with the scarf on, and Mary McLaughlin had presented it at trial.

When the trial was over, the foreman told reporters the jury had seen redness and swelling in the photo. They had debated finding Clare not guilty, but couldn't completely discount Anne's and Frederik's testimony. Still, they found that Clare had truly believed she was protecting her sister, and they considered her state of mind to be a mitigating circumstance.

Instead of fifteen to twenty-five for attempted murder, Judge Berman sentenced Clare to two to four years for a Class E assault. She was driven straight from court to Bedford Hills Correctional Facility, New York State's only maximum-security prison for women.

Stuck in her cell, Clare had felt tortured by memories of being at the Montauk house that morning, knowing Anne had been ready to pack up the kids and leave—in contrast with how she'd been on the witness stand, stiff and wooden, never meeting Clare's eyes, saying she couldn't imagine what threat Clare had perceived, that she had gone after Frederik for no reason. But the worst part for Clare came afterward, when she never once heard from her sister. It felt like hell.

After Clare's release, early days on the Internet, she found Frederik's Web site; his bio said he lived and worked in Ebeltoft, a coastal town on the Danish peninsula of Jutland, known for its glass museum. It mentioned a wife and children, but gave no details.

Now the cats wandered into the living room and settled in their favorite spots, cleaning their whiskers after dinner. Clare ran her thumb over the envelope's raised wax seal. Perhaps Anne had given the ring to Grit on her twentieth birthday.

The letter had been postmarked two days ago, Scarborough, Maine. She tried to imagine why Grit might be up there instead of in Boston at Emerson College, heading toward the end of the fall semester.

Clare couldn't sit still; she needed to move, get some air. It was nearly dusk, a perfect time to head back to the park and pursue what had become her owl-stalking, night-exploring obsession; besides, she could probably make it in time to watch four long-eared owls, residents of Central Park's Cedar Hill, fly out for the night. But instead she texted Sarah: Meet at Clement's?

Five seconds later, Sarah's reply: Hell yeah!

Clare pulled on her jacket, stuck the letter in her pocket, and locked the door behind her.

Stepping outside into the cold, she stood on the brownstone's top step, saw people hurrying by, and found herself studying their faces. Would she recognize Grit? She scribbled a note for her, saying she'd be home by eight, and stuck it in the brass frame above the buzzers.

As she headed down Tenth Avenue to Clement's, her local pub, the scars on her hand began to ache and she realized a long-buried thought had come to the surface, the question, after all these years of silence. When Grit arrived, Clare could ask if her sister was still alive.

Sean Kilroy stood behind the long mahogany bar, pouring Guinness right: He filled the glass halfway, let the dark magic settle, and then resumed his pour, ending with a half inch of creamy head.

Clement's wasn't even an Irish bar, not like Paddy Reilly's or Connolly's—it was named after Clement Clarke Moore, the rich Anglo-Saxon landowner who'd once farmed the plot on which it stood—but it served Guinness and therefore was lucky to have Sean as head bartender.

And who should come through the door but the resurrected angel Clare Burke. She had powder-white skin, long dark hair with a silver streak, blue eyes with the depth and treachery of Clew Bay.

The ugly burn on her right hand looked as if she'd reached straight into hell and stayed there awhile.

"How's it going, Clare?" he asked, fixing her a generous Talisker single malt, neat.

"Good, Sean. You?"

"Not so bad. You meeting Sarah?"

"Yes, she'll be here soon."

Sean nodded and edged down the bar. Clare came in for company, but he knew how to read her mood and when she wanted to be alone. He watched her take the laptop from her bag and open it up, blue light reflecting on her face and making her skin look almost transparent.

Clement's cheap owners nonetheless supplied free Wi-Fi, so when Sean had served Clare, he went to the computer behind the bar, mainly used for setting up playlists, managing the night's music—Bon Iver's For "Emma, Forever Ago", right now—clicked favorites, and came upon Clare's blog.

Many nights she came here, either alone or to meet a friend, and wrote about her day spent in nature—Strawberry Fields, the Ramble, Evodia Field, the Lake, Swindler Cove Park, Ebbets Field, Rockaway Beach, and Saw Mill Creek on Staten Island—the only borough, as she wrote, where Chuck-will's-widows still nest in the salt marsh and call through the summer nights.

She seemed to love raptors, nocturnal birds, and herons more than any others. Her posts were beautiful, spare impressions of what she saw and felt, more poem than essay. He drank in her photos, still and mysterious, as if taken by a wild creature instead of a human woman.

"You could just ask me about my day," she called, smiling from down the bar.

"I'd rather read it and look at the pictures," he said.

"Why don't you come out with me sometime?" she asked. "I'll show you where the owls roost."

"Sure, just tell me when," he said, but he knew the game they played, with her always inviting him and Sean always saying sure. There was nothing between them, not like that. She was older than his oldest sister; in fact, maybe that was the charm because in spite of their age difference, he and Eileen had been the closest in their family of seven.

Clare had to be closing on fifty, if you added it all up, the details of her life and all she'd been through, but she looked thirty-five. Most people would never guess she'd done time, but Sean could tell. Prison usually bled the life out of a woman, burned off her beauty and intelligence, left her looking bitter. His cousin Darlene, who'd gone in and out for kiting checks over a period of fifteen years, was forty-five but looked like a wizened winter apple.

Not Clare; she had a mysterious inner glow. Soft smooth skin, eyes that saw everything—but sometimes, right in the middle of a conversation, she'd lose her train of thought, seem to forget what they'd been talking about, and when she raised her eyes again they'd be blank. That was prison.

He'd watched her with Paul, lately, seeing how she still held herself back. They met here sometimes, leaned in close over the candle while they talked about—what? Birds, no doubt. Sean knew the signs of romance—every bartender did—and he saw them between Clare and Paul. She guarded herself, though.

Sean made a couple vodka and tonics, poured a round of Pinot Grigios, spiked an Irish coffee. Two guys, art handlers from the look of them, ordered beers and while Sean pursued the art of the pour, he waited for the first half to settle and stared at the photo Clare had just put up, yellow owl eyes peering out from thick pine boughs, no other part of the bird visible.

Clare never gave away the locations of owls. The birds slept all day and were too vulnerable to idiots, but she'd written that the tree was on a well-trod path in Central Park, which meant to Sean that the owl was hidden in plain sight, just like the blog author herself. Serving the leather jacket art-handler guys, he glanced over at Clare. Sarah had come in, and they were hugging.

Sarah Hughes had come straight from Prada, where she sold clothes, and where one dress could cost more than all Clare's optics put together. Right now she was dressed in her work uniform: a finely tailored white cotton shirt, straight pants, and cropped jacket in black tech fabric, a Prada creation that reminded Clare of shark's skin: *real* shark's skin, not the material.

"Perfect timing—you caught me coming out of the subway," Sarah said, hugging Clare. "Long day, sore feet. What's up?"

"Sarah, look what came," Clare said, placing the letter on the table.

Sarah checked the return address and ran her thumb over the raised sealing wax. "Holy shit, *Anne*?"

"No, it's from Grit."

"You're kidding."

"Read the letter."

While Sarah smoothed out the sheet of stationery, Clare leaned in. The two friends were so absorbed in the letter they failed to see the young woman, hair tucked under a black wool cap, sitting at the end of the bar. Sean offered to refill her club soda, but she shook her head, impatient for him to get out of the way. He was blocking her view of Clare.

THE SILVER BOAT

Luanne Rice

Ever since she was a girl, Dar McCarthy's favorite constellation has been "the Pleiades—sisters clustered together" (p. 35). Now, decades later, closeness with her younger sisters, Rory and Delia, continues to define her—almost as much as the loss of their father, who abandoned them when Dar was just twelve years old. So when their mother dies and the three sisters can no longer afford to keep the family home on Martha's Vineyard, they gather for a final visit to clean out a house filled with memories. Each is grappling with a private grief until a bundle of old letters hints at a different ending to the tragedy that has marked all their lives.

"Back when they'd been kids . . . every boy on the Vineyard had wanted Rory" (p. 25), but it was Jonathan Chase—the scion of another eminent Vineyard clan—who won her. After a rocky start, they settled down and began to raise a family. But Rory is still reeling from her mother's recent death when she discovers that her marriage is not as solid as she'd imagined.

Delia, the youngest, put down roots farthest from the Vineyard. "Jim, Delia's husband . . . considered it too snobby" (p. 13) and usually skipped the family get-togethers to stay at home in Annapolis. So Delia would come with their only son, Pete, who grew to love the ocean and its wild beauty—until he fled a paternity suit two years ago. Delia's been nursing her heartache ever since.

Unlike her sisters, Dar has always been a loner. She returned after art school to live in a cottage on the perimeter of Daggett's Way, the main estate. There, Dar cared for their aging mother, Tilly, and created a successful series of graphic novels featuring Dulse, a water spirit with two sisters. She also drank until she hit bottom and was saved only by AA and the fear of losing her muse.

In the midst of their packing and memories, Dar unearths some letters from Michael McCarthy, their father, to their mother. Michael was a penniless Irishman who came to the Vineyard in search of land he believed to be rightfully his. He fell in love with Tilly, but Tilly's mother, Abigail, accused him of being after the family property. She continued to scorn him even after the girls were born.

For a time they lived on Abigail's largesse and Michael's scant wages. Then he built the *Irish Darling* and sailed the boat solo to Ireland. He wrote: "I won't come back home until after I retrieve what I'm owed" (p. 89). He sent word of his arrival, but never returned. Inspired by his letters, the three sisters embark on an Irish adventure that will transform both their past and their future.

ABOUT LUANNE RICE

Luanne Rice is the author of twenty-nine novels. She lives in New York City and Old Lyme, Connecticut.

A CONVERSATION WITH LUANNE RICE

You made your writing debut in 1985 with Angels All over Town. The Silver Boat *is your twenty-ninth novel. How—if at all—has your writing process changed over time? Have the Internet and other technological advances affected your writing experience?*

In many ways my process has changed very little. My novels always begin with a character. I wait for her to tell me who she is; often she inhabits my dreams. Once I know her name, I'm ready to start writing. Although I now work on a MacBookPro 15, I still like to write the earliest scenes on a yellow legal pad with a fountain pen. The Internet makes research go faster, but something is lost. It's too easy to search for information, take what I need, and move on. I prefer to do research from books, getting lost in the background and immersed in the realm of whatever I'm trying to learn.

The importance of family is a recurring theme in your novels. How did your own upbringing influence your decision to become a writer?

My family was loving but complicated. Our house was filled with secrets and bass notes. As a child I was a detective, listening at walls and going through drawers, looking for answers to what was wrong. My writing has been my lifelong solution to figuring things out, finding the love I know was there, learning everything I can about the way families work, ways of loving and trying to be happy.

"Was that the inspiration for Dulse's latest adventure? Dar wasn't sure. She only knew that her ideas came from deep down, experiences and emotions of her own" (p. 282). Part of what makes your novels so heartfelt is that each of them comes from a deeply personal place. What was your inspiration for The Silver Boat?

The answer has three parts:

a) Like the McCarthy sisters, my sisters and I had to face what to do with our beloved family beach cottage after our mother died. It was an immense challenge. The house contained so many ghosts and memories. My grandparents had built it; no other family had ever occupied it. It sits on a granite hill, and the top step still has three pennies placed there by my grandfather in 1938, the year it was built. We put it on the market for ten seconds—selling felt unthinkable. My sisters were very generous and let me buy them out. I still want it to be the family house.

b) My father had a way of disappearing. Not forever, like Michael McCarthy, but frequently, and without explanation. I've been writing my way into that situation my whole life.

c) The silver boat actually exists.

Harrison is such a glorious character. Is he based on someone you've known?

Yes, but like the character, he would want to remain a mystery.

In your blog, you have a section called "Advice to Young Writers." What is the one bit of advice that you consider most important to a writer just starting out?

Write every day; don't worry what your parents, true love, or teacher will think; go to the library, find the shelf where your book would be, and imagine it right there.

In an alternate universe, is Luanne Rice still a novelist, or is there a "road untaken" that the other Luanne has followed?

One of the best parts of being a writer is that I get to take all those roads; for months on end I've lived the lives of an oceanographer, gardener, sculptor, anthropologist, veterinarian, actor, beachcomber, researcher at the Louvre, and many more.

Poetry always has a prominent supporting role in your novels. Who are your favorite poets, and why?

W. B. Yeats for the language, beauty, mysticism; Eavan Boland for her strength and evocation of Dublin; Mary Oliver for her connection to nature and the sea; Jim Harrison and Ted Kooser for their friendship; my sister Maureen Rice Onorato because her work is tender and powerful.

Dulse is another name for a type of seaweed also called "Irish moss." Why did you give her this name?

Dulse's element is water. She is a fluid character, flowing in and out of fantasy and dreams. She leads Dar deep into her own subconscious, allowing her to bring forth things buried inside, answers she didn't know she had.

I chose the name because it's beautiful to say. Also in honor of the seaweed that fills tidal pools, hides sea creatures, smells like life and death, and because I love its Latin name, *Chondrus crispus.*

Also because the short story "Dulse," by Alice Munro, affected me greatly when I first read it in *The New Yorker.*

You describe Dulse and her world so vividly that the reader can really picture the pages. Is there a graphic artist whose work inspired Dar's?

My niece Amelia Onorato inspired me and helped me research the character. She is a writer and an artist, getting her master's degree in cartoon studies, and working on her first graphic novel.

Have you found the seed of your next novel yet? If so, could you share a bit of the story?

It starts with a crime, continues with an unexpected visitor, threads of estrangement, lost love, and the kind of deep love a person can have for someone she's never even met.

QUESTIONS FOR DISCUSSION

1. Which boat is the one referred to in the title? How does it drive the events of the novel?

2. Discuss the ways in which their father's abandonment played out in the lives of each of the three sisters. What does the trip to Ireland represent for each of them?

3. Michael McCarthy loved his daughters, yet he felt compelled to leave them to find and claim his rightful legacy. Do you believe a mother would have left her children under the same circumstances? Do most men today still feel they need to be their families' main provider?

4. Dar's and Pete's respective experiences with alcoholism and drug addiction wreak damage beyond their individual lives. How does a history of substance abuse affect a family?

5. Would Dar have been an artist and writer if her father had not abandoned them? Is suffering an inherent part of the creative process?

6. Why did it mean so much to Cathleen McCarthy to meet Dar and her sisters? How does that affect them? Does the fact that their father had an affair with Cathleen diminish your opinion of him? Why or why not?

7. "Hence Bluepool's waving groves delight/Amuse the fancy, please the sight/And give such joy as may arise/From sylvan scenes and azure skies/The weary here in safe repose/

Forgetting life's attendant woes/May sit secure, serene and still/And view with joy yon famed hill" (pp. 161–164). How does this poem—partially quoted by Cathleen and engraved on the Dalua Bridge—tie into the novel?

8. " 'No, it's not that,' she said quickly. But he saw her look around. He felt how ashamed she was of all this, and was ready to drop it, just drive her home" (p. 222). Was Pete correctly interpreting Delia's feelings about going with him to the AA meeting? Why is it important to him that she be there?

9. "Dear R & D, I know it's beside the point, but we now have an offer from the Rileys. I took the liberty of burning it" (p. 248). Of the three sisters, only Dar wants to keep Daggett's Way. Rory and Delia see it as a beloved white elephant and imagine how helpful the money from its sale could be for their families. Might Dar feel differently if she had children of her own? If you are a parent, did your priorities change once your child was born? How?

10. What role does Harrison play in the novel? Why does he choose to live "off the grid" in Martha's Vineyard over a more conventional life elsewhere?

11. Ultimately, the sisters decide to sell Daggett's Way, but donate the even more valuable land grant. Why?

To access Penguin Readers Guides online, visit the Penguin Group (USA) Web site at www.penguin.com.